Potentates

By
Amos

Potentates is a work of fiction. All characters and incidents are purely fictitious, the creation of the author's imagination. Any resemblance to actual persons or events is purely coincidental.

Copyright 2005 by Randall A. Chapman

ISBN 0-9761296-0-4

For information contact:
amosauthor@yahoo.com
potentatesbook@gmail.com
P.O. Box 944, Chester, SC 29706

Library of Congress Control Number: 2005908125

Printed in the United States of America

This book is dedicated with love to my mother Theresa Chapman, who worked so hard to meet my needs when I was growing up. She was a great mother and grandmother and always helped the elderly and the sick. She had a kind word for everyone she met.

Chapter 1

My name is Reginald Howell, but I have been called Ren ever since I can remember. I am at the crossroad of my life now. Today I was reading some newspaper commentaries about the Enron and World-Com scandals. These scandals have renewed my own fears that what I have done, what I have been a part of, what I am still a part of, may be discovered. Before anything happens to me or to my mind, I want to—I need to—tell the story of my life. So, I sit here, putting these secrets into a journal. When my story has been told, when the truth has been put down on paper, I will lock it away in my private safe deposit box, which only I know exists.

I have spent the major part of my adult life working for a politician by the name of Margaret Stewart Hall. Margaret's childhood was uneventful. She grew up in a small South Carolina town called Richmond. Her father was the manager of the local shoe store, and her mother had a part time position as a teller at the local savings and loan bank. Since she was an only child, Margaret's parents doted on her, and she quickly learned how to shrewdly maneuver them to get her own way. Margaret always thought of her childhood as dull. According to Margaret, her most eventful happening during grammar school was winning the regional spelling bee in her

fifth grade year. The only other memorable event occurred in her senior year of high school when her cheer-
leading squad won the state championship. Margaret
was, of course, the captain of the squad. After high
school she was off to the University of South Carolina,
where she earned a bachelor's degree in business and
graduated cum laude.

By the time Margaret graduated from college, she
had already come to the realization—thanks to a series
of past sales jobs—that she had a talent for selling. She
was soon working in Waverley, a suburb just southwest
of Greenville, for Evans Corporation, a fast-growing
company which sold computers to industrial companies. Within a year Margaret had moved from a sales-
person to the position of regional sales manager. To im-
press her boss, she went after government contracts on
the side, acting as a self-appointed lobbyist for Evans.
The corporate management of Evans doubted that the
company was big enough to get state contracts but was
willing to let Margaret try as long as she did her regional sales job. The corporate director joked about how
Margaret was going to make them all rich, but within a
year, Margaret had landed a major state contract. No
one joked about her ability at Evans Corporation from
that day on.

Over the next two years, Margaret made Evans
Corporation millions. She loved dealing with politicians
and negotiating for government contracts. She loved
maneuvering and manipulating the bureaucrats into
buying Evans computer systems for state offices,
schools, libraries, or, for that matter, anyplace that the
state had a need for one. Sometimes this included a department that had excess money and needed to spend it
for fear that if the total budget was not spent, it would

be cut the next year. Therefore, computers were purchased, complete systems that, most likely, would never see the outside of a state warehouse until years later when an auctioneer would sell them for pennies on a dollar as surplus merchandise. This was a good thing for Evans Corporation because the service warranty contract would never be enacted, saving the corporation millions of dollars. Margaret once told me about a board meeting at Evans at which they actually discussed producing a computer system that did nothing but that could be built cheaply. These computers would be the ones that went to the state warehouses, thus enhancing profits even more.

Margaret thrived on these deals; the more tainted they were, the more excited she was. She was amazed at how cheaply and easily the politicians sold favors. Airline and sport event tickets were routine, even personal computers for the home, but once when a senator just asked for a suit from a local department store in exchange for securing a $200,000 contract, even Margaret was shocked. She would have readily given him a suit from the best tailor in South Carolina. Evans Corporation had accounts to take care of such matters, and part of Margaret's job was to spend this money to keep the politicians happy. Margaret did what she told the other sales reps under her command to do—sell. She did not care how they sold, just that they sold.

As Margaret watched the politicians maneuver in the House of Representatives and the Senate, she saw herself in a new light. She was smarter than they were, much smarter. She was also stunningly beautiful. Her oval face boasted a flawless complexion and large hazel eyes with long lashes. Margaret was tall at five feet eight and her figure was trim, yet shapely. Her most outstanding physical asset, though, was her thick shoulder-length chestnut hair. She was always dressed impeccably. Margaret was a most appealing woman, and no man ever walked by without turning around to look at her. She always radiated a sociable and cultured presence, yet, if anyone really took the time to look into her eyes, into her soul, he was struck by the undeniable feeling of coldness and disdain he saw there.

Margaret began to make plans for a new career. She began looking into running against Robert Eaton, the state representative from her hometown district; however, she soon came to the realization that the numbers were not good. Eaton had beaten his last opponent, a local businessman, by capturing seventy percent of the vote. Margaret decided to bide her time till a position came open that she could win. She had made her decision, though. Someday she would be a legislator, maybe even governor. She continued to search for an opportunity to enter the political arena, but if the risk was not acceptable, she would begin a new search, even more diligently. She was willing to move to a new district, give up her job; whatever change was needed, she was willing to do. She was like a famished eagle, soaring over the landscape seeking a rabbit to swoop down upon and consume without the rabbit even having a chance to struggle. Once, as Margaret drove through the foothills on her way to a meeting, she did, indeed, notice an eagle poised on the wind. It controlled the sky she thought, and, therefore, it controlled the land below. No one had ever heard of an eagle starving to death. To be an eagle was to be in control. She never forgot the eagle as it swooped down effortlessly, speared the rabbit with its talons, and snapped the furry little neck. Margaret's code became "look at the big picture." She was sure the opportunity to enter the political arena would appear, and then she would swoop down and take control.

As Margaret went about her work selling computers, she came into contact with a state representative, a young lawyer by the name of Mark Hall. At six feet, three inches, he was a handsome man. He had an athletic body, and his dusty-blonde hair, which always appeared a bit disheveled, and blue eyes hinted at his fun-loving and eager-to-please nature. But what Margaret found most appealing about Mark was his naivety, for this meant she could easily control him. The partners in the Greenville firm that he worked for, Dudd, Stevenson, and Marro, were all too busy making money to go to the state capital, so they put what they liked to refer to as their "young turk" into the state representative seat. This was accomplished by using the law firm's political connections and money. The firm's connections were so good that Mark easily beat two other candidates. His job, as far as the partners of the firm were concerned, was to be present when clients went before the state boards. The members of the board were appointed by state legislators; therefore, the presence of any legislator at a board hearing—in this case, Mark's presence—meant that the decision easily went the way the client of the state rep desired.

Representing clients who had cases with state boards meant that the law firm Mark worked for would get a favorable decision, too. Of course, the firm charged thousands of dollars to make this happen. On one occasion when a client complained about what he was being charged, Mr. Stevenson laughed. "He's our turk and that's what we get for him" was his reply. The cases that came before these boards mostly regarded state mandated regulations, such as environmental laws, insurance laws, public utility laws, and consumer laws. The list was endless. Mark's job was to make sure that these corporate clients got a favorable hearing, which they always did. The duty of the newly elected partner of the firm, Tom Marrow, was to deal with corporate clients. However, he spent most of his time making sure Mark Hall's position as state representative made the firm "big bucks," the phrase Mr. Dudd used to refer to the huge fees these corporate clients paid.

When Marrow did not have enough corporate clients who needed Mark's special help, he would transfer Mark to Workmen Compensation cases. The routine was almost ritualistic. Mark would appear before the Labor Board with his client and speak for half an hour; then the board would sequester itself for an hour and return with a favorable decision. Mark's speech was merely a formality. The decision would have been favorable simply because Mark showed up with the client. The members of the board, who got paid well for their services, knew that their jobs depended on serving the lawyer-legislator. If they didn't, when their term ended, the lawyers would make sure they never got appointed again.

This arrangement cost businessmen of the state millions of dollars in insurance premiums to protect themselves against illegitimate accident claims from employees. Legitimate cases became less important, leaving the cases of these victims mixed into a pool of illegitimate claims. This, more often than not, led to unsatisfactory results for the legitimate claimants. The lawyers who were involved laughed about the situation and the businessmen snarled. In the end, though, the businessmen knew that they needed these political lawyers to protect them in other ways, so they went along with the system and charged off the cost to the consumer.

One might hope that Mark would seek to justify this behavior and sooth his conscience with the idea that he would someday introduce a great bill into the legislature and get it passed into law. Or, at the very least, one might hope that he would support the effort of some other legislator who was working toward this honorable task. But this was not the case. Mark did not have to worry about such lofty goals or, for that matter, even to read the piles of information that he received on each proposed piece of legislation. The law firm's partners had already dictated how he would vote.

Late each Friday afternoon during the legislative season, the partners would meet to discuss any proposed legislation. Their decision was based on negotiations that went on with other law firms across the state which also had their own "young turks" in the legislature, although some of them were not so young anymore. Votes were traded and bargained for, based on the needs of clients and how much these clients were willing to pay. On any given day a bill could be turned into law if a client had enough money. In most cases, though, the client wanted sincere legislation from honest legislators "killed," and on any given day, in most cases, this could be done.

Mark was not invited to these Friday meetings. On Monday morning in his mailbox at the law firm, he would receive a memo outlining how he was to vote on each piece of legislation that would come before the representatives that week. A note at the bottom of the memo always reminded Mark that if anything else, unannounced, was to come up before the House, he was to call Tom immediately. This system was great as far as

Mark was concerned, for it left him plenty of time for socializing—which he loved to do. The only person disgruntled with this arrangement was Miss Plincey, an older woman who had been a secretary with the firm for years. It was she who had to stay late Friday afternoons to type the memo, which she referred to as the "blasted thing." She "earned" the job because the partners knew she was loyal and discreet.

Mark met Margaret for the first time at a thousand-dollar-a-plate fundraiser for the governor. She was twenty-six and he was thirty-two. When their eyes met across the room, there was a mutual attraction. The relationship developed quickly and had plenty of romance. Mark and Margaret were married six months later. The marriage started off prosperously enough, two people in powerful positions, making lots of money. They bought a nice four-bedroom house in Waverley.

Within a year, a son, Mark Jr., was born and a year later, a daughter, Tammy. During both of her pregnancies, Margaret only took six weeks off for maternity leave. Mark and Margaret were so busy with their careers that they hired a nanny to watch the children. At first a schedule was arranged so that the children could see their parents for a few hours each day. Mark was fairly consistent, but Margaret found it difficult to make it home before the children went to bed. Margaret's tardiness often caused problems with the nanny, resulting in arguments. Within four years they had gone through several nannies.

Finally, an older woman named Margie was hired to care for the children. Margie had more interest, however, in her dog, a small white poodle, than she did in the children. In Margie's perception everything was fine as long as the children did not disturb her routine of phone calls in the morning, soap operas in the afternoon, and rented videos in the evening. Mark came home many nights to find that the children had not been bathed nor fed an adequate dinner.

But there were some good times for Mark and Margaret and the children, too. These times usually occurred on Sundays when the family would take time to relax. There were riding excursions at a nearby horse ranch and trips to amusement parks, local fairs and rodeos, and, Mark's favorite, the movies.

After Margaret had her second child, she let it be known at Evans Corporation that she had no intention of having any more children. She began to be rapidly promoted now that the board understood that she was going to be fully committed to her job. Within three years, she was made vice-president of Evans, which was now doing a tidy seventy million dollars in sales. This was quite an accomplishment for someone who was only thirty-four years old.

Margaret now found her job at Evans wholly intertwined with politics, not only in South Carolina but also in many surrounding states where she lobbied governors, state senators, and state legislators. She had an endless energy for politics and truly loved all aspects of her job—the negotiations, the meetings, the parties, the manipulation. Every successful deal made her more vital to those with whom she did business and gave her a new sense of power. Margaret thrived on politics and the power it gave her to control others.

The next step was inevitable for it had germinated long ago. Margaret began to speculate on how she could get her husband's state representative seat. She could go to her husband's law firm and secretly ask them to make him a partner in trade for a contract to do the legal work for Evans Corporation. This would be a mighty lucrative contract for the law firm. If her husband were a partner, he would be too busy to be state representative; then she could convince the firm to support her in the next election. The only reason she did not move on the idea immediately was that she might appear too manipulative and pushy to the law partners. The thought that her husband might have objected never occurred to her. Besides, long ago Margaret had decided her career should come first. Mark, she had learned, was just not aggressive enough. As for the children, there were always live-in nannies.

Two years later, though, when Margaret was ready to make her move for her husband's representative seat, something unexpected happened—Senator Caldon died of a heart attack. The political operatives jokingly said that he died from his "excessive consumption of sugared jelly donuts." Nine months previously he had been re-elected to represent the district where Mark and Margaret lived. Margaret took this as an omen; it was her chance to get into politics as an elected official. Her husband would naturally be in line to move up to the Senate, but if she moved quickly, she could have the Senate seat herself.

That evening, over a nice candle-lit dinner, which promised much more to be offered later, she presented her proposition to her husband. He would stay state representative so that there would be no chance of them losing what they already had and she would become a candidate for the Senate seat. Mark was seduced into agreement, and a few days later, Margaret met with the partners at her husband's law firm. After making many promises, she received their backing.

Then, Margaret went to the Board of Directors of Evans Corporation to get their support. She agreed to continue with her lobbying activities as a paid consultant to Evans, but she resigned as vice-president. Margaret got Evans to make a considerable donation to her campaign fund, and she was given the use of one of the several condominiums that the company owned in Columbia. Evans maintained these condos as a perk for its clients and favored politicians to use on a sporadic basis, but the Board agreed to let Margaret use one for as long as she was in the Senate. This would save Margaret a tremendous amount of time from traveling back and forth between Waverley and Columbia, as well as money. The Board of Directors was totally satisfied with this arrangement for two reasons. First, if elected, Margaret would make sure that Evans received government contracts, and secondly, she would be able to introduce lobbyists from Evans to key legislators who sat on the right committees. Margaret had everything worked out. Unofficially she was now a contender for the South Carolina State Senate.

Chapter 2

The special election to replace Senator Caldon was two months away. The first thing Margaret did when she started her campaign for the Senate seat was to go after the money from the Political Action Committees, known as PAC's. She knew that if she tied up the PAC money, the press would see her as a winner. She moved quickly to put the momentum on her side. She boldly sold her potential future influence to anyone willing to buy, from the Chiropractic Association to the Developers Association. She became a political prostitute. She was willing to meet whatever the need was as long as there was enough money involved. Margaret's private slogan was "no money, no services."

In that two-month period Margaret visited over one hundred special interest groups and associations. The lobbyists from these groups were glad to see her, and these visits gained her $113,000 in campaign contributions. By getting in early and raising a lot of funds, she discouraged other political office seekers from entering the race, people who might have beaten her. Some county council members hinted that they were going to get into the race, but they were nowhere to be found when it was time to file their candidacy. The only soul willing to run against Margaret was a retired Methodist minister named Sam Murray, who had moved into the Senate district only a year before, and he had no political experience. The two thousand dollars in his savings account is what he had to spend. Within two weeks of Senator Caldon's death, Margaret's campaign was in full swing. She had been preparing for this opportunity for years, so she was ready to move quickly. She gathered together people with political power by promising to appoint them to boards and commissions.

Margaret had also hired Harry Jameson as her campaign manager. Harry was five feet six inches and was a little heavy at 180 pounds. He had a headful of curly red hair, which indicated his Scottish heritage. Harry was recently married to a woman named Janet, who was not the least bit interested in politics. Since Harry worked such long hours, she spent a lot of her time with her family. Her father owned a transmission shop, and Janet worked there as his bookkeeper.

Harry had worked with Margaret at Evans Corporation as a salesman. Margaret had convinced him that a great opportunity awaited him working for a senator. His only previous political experience had been working for a congressional candidate as a volunteer when he was in college. The political involvement had excited Harry and he found his sales job rather routine, so he was an easy target for Margaret. Harry took a substantial cut in pay to go to work for Margaret, but she promised him a good salary and great benefits when she was elected. Margaret felt good about hiring Harry. He was five years younger than she and he was accustomed to her being the boss, so it was easy for her to dominate him. Harry had a great personality, and people found him easy to talk to. He was very articulate, organized, and meticulous about getting paperwork and details taken care of.

Harry did Margaret's scheduling, made sure volunteers were making phone calls, and reassured those supporters who were seeking state board or commissioner positions. There were also job seekers who wanted to be state employees when Margaret became senator. More importantly, Harry was in charge of organizing the black votes. This was done by searching out the leaders in black neighborhoods and rural areas. Each leader was given an amount of money, usually $4,000, but the amount might vary based on the number of votes the leader could influence. He would keep $500 for himself and then distribute ten dollars to each of his neighbors who agreed to vote for Margaret.

This money was referred to as "bag money" because in the past it had been delivered in brown paper bags. Negotiating all of this out with ten or more different neighborhood leaders was quite burdensome. Every leader always felt as if the others were getting more money than they should. Some of the leaders would also demand a few hundred dollars for their respective churches. This worked in the leader's favor, making him appear even more powerful. It was also a means of keeping the practice of bribery "straight" with God. The bag money, if successful (and it always was), would produce at least 3010 votes; this would easily decide the election.

There was also the Hispanic community that was part of the senate district. Bag money was used there too, giving the potential of another 2840 votes. The minority groups' distrust of government made this bag money system all possible. As far as the minorities were concerned, everyone involved in the political system was crooked. The bag money was just their share.

One of the other details Harry had to take care of as campaign manager was to make sure that the Black and Hispanic leaders hired drivers to carry people to the polling sites. The leader got sixty-five dollars for driver he hired. He would then turn around and hire drivers for twenty-five to forty dollars each. More profit for him. The leader was also given a lump sum of money to rent vans and pay for gas. Sometimes the leader could get away with convincing some of the drivers that the candidate would be "good" for the community and get them to drive for free. Sometimes the vans were borrowed or rented from churches, giving the leaders another power boost.

Of course, not all the money went to the church—the deacons and trustees of the church had to be paid too. The real key to Harry's job was to know the "right" minority leaders. Approaching the wrong leader could mean big trouble because there were some minority leaders who despised the whole vote-buying, bag money process.

Harry had his own long-range plans, and working for Margaret was just the beginning. If Harry could work his way up the ranks as a campaign manager, he could one day be working for a United States congressman or even a governor. Candidates running for these bigger seats had what Harry liked to refer to as "real money." This meant that the campaign manager did not take care of the bag money. There were separate "bagmen" who took care of the "dirty" money. The campaign manager just made sure that the bag money was delivered, but he did not actually carry the money around to the various leaders.

Harry didn't think his prospects for the big times were looking good with Margaret. He had nicknamed her "the bitch" because of her constant pressuring and complaining. Margaret would get upset at him for giving out an additional thousand dollars to be distributed to black churches. She just could not understand that the conscience of these black leaders was put at ease when a little money was given to the church. Once over a beer at a local bar, Harry told a friend that "the bitch" did not understand because she herself did not have a conscience. Margaret's nickname, "the bitch," stuck with the campaign workers, and she never would be rid of it. She knew about the name, but she pretended she did not. Secretly, she was proud that she was perceived as being tough. As long as the workers knew that she, "the bitch," was in charge was all that mattered.

While all of this was transpiring, Rev. Murray was out working the district, going door to door, talking with people. It was apparent to everyone that he was gaining momentum. A victory for Margaret seemed more and more uncertain. Rev. Murray was honest, intelligent, and well-received by people. He constantly talked about the need for better education and more recreational activities for children. Publicly Margaret always responded, "I am a mother. I know what children need." Privately, however, in the sanctity of the office among her loyal campaign workers, she would say, "I'll let that bastard preacher have every child's vote in the district; too bad they can't vote!"

As the election neared, the numbers seemed too close to Margaret. She had planned for this political seat for years and she was not about to lose it now. So, she called Harry into her office and together they made a plan. Harry had gotten hold of a picture taken of Rev. Murray with his arm around a prostitute. The picture had been taken at a soup kitchen where the prostitute had gone for assistance, and Rev. Murray had been volunteering his time. The picture was innocent enough, taken to promote the mission program, which operated the soup kitchen. Harry's job was to secretly have a flier made of the picture with the caption "Who is the prostitute with Rev. Murray?" These fliers would be distributed anonymously and stealthily so that they would never be connected to Harry or Margaret.

The distribution of the damaging photo was set for three days before the election. Harry would also bribe a reporter at the newspaper to get the photo, along with a speculative story, into the paper the morning prior to the election so that Rev. Murray would have no time to react to or refute the allegations. Margaret's victory would be assured.

On election night the results were just what the political predictors thought they would be. In the white precincts, Rev. Murray got 58% of the white vote, but when the black and Hispanic precincts came in, Margaret got 87% of the vote. The total of all votes gave Margaret 273 more votes than Rev. Murray. Now, at age thirty-six, Margaret Hall was a South Carolina state senator.

Although officially she was now Senator Margaret Hall, for the people that worked the campaign as paid staff, she was still "the bitch." Throughout the entire campaign not one of them had been paid a compliment, not one of them had received an acknowledgement of the long hours put in. Publicly, in front of the television cameras, Margaret accepted her new job gracefully. The next day, however, when she stood before her campaign workers—who were anticipating a big thank you—Margaret just snarled, "I bet you all expect big paying jobs now!" A young girl named Susan, who had spent her evening convincing her mother, father, aunts, uncles, and anyone else she could find to vote for Margaret, burst into tears. Margaret just walked out of the room. Harry was astounded by this at first, but then he tried to rescue the situation by saying, "She's tired. You all did a great job; we'll be calling on you."

Chapter 3

The race for the Senate seat may have gone Margaret's way, but her home life was a disaster. She and her husband were barely on speaking terms, and the relationship was more like a business partnership than a marriage. Both of the children were physically adorable. Mark Jr. had Margaret's chestnut hair but his father's blue eyes. Tammy had both her father's blonde hair and blue eyes. Unfortunately, the children's mischievous antics were no longer amusing. They had become impossible to discipline.

When Margaret or Mark came into the house, the children would start their mischief with a passion to get their parents' attention. Once they even climbed out the attic window of the two-story house onto the roof. Mark rushed to the garage to get an extension ladder to rescue them. Margaret stood at the bottom of the ladder, screaming orders at Mark as he coaxed the children from the roof. Another repeated prank would be for the kids to unplug the refrigerator or to alter the temperature control dial to its lowest or highest setting, causing everything liquid to freeze or everything in the freezer to thaw.

To make up for the time not spent with their children, Margaret and Mark showered them with gifts almost on a daily basis. Within a few days the toys would be broken or lost, but the children did not perceive this to be a problem because they knew there would be a new toy to replace it the next day. The principal of the school called so many times about Mark Jr.'s behavior that Margaret finally used her political clout to get the principal fired. There were no more calls from the school, but the firing of the principal did not solve Mark Jr.'s behavioral problems.

At this point if the parents would have just settled down to a normal life style, Mark Jr., who was seven, and Tammy, who was five, might have been guided out of their troublesome past. Unfortunately, their parents' career interests were more important than their children. Mark was now trying to become a partner in the law firm, and Margaret had a state Senate office to run.

Harry had moved quickly to find other employment in his chosen field as a political operative, but Margaret had moved more quickly. She put out the word to Harry's prospective employers that he was very unreliable and had almost lost her the election. Soon Harry saw the writing on the wall—he was going to have to stay working for "the bitch" if he was going to remain in politics.

Normally, Harry would have been offered the job of office manager. Margaret did not see it that way, though. She gave Harry a job doing research. What Harry was really doing, however, was checking which political action committees would give the most money in campaign contributions if Margaret cast her Senate vote a certain way. This was a taxing job because on any given day before a vote, one side or another might be willing to raise the ante. Harry had to be extremely careful not to sell out too soon.

It was the office manager's job that got me involved with Senator Margaret Hall. I, Ren Howell, answered an ad in the classifieds of the *Columbia News*, and after having a short interview with Margaret, I was promptly made her office manager. I was surprised that I was hired because I had no experience and no great desire to be involved in politics. I needed a job desperately, so I had been applying for anything for which I might, in some small way, qualify. Of all the jobs I had applied for in the last few weeks, this was the one I most expected to go nowhere.

I accepted the task before me for no other reason than that all of my funds had been depleted and I needed money to pay the rent on my three- room apartment. You see, I was originally from Boston and had gone to twelve years of Catholic school and then a Catholic college. After college I joined the Peace Corp for a number of years. My friends were not surprised at all when I enrolled in the seminary to become a priest. After being ordained, I was assigned to a church in South Carolina to assist Monsignor Daniels, who was the administrator of a Catholic boys' home. For ten years I was very happy with my position. Then, one day I returned from work to the rectory and found the monsignor in bed with a young boy. When I reported him to the bishop, I was labeled a troublemaker, and shortly after that I was asked to resign. I left the priesthood angry. The world was an ugly place and I wanted to get even with all the bad people–at least those that I perceived as being bad.

Margaret had instantly realized how angry I was and decided that this anger would be a powerful tool for her to use. I did not know what to do with this anger, so to have someone in my life who could direct this force that lived within me was a relief. As office manager my job should have been to make sure Margaret's constituents got their needs met, but my real job was to make sure Margaret got re-elected. Anyone who got in the way of that objective was the enemy and had to be destroyed. The only constituents Margaret really cared about were the ones who could provide money or a large block of votes.

I remember one time an older black man, perhaps in his late seventies, drove one hundred miles to the Senate office in Columbia to plead for his son who had been put in jail but no formal charges had been pressed. I had learned that this was not an uncommon occurrence in the state. The whole matter was ignored for weeks, and I began receiving daily phone calls from the distressed father. When I finally pressed Margaret about what we should do, her response was brusque, "I'm supposed to care that some nigger's kid is in jail?"

About a week later when I was talking to Harry, we discovered that the father was one of the black leaders who handled the bag money in his area. When Margaret heard this, she immediately made the calls to the "right people." Within twenty-four hours the young man was released and safely at home with his father. That evening Harry and I went to a lounge and laughed about the situation. Harry kept saying that there was justice in the world, justice for a bagman's son. Each new beer brought the words back to his lips and always with a painful laugh. At the end of the evening as we were ready to depart, Harry looked me straight in the eye and said, "Ren, we done good today—the devils we are." His words stunned me. I managed a faint laugh, but those words haunt me till this day.

I had been working for Margaret for about six months when she said, "We need to have lunch. How about Friday?" I knew instinctively that something was up. At lunch that Friday Margaret told me her marriage was on the rocks and Mark had filed for a divorce. Mark was going to stay in the house in Waverley with the children, and she would stay in the condo in Columbia until things were settled and the divorce was finalized. The office (meaning Harry and I) needed to do some immediate damage control. The fact that the marriage was breaking up was no surprise to me, but what she confided thereafter left me in shock and fear.

"Ren," she said, "I want to create a new image for myself. I know everyone thinks of me as the super-professional woman. But, I think it's worn thin."

I didn't know what she wanted me to say. "Well, what do you want for an image?" I asked.

"I want to present myself as a devout Christian woman."

My head swirled with disbelief. How could "the bitch" ever pass herself off as religious, let alone Christian? After all, the only person Margaret was concerned about was herself.

"I'm going to start attending church. Not one particular church. I think it's best if I float around. Go to a lot of different churches. That way I'll cover all my bases. It's best that I not be connected with a particular denomination. I don't want to alienate anyone, you know. Exclude any votes, right?"

Disagreeing with Margaret was not a wise move. I knew that much. So, I simply said, "Well, that might be a good way to start."

She went on to say that running against a minister had made her look bad, which made the thought immediately come to mind that Abraham Lincoln had run against a preacher in his Congressional race, beaten him, and seemed to have survived the experience just fine. As this thought that was going through my mind,

Margaret looked straight into my eyes and said, "Ren, it is your job to make me a Godly person."

Suddenly I realized why she had hired an ex-priest with no political experience as her office manager. I was on the verge of laughing when I realized she was dead serious. Even more ludicrous, I found myself agreeing to the proposition.

Over the next few months Harry and I tried to establish Margaret as a victim, as a person who had been abused by her husband and now he was divorcing her. Unfortunately Mark's law firm had gotten the jump on us and their news releases were good. Mark was concerned about the children. Margaret had no time for them and no time for her husband. Mark did a press conference, which was aired on the local evening news. He pleaded for his wife to resign from the Senate and to stay home and care for the children. The "divorce situation," which was how Margaret referred to the breakup of the marriage, was clearly not going her way. Mark's lawyer was trying to get Margaret legally removed from their home and temporary custody of the children given to Mark. Margaret's lawyer knew the judge, however, and had the hearing delayed for sixty days.

A few days after Mark's press conference, Margaret summoned Harry and me into her office. She kept repeating that something drastic needed to be done, pushing us for ideas.

"Well, gentlemen, we need to come up with something and quickly. Mark is making me look the villain, like an unfit mother, too busy for her children, let alone her husband."

"We could get a picture of Mark with a prostitute," Harry suggested. "That wouldn't make him look so sympathetic."

"No," snapped Margaret. "That's not serious enough to turn the public's opinion against him."

Harry kept pushing the idea. When I saw Harry's idea was not what Margaret had in mind—and having none of my own—I asked her what she thought. She answered so quickly that I knew she had come into the room knowing what she intended to involve us in. Asking our opinion had just been a formality.

"No, a female won't do. I want a picture of Mark, naked with a man."

Her scheme was for Harry to hire a "dirty tricks" guy for $10,000. The guy would fly to San Francisco, where he, in turn, would hire a gay male, who, for the sum of $3,000, would come to South Carolina and hide in Mark's bedroom. A cameraman would also be hired for the sum of $1,000. When Mark came home and got undressed, the gay male would come out of hiding, and the cameraman would burst in just in time to get the picture. Margaret was going to take the nanny and the two children to Orlando, Florida, on a vacation trip during the time this was scheduled to happen, ensuring that no one else but Mark would be home.

After the compromising picture was in Harry's hands, he would have a private detective sell to a newspaper, saying he had acquired the picture while doing an investigation. Once the picture was released and stories started appearing, Margaret would hold a press conference. She would reluctantly disclose that she had known her husband was gay for years, but, as an act of faith, had hoped he would find God and change.

Harry and I argued against this plan. Harry did not believe the picture could be taken with success. I agreed. Before the "perfect" picture could be snapped, a fight was sure to break out. I thought Mark would punch the homosexual. Margaret had an idea. Mark always had vodka and orange juice when he came home in the evening. The orange juice could be spiked so that he would be conveniently "drunk" by the time he got to the bedroom. Harry said he knew of someone who could get the right dose of drugs to accomplish the task. He would appear intoxicated but he would not pass out.

Although the plan was not approved in any formal capacity, it was clear when we left the room that Harry would begin working on finding the "dirty tricks" guy. For better or worse, this scheme was about to unfold. I did not hear anymore about it until two weeks later. Harry pulled me aside and whispered that we needed to have an emergency meeting.

At first the plan had gone smoothly. Harry had hired the "dirty tricks" guy, whose name was Ralph, and Ralph had hired the gay guy and cameraman. The problem came when Ralph realized that he had to pay for them out of his $10,000. Ralph had started to get really nervous about the whole deal and was now demanding that he get $15,000 instead of the agreed upon $10,000. He wanted $10,000 for himself, $3,000 for the gay, $1,000 for the cameraman, and $1,000 for expenses.

We knew that we couldn't take that much out of our regular Senate account. We feared the transaction might be noticed in case of an audit or investigation. We sure did not want to be in a position of having to explain why that much money went to a "political operative" in another state. We did have money in the safe that had been set aside for political activities, money that we did not want to be public or have to file a disclosure paper on.

The total amount of these funds was $5,000, which we really had already committed to secretly investigate other senators whom Margaret disliked. Now it would have to be used for the set up. This money had accumulated from contributions that came to us in the form of cash. Harry would stack the money in a bag and the bag would go into the safe, which was in a locked closet in his office. Contributions that came in the form of checks were recorded into the bookkeeping system and deposited into our Senate account at the bank. Of course, those who contributed cash were favored over those who contributed checks.

We decided the only way we could raise the other $10,000 we needed was to find someone who needed a favor from a senator. Harry said that a lobbyist for AME, Inc. had been calling regularly. AME manufactured poker machines and wanted a senator to introduce legislation into the Senate so that convenience stores, bars, and restaurants could install the machines and pay off customers who won. Margaret had been against introducing the legislation because gambling did not fit her new "Jesus image," as she liked to call her new political posturing. It was a phrase neither Harry nor I could ever get used to. When Harry was alone with me, he would refer to this new image as the new "religious bullshit thing."

Margaret was already in Orlando, or at least on her way, so Harry looked at me and said, "It's your call; you're the office manager." Deep down I still did not really believe that Margaret was truly serious about this new image. I looked at Harry. "God damn it! All right, get the money but tell them we won't introduce the bill, just support it when it comes to the floor for a vote." I surprised myself with my own words because I never cursed, especially misusing the Lord's name. I suddenly realized how much Margaret had changed me. I was becoming what I despised—a hypocrite with no core values.

The plan to set up Mark seemed to be going along without any more hitches; then Ralph got nervous again. He was supposed to fly back to San Francisco with the gay guy and photographer; instead, he just dropped them off at the airport. On the flight back to San Francisco, the homosexual told the photographer that he got $3,000 for the scam. The following Monday morning Harry received a call from Ralph. He, in turn, had received a call from the photographer, who felt he had been ripped off because he had only gotten $1,000. Harry reached Margaret at her hotel, had a quick conversation, and decided to send Ralph to San Francisco with the additional $2,000 and a message. Margaret's exact words were, "Tell the bastard that if one word of this leaks to anyone, the next $3,000 will go to hire a hit man."

Four days later the first news story came out. The article stated that the real reason Mark wanted a divorce was that he was in a relationship with another man. The news story devastated Mark. He tried to avoid the press, but the more he ducked them, the guiltier he looked. Meanwhile, Mark's law partners immediately began to distance themselves. Mark was at a loss because, in the past, his partners had always made all of the political decisions, even telling him how to vote in the legislature.

One reporter, Skip Keen, whom I did not personally like, made the statement on the six o'clock news that it was obvious that Representative Mark Hall was guilty as accused. I would have loved to have made a fool out of him by going to the press and confessing the whole scam. I did what a good political office manager does in times like this, though, and I laid low. When a reporter caught up with me to ask about Mark's homosexual affair, I said, "No comment. It's a personal matter between Senator Hall and her husband." I knew if I said more, I would sound guilty. The reporter didn't bother me anymore because our Senate office was, at best, just a side attraction; what he really wanted was Rep. Mark Hall.

Margaret called a meeting about a week after the story broke about Mark. She told Harry and me to set up a press conference for Wednesday morning. When we asked her what she was going to say, she dismissed us both and in a disgusted tone said, "Don't worry about what I'll say. I'll take care of it." Harry tried to pursue what "it" was, but all Margaret made was a terse comment that Mark's getting in the way of her political career was going to stop. Harry did not press her any further. I knew Harry was not about to beg Margaret to tell us what she intended for the press conference. We would know when Margaret wanted us to know.

For the next few days, the reporters were constantly calling. Neither Harry nor I could tell them anything because we truly did not know anything. We just kept reassuring them that it would be a big story and that they needed to be there. At the time I would never have guessed how big of a story the press conference was going to be.

Margaret never came to the office until three o'clock Tuesday afternoon. Harry and I were surprised by Margaret's disappearing act because it was customary for us to spend a few hours prepping her for a press conference. Harry and I would fire questions at her as if we were reporters to prepare her for what was coming. If her answer was not sharp and clear enough, the three of us would work on the answer until it was exactly what we wanted the reporters and public to hear. Then, Margaret would memorize the answer and repeat it back to us just as she would do at the press conference. We would sometimes spend hours prepping for these press conferences in order to appear to be giving an answer but, in fact, not really answering at all.

On one occasion Margaret had voted in favor of a toxic waste plant, which would primarily dispose of waste from other states. The plant or, more accurately put, the dump was extremely unpopular amongst the citizenry of South Carolina. Unfortunately, C & X Waste Management, Inc. had given such large political contributions to so many South Carolina legislators that the fact that the people were against the plant did not have much weight. C & X had bought and paid for the legislature, and the plant was going to be built in South Carolina.

The president, Clyde Sims, knew the plant would become a political football, so he had already ensured himself that the legislature wouldn't back out by "assisting" their family members. Family members with businesses received contracts from C & X, purchasing everything from nuts and bolts to computers. The wives of three different state legislators received contracts, one for accounting services, one for insurance, and one for food catering. A brother of a state senator was given a contract as a business consultant, a real step up from his previous job as an assistant manager of a local clothing store. The mother of another state representative, who was president of a small charitable organization, was suddenly looking at the biggest single donation check the charity had ever received.

The list of family members who benefited from C & X went on and on. Our office, with Margaret's permission, had accepted a large cash donation. We knew the press would ask questions when Margaret voted for the waste dump, so we crafted her answer to make her look good. Margaret was quoted as saying, "They closed down Coy Manufacturing, Inc. Forty jobs were lost. The people of this state need jobs. How could I vote against the jobs that C & X is going to bring to South Carolina?"

Of course, there was no mention of the cash in the safe. There was no mention of the scholarship program C & X Chemical was setting up for the children of legislators. What was most amazing of all, though, was that not one reporter asked how the jobs at C & X waste site were going to help the former employees of Coy Manufacturing when the two sites were 150 miles apart.

Harry and I left the office Tuesday evening not knowing what was going to transpire next. We went to a local bar, had a few drinks, and tried to analyze the situation. We could not figure out why Margaret, who had always spent a few days preparing for a press conference, suddenly avoided the office and necessary preparations when the most important press conference of her career was about to happen. The only conclusion Harry and I came to was that the divorce situation had gotten the better of her and the stress had become too much. We left the bar, having drunk too much, sure that disaster loomed before us.

Potentates

Chapter 4

On the day of the press conference, we finally found out where Margaret had been the day before. She came in with a self-assured attitude and called Harry and me into her office. As soon as the door was closed, she announced that she was having her husband arrested for molesting their son. Suddenly I realized that once again she had outsmarted me. For weeks Harry and I had thought that Margaret's plan was to ruin her husband with the picture of him with the homosexual. As always, though, she had kept part of her plan secret. She knew, or at least suspected, that Harry and I would not go along with her plan to falsely frame her husband for child molestation. She had secretly and maliciously let us set Mark up in this sex scandal so that it would seem believable that he really was capable of molesting his own son.

Harry started shooting questions at her. "How are you going to pull this off with the press? Do you think the police will buy the story? What is Mark Jr. going to say?"

I looked at Margaret, stunned. My one thought was how could I stay working for this woman? Finally, in the middle of one of Harry's questions, I blurted out that I did not want to be involved in this. "It's crazy!" I asserted.

Up to this point Margaret had just sat there with an amused half-smirk, half-smile on her face. Her expression turned to rage, though, when she heard what I said. She leaped to her feet, pointed her finger at me, and in a barely controlled voice said, "You already are involved.

You set all this up. Just remember, Mr. Howell, you are the office manager. You take the fall if it goes bad."

She had never called me Mr. Howell before. It had always been Ren. Just looking at her sent a cold chill creeping through my body. I looked away but I could still feel her piercing eyes on me. When I looked up again, she said, "Why are you getting so holy? We're just *accusing* someone of child rape. Your Catholic priests *actually* rape them."

A look of calm satisfaction came over her face. "Look. I have Mark Jr. convinced that it actually happened. I told him that I would take care of him, that I would take care of everything. The kids are out of town. I had the nanny take them to Florida, to Orlando. The police have already talked to Mark Jr. and he's given them an affidavit. Mark's ass is going to jail—he should never have messed with me. Excuse me. I should watch my language. It's not fitting for a Christian lady to cuss like that. Ren, I want to speed up the God stuff. We need to change my image. The public will eat up my finding Jesus right now with my child being molested and everything else."

I sat there for a moment, dumbfounded. The bitch was trying to turn herself into a saint. Harry could not stand the silence that had erupted, swallowing the room. He gave me a slight nod and said, "Let's go; we've got work to do."

The press conference went amazingly well. Margaret read a statement which basically detailed how she had come home one day and found Mark and Mark Jr. in bed together. "I didn't actually see anything happen, but I knew then that something was wrong. It was terrible," said Margaret and her voice slightly trembled as she spoke.

The press asked a few questions. You could feel the tension of each reporter. Not even the vultures who loved misery were comfortable with this story. Margaret answered each question in a forlorn voice and forced some tears from her eyes. The press conference was over when she bit her lip as if fighting back a total breakdown and whispered to the reporters, "You understand—I've got to get back to my son."

Margaret left for Florida after the press conference, and we expected that we wouldn't see her again for two weeks. For the next few days following the press conference, reporters kept calling with back up questions. It was clear that they had bought the story completely. Harry was terrified that the press would pop the obvious question—where was the nanny when these sexual acts were supposed to be happening? But, they never did ask. Fear was with us always during these days, but there was also a feeling of being "high" on the idea that we could fool the whole world and nobody knew the truth. This "high" would go on for years. It was the genesis of us seeing ourselves as invincible.

Mark's arrest happened on the evening of the fifth day following the press conference. The police and district attorney had waited until then because they wanted the area to be swarming with reporters. They had two reasons for doing this. First, it was good press for them. Secondly, a jury that saw Mark on television, being taken away in handcuffs, would find it easier to convict him. The police were also having some difficulty figuring out what to do with Mark once he was arrested. They did not want to put him into the general holding tank for fear that, as a despised child molester, he would be accosted or even killed, but they also did not want to appear as if they were giving him special treatment. It was finally decided that he would be put into a single cell, separate from the other inmates.

When the police finally arrived at Mark's house, there were, indeed, plenty of reporters and cameramen just as they had expected, but there was also an angry mob of about twenty people. One man in the mob was actually screaming, "Let's hang him!"

The police had to disperse the crowd before they could even get near the front door. They knew Mark was inside because there had been an unmarked car keeping him under surveillance since the day Margaret had told the police her accusations against her husband. The police had also tapped Mark's phone to monitor his calls. Just a few hours before, he had called his mother and father.

When the police knocked on the door, Mark did not answer. They tried phoning him in the house, but he still did not answer. With the throng of press waiting for a show, the police decided they had better move quickly. They called for more back up, and six state troopers arrived within twenty minutes. They tried to kick the door in, but it was so securely locked, it would not give way. Then, a window next to the door was broken, and a police officer climbed through. He unlocked the front door, allowing a barrage of officers, weapons drawn, to flood in. When the window had been broken, the alarm system had gone off. The noise was loud and overbearing and was obviously distracting the police officers, whose faces seemed to squint in pain as they moved methodically through the house.

Suddenly, trying to be heard above the din of the alarm, two police officers simultaneously bellowed, "Up here!" Each officer witnessed the same grizzly sight as he arrived—a man lying on a bed with thirty percent of his head blown off. It was later speculated that Mark had gone down into his basement workshop and, using a hacksaw, had cut eighteen inches off the barrel of a shotgun. He had then gone upstairs into his bedroom, loaded the gun with two shells, aimed it at his temple, and pulled the trigger. Margaret's worries about Mark's interference were totally ended.

I was watching a ball game on a big screen television in a bar when I heard the news. The game was interrupted for a special bulletin. I tried to act cool, but by the time I made it out of the bar to my car, I was physically shaking. "Hell, they're going to charge me with murder; hell, they're going to charge me with murder; hell, they're going to charge me with murder." The phrase kept circling in my head. The emotional pressure was so great I could hardly breathe and I thought my heart would thump out of my chest. I was filled with guilt. Pure guilt. We had set Mark up. I was part of the scheme. Somehow, I had become enmeshed in all this, and I didn't know how it had happened. I kept telling myself, "You are not an evil person." But, the more I said it, the more evil I felt. I was petrified. The only thing I could think of was to get away, but I couldn't move.

Ten minutes later my hands stopped trembling enough so that I managed to unlock my car and get in. I drove back to my apartment and threw some clothes into a suitcase. When I left my apartment building a few minutes later, I cautiously peered up and down the street, half expecting the wail of sirens and police jumping out to handcuff me. I got back into my car and drove to the interstate. I took the ramp heading north. The police would probably expect me to head for Florida, to take a boat, so I would do the opposite. Just go is all I could think.

As I drove, the hum of the engine and the monotony of the passing highway began to lull my racing mind. I began to think more clearly. Who knew about setting up Mark? The scam guy Ralph, the photographer, and the gay guy. But they were all in California and wouldn't be under any pressure from the police. Ralph did "dirty tricks" for a living. The other two worked for Ralph regularly. When Harry hired Ralph, he had been told that he was the best in the business, a real professional. Supposedly he had set up a major presidential candidate by having a beautiful girl lure the guy to a party on a boat named *Monkey Business*. Ralph had even had enough foresight to name the boat that because of the irony. The press carried the story over and over till there was no life left in it—or the poor guy's political career. Yes, these guys were professionals. I did not need to worry about them. The only other people who knew that Mark had been set up were Margaret, Harry, and I. The bitch would hold her cool; she always did. Should I go to the police before Harry did? Maybe I could make a deal and walk if I cooperated and gave evidence first. Maybe a little community service at worst. But, what if Harry didn't say anything either?

I made a decision. I didn't want to use my car phone so that it could be traced, so I exited the interstate and found a pay phone. I had to find out if Harry had heard about Mark's death. Harry answered the phone on the first ring. As soon as I said, "Harry," he interrupted with, "Where the hell are you, Ren?" I told him that I was a hundred miles north of Columbia.

"Don't say anything over the phone," Harry cautioned, "just in case it's bugged."

We agreed to meet in the parking lot of a motel we both knew which was an hour's drive north of Columbia. That meant it would take me forty-five minutes to get there. I would have time to get a cup of coffee before Harry would get there. My nerves needed the caffeine.

When I got to the motel, Harry wasn't there yet. I sat in my car, thinking. What if this was a trick? What if Harry was setting up a trap? Any moment I could be surrounded by police. I was momentarily blinded by headlights. Suddenly I saw Harry's mini-van, headlights flickering, as it hit the speed bumps and headed toward my car.

We decided not to get a room at that motel, just in case Harry's phone had been bugged. Maybe our caution was just the result of our guilt. We felt like criminals so we thought like criminals. We got back onto the highway and drove north for two more exits. The only motel was a dilapidated place called the Tex-E-South. We each rented a room, spacing our registration time about fifteen minutes apart. Harry went first.

I put my suitcase in my room and then went to Harry's. I knew which room was his because his car was parked directly in front of the door. Even though there were no other cars around, I still glanced about before slipping into his room. He held a bottle of Kentucky whiskey in his left hand. He filled a plastic cup full.

"Do you want a drink?" Harry asked. "Because I sure do."

"No," I said. He sure appeared much calmer than I was. In my mind I was trying to decide if his demeanor was calmer or if he only seemed so because of the whiskey. We talked about our options, but the bottom line was that we had to talk to Margaret. We could drive to Florida or fly. But, Margaret had not given us a clue as to where she would be staying, only that she was going to Orlando. Harry and I finally decided to go back to the office and wait for her to call. There was a private phone there to which only Margaret, Harry, and I had the number. The three of us used this number when we absolutely had to get through to the office or when we wanted our privacy guaranteed.

We left the motel rooms two hours after we checked in and drove back to Columbia. The city streets were deserted at this time in the morning except for the homeless who were always present. We parked our cars a few blocks from the office so that no reporters on the prowl would know we were there. We also kept the lights off. We groped our way back to the conference room, the only room without windows. Once we were ensconced there with the door shut, we flicked on the lights. I told Harry he could take the sofa; I took the lounge chair. Harry was asleep within minutes. I stayed awake about an hour, my thoughts just tumbling around in my head, before I started to doze off. I awoke at 8:00 A.M. Harry was already watching the Channel 9 news. The press's angle on the story was that Mark, a guilty man, was unwilling to face his punishment so he committed suicide. There was no mention of the possibility that Mark could be innocent.

At 9:10 A.M. the phone rang. Margaret did not waste any time on cordial greetings. " Ren, I want you to get Mark's funeral arrangements made as soon as you can. His home town was Temple. Just call someplace. Let's get the bastard in the ground. And tell Harry to rent a nice house in Columbia for the kids and me. Have some furniture moved in and the lights turned on.

Get me an unlisted phone, too. Also, tell Harry to pick me up at the Columbia airport Thursday night at 7:00 at Gate 6. Don't speak to the press about anything except to say I am in tremendous grief. Oh, and you can tell them what the funeral arrangements are. Family only at the wake." She hung up as abruptly as she had begun.

Temple was a small town just outside of Spartanburg, so I got a phone book for Spartanburg, went through the Yellow Pages, and picked out a funeral home that sounded prestigious. I called and made arrangements for the burial. The funeral director would take care of transporting the body. Then, I called the coroner's office to let them know what was happening. I was a bit surprised to find out that Mark's parents had already claimed the body. I figured I had better let Margaret handle this.

On Thursday, I went with Harry to pick up Margaret at the airport. She had left the nanny and the children in Florida. When Margaret disembarked from the plane, she was not alone. She had her arm looped through the arm of an unfamiliar man. I could only describe him as a bit sleazy looking, over-dressed in a three-piece suit that was too tailored to fit his personality, which reflected that of an overburdened salesman. Margaret introduced him to us as Dave Blair, a computer company executive from New Jersey. She had met him in the airport lounge in Orlando and was so pleased to learn that having completed his sale in Orlando, he was also boarding the plane to Columbia, where he was going on business.

Margaret did not act the least bit nervous or upset. It was apparent that she had said nothing to her new-found friend about the suicide of her recently deceased husband. We all got into the Cadillac, Harry and I in the front and Margaret and Dave Blair in the back.

"Harry, take me to my new home," Margaret commanded.

Harry reached into his pocket and handed her a house key. Then he started the engine and we drove for several miles in silence. I worried that we might be stopped by the police since the car had a state senator's license plate. The car would be easy to spot. Exactly why the police would want us, I didn't know. The press had totally swallowed the story of Mark's guilt and consequential suicide. I knew I still wasn't thinking clearly, that I was still shocked about Mark's suicide and remorseful for my part in it. My mind was convinced that someone ought to punish us for what we had done. Actually, at that moment punishment would have offered relief.

When the silence became too obvious, I began to make small talk.

"Great weather we're having, isn't it?"

Neither Margaret nor Dave Blair responded.

I tried again.

"Have you seen the new First Federal building going up downtown?"

This time Harry answered with a "yeah," but that was it. I was curious as to why there was total silence in the back seat. I turned slightly, trying to catch a glimpse of Margaret. I almost choked on my own breath. Out of the corner of my eye, I could see Margaret with a set of arms around her. I could see neither person's face, but I knew instinctively that they were kissing. I wanted to vomit.

When the car pulled up to Margaret's new house, I was surprised by the choice Harry had made. The house was a modest brick structure. The only feature that set it apart from any other brick home was a nice set of columns, two stories high, giving the house the look of an old colonial.

Margaret and Dave Blair got out of the car and headed for the front door. She said not one word to either Harry or me. When it dawned on me that we were not going to be invited in, I jumped out of the car and literally ran down the front walkway. How could she not want to talk about what had happened?

"Senator Hall, could we have a word with you in private?"

The second I called her senator, I regretted it. I realized that I did not know if her friend knew she was a senator. Margaret handed the key to Dave Blair and walked toward me.

"Mark's parents had already claimed the body before I got all of the arrangements made," I blurted out.

I was expecting Margaret to start reprimanding, even screaming that I was incompetent. Instead, she gave a slight wave of her hand and said, "Good. I won't have to pay for the bastard's funeral." Then she pivoted and started back down the walkway.

I was stunned, speechless. For the first time I took notice that the computer executive was having a hard time getting the key in the lock.

"But...but should I call a press conference?"

"Sure, call a damn press conference for tomorrow afternoon, Ren."

The clipped words were just tossed over her shoulder at me. And by the time she said them, Harry had gotten out of the car and unlocked the door of the house. Margaret and Dave Blair went into the house, shutting us out. Harry and I got back into the car. As we backed out of the driveway into the road, Harry looked over at me.

"She really is a bitch. Her husband just committed suicide, which she orchestrated. He's not even in the ground yet, and she's screwing another guy."

"She is a bitch," I agreed. "And we have to get a news conference together for her by tomorrow afternoon." I didn't want to think about what was going to happen in Margaret's new house after we left.

I tried to get Harry to talk about the press conference, but he could not get his mind off Mark being in a coffin.

"It's our fault. We helped put him there." Harry said this at least three times. I knew he was scared of being discovered but I was glad that he was voicing his feeling of guilt. It made me feel better. I had felt the weight of guilt the instant I had heard about Mark's death.

Harry had driven me all the way back to my apartment and still nothing had been settled about the press conference. We agreed to meet early in the morning to work out the details.

In the morning Harry and I decided it would be advantageous to wait a few days after the funeral to have a press conference. We called Margaret and she actually seemed pleased about putting it off. For the next few days, Harry remained in the office, answering the phone. Most of the calls were just from reporters. As for myself, I spent much of my time in a local bar called Hoppers. Keeping a bit drunk helped me to keep the guilt of what we had done at bay. Margaret stayed shacked up in her house with her computer executive.

Harry also had the job of going to the store each evening for Margaret. It was decided that she would not venture from the house until after the news conference.

The media had no idea where she was and we wanted to keep the new house a secret as long as we could.

In the morning two days before the press conference, I went to Margaret's house so that we could plan the strategy. I pulled into her driveway and just sat in the car for a while. I thought, "I have to quit this job! For $37,000 a year this is hell. Hell, doing this for any amount of money is absurd!"

When Margaret answered the door and let me in, she was overly friendly.

"Ren, how good it is to see you. Come in, come in. We've got a lot to do. Do you want anything? A drink? Coffee? A soda?"

"No, not right now."

I did not see Dave Blair hovering anywhere. Maybe he had gone back into whatever hole he had crawled out of. Margaret listened intently to what I had to tell her. She did not interrupt once. That was unusual. When I finished speaking, she looked at me intently as only she could do. "Ren, I think we need to end this mess with a big bang. I am going to finish the press conference by saying how much I loved Mark and that I had been hoping all along to restore our marriage. Then I'll start crying. I've been practicing for four days. I think I've got it down."

Before I could say anything, Margaret began to cry. Tears began to trickle from her eyes. Her face showed sorrow, passionate sorrow. She was good. She was really good. I couldn't believe it. I knew my mouth was hanging open. Then, almost as soon as she had begun, she stopped.

"Ren, when I begin to cry, I want you to step in and introduce yourself as my office manager. Tell the press that there will be no more questions, that I am still in too much pain and shock. Then give me thirty more seconds in front of the microphone, and I'll say, 'Jesus, help me' and then lead me away. Better yet, get that old lady who helped out on the campaign—what's her name—Mrs. Lee—that's it—to reach out for my hand and lead me away. People will think she's my grandmother. That will look really good. That will make the finale of the news conference so dramatic I bet we'll be the lead story on the evening news. They love that kind of stuff. Nobody will care what I said. All they'll remember is me, the Senator, the loving wife, bereft, tearful."

I know my mouth was still open. Margaret was revved up. She loved this scheme.

"Ren, if I do this as well as I think I can, we'll get votes you can't even imagine. Every woman that has ever been wronged by a man will vote for me. Multitudes of men will vote for me because they will feel guilty about their dirty little secrets. And, by God, I'll get all the Jesus lovers. The possibilities are endless!"

My head nodded in agreement, but my stomach ached and a voice inside me was saying I needed a shot of whiskey. The whole mess made me physically ill. I had never had a drink of alcohol before I started working for Margaret. Now, the guilt was unbearable without some alcohol to dilute it.

Margaret made some small talk which didn't really register with me, and then her eyes held mine again.

"Ren, I know we have been through a lot lately, but you haven't been doing what I told you."

I looked at her quizzically.

"You haven't been making me look Christian. I want people to see Jesus Christ when they see me. Ren, do you know how many Jesus lovers there are in South Carolina? Enough to win any office. I worship the Senate. It's my god, but out of the corner of my eye I can see another god, a better one. One with more power. Ren, stick with me. I promise you that we're going places."

I just stared at her and mechanically moved my head in agreement. She scared the living daylights out of me. "I'll have Harry and the office staff start working on the press conference."

Margaret looked at me again. This time her eyes were cold. I could never figure out her eyes. I turned my head and averted my eyes to look at a clock. I could not stand the pressure of looking at her. I knew she was staring at me as she spoke.

"Father Howell, the hell with Harry. You do it; you're the man."

What in the world was she talking about? Why was she calling me Father Howell?

"Ren, you better get back to the office. You have a lot of work to do."

I didn't say a word, but my mind was racing with thoughts. Turning Margaret into a religious person, making her look like a believer in Jesus, was one monumental task.

When I left Margaret's house, I did not go to the office. I headed straight to a bar. Hell, I could not believe what I had just heard. What a bitch, what a liar, what a schemer she was! I couldn't even think of words that would adequately describe her. As I sped toward the bar, I listened to a country music station. I turned the radio up trying to blast the image of Margaret out of my mind. But, Margaret never left my mind until after my second double at the bar, and only then because the bartender engaged me in a compelling conversation about baseball.

The press conference went amazingly well. The media swallowed the whole of Margaret's story as if her version was nothing but the truth. When Margaret started crying, doing her "Jesus scene," I actually saw reporters with tears in their eyes. It was unbelievable. My stomach began to bother me again.

After the press conference I was stuck with the job of bringing Margaret to the airport. Harry was busy hustling reporters to get as much good press as he could. When Margaret first got into the car, we made some small talk, mainly about the press conference. Then there was silence for the rest of the drive. I would sure be glad to get her on that plane to Florida so that I could get a drink. I needed one badly. I was glad that Harry had gotten her bags from the house earlier that day so that we didn't have to go there first before we headed for the airport. I wondered if Margaret had told the kids yet about their father. The bitch had probably told them over the phone; how impersonal but how like her.

At the airport I got the luggage out of the trunk. I checked in the bags at the counter and left Margaret sitting in the lounge area waiting to board the plane. I was ready to leave.

"Ren, we are going to take this all the way now. Everything is gone that stood in my way. Father Howell, you get working. I want people to see me as a super Christian woman by the time I get back. When they say Senator Hall—I want people to think Jesus."

That's all she said. I didn't know what to say. What was all this "Father" stuff about? I hated it when she called me Father Howell. I thought about creating a scene and screaming not to call me that, but, of course, I didn't. Instead, I gave her a "thumbs up" signal and said, "Just like Jesus." Margaret dismissed me with a mere wave of her hand. I obeyed and walked away.

I did not wait to drive back into the city to my regular bar. I needed a drink now. I headed for the lounge at the airport. My brain was so distracted that I bumped right into a woman and had to apologize.

Was Margaret crazy? She was lucky not to be sitting in jail, and all she was thinking of was more power, a higher position. I was ashamed of my own last comment to her. "Just like Jesus." Why did I say that? How could I say that? I kept running her words through my mind, over and over. I couldn't make any sense out of them. As I sat on the barstool, I finally told myself that she was just a power-hungry bitch and tried to let that resolve the conflicts in my mind.

Potentates

Chapter 5

When Margaret returned from Florida two weeks later, she was unusually happy. Plans began to be made for her next Senate campaign. We constantly went over names of possible opposition candidates. Names came and went, but it was difficult to create a campaign strategy because we did not have any idea who the opposition would be. We stayed in close contact with our base group of supporters, and Margaret spoke at churches in the district, mostly black churches with black congregations. The preacher would allow her to speak for five minutes before the official service started. Our goal was to have her say *Jesus* ten times in those five minutes.

Harry and I, meanwhile, worked the phones, doing what we referred to as "friendly calls," which meant calling business people to remind them of the favors Margaret's office had done for them. Over the past two years, we had been able to get the state to award jobs to several contracting companies, ranging from houses to state buildings to bridges. Margaret had also cast the deciding vote against usury laws. This action had gotten the bankers and small loan companies on our side. The insurance companies were with us because we had kept a consumer advocate from getting a seat on the state insurance board. The chemical companies loved us because Margaret had never seen a chemical she thought was dangerous. The list seemed endless. Hundreds of calls had to be made each month.

A month later we found out that Margaret would have no opposition in the primary election. What astounded us even more two months later, though, was that there was not going to be any opposition in the general election either. Six months earlier I had been getting my resume updated, ready to look for another job because I had never really considered the possibility that Margaret would win the Senate seat again. Of course, I knew all the sordid details that the public didn't. Now, six months later, everything had changed. We used the opportunity to go after money from every corporation we could find. We told them that the election was a sure thing. Our saying became "you can have a friend in the Senate with no risk." The office was making an all-out effort to build up the campaign war chest as much as possible. We were relentless and no amount was enough. So, the money poured in.

A surprise did come about three weeks before the general election. The mayor of Waverley, Steve Byers, began to mount a write-in campaign for the Senate seat. In realistic terms, the write-in campaign had no place to go. We knew it was going to be extremely difficult, if not impossible, for Byers to get enough votes as a write-in candidate, but the Byers's candidacy did force us to take the election semi-seriously.

Margaret, Harry, and I held a closed meeting in Margaret's office. We decided to be on the safe side and deliver bag money to key black leaders. These leaders would keep their share of the money and then would use the rest to "persuade" members of their neighborhoods to vote for the candidate who had given the money. We tried to keep the bag money to a minimum. The black leaders, however, knew that we needed them, so they asked for the same amount they had received in the last election.

Margaret hated to be manipulated so she considered her other options. One was for Harry to give Byers money to stay out of the race, but no practical way could be found to approach him. We also considered getting the governor to appoint Byers to head some state board position, but the governor wanted too much in trade—he wanted to control Margaret's Senate votes for a whole year. We had made promises to too many corporations, in exchange for their support, to capitulate. We even considered a double-cross—let the governor make the appointment and then Margaret would still vote the way she had promised the corporations, but we were afraid we would get caught in the middle. In the end, after much negotiation with key black leaders, we agreed to the same amount of bag money as the last election.

We thought we had everything worked out, but when Harry went to deliver the money, there was a new problem. Three of the black ministers would not take any money and began to speak out against the bag money system. We were seriously worried for a while, but Harry left the office early one morning and said he would take care of the matter. Within a few days I heard that a sizeable number of the church members of these three outspoken ministers had threatened to leave their respective churches and join other churches. The three black ministers had been silenced. I never did learn for sure how Harry managed that one, but I figured he had bribed some church deacons. I didn't want to ask, and, for some reason, I really did not want to know.

When Election Day finally came and was over, Margaret had gotten 62% of the vote. Byers's write-in campaign got 14%. The most revealing statistic, however, was that 24% of the people who had voted in the election had refused to vote for the only name on the ballet; instead, they had opted to leave it blank. It had always been my intention to quit my job as office manager after the election and find new employment, but, somehow, I lingered on. Margaret had a hold on me, one I did not even understand.

We got to rest for about three weeks after the Senate race was over and the victory was Margaret's. Then, Margaret became obsessed with Harry finding out what the numbers were on the past lieutenant governor's race. So, Harry did the numbers. This required finding out where the votes came from—how many of the votes were rural, how many urban. What part of the state had former lieutenant governors come from? How much money had the candidates spent? How many women had voted and how many men? What age were the voters? And so on and so on.

For six months Harry compiled the data while I tried to handle constituent services and scheduling. Margaret continued to build her Christian image in her spare time by visiting churches all over the state. She had memorized a few Bible passages, and these scriptures, along with the word *Jesus*, became her new language. She began to take voice lessons so that she could get up before a congregation and sing "Amazing Grace." It was all so totally phony to me, but I soon began to realize that most people, especially those in the churches she visited, were not so cynical.

I was also having a hard time understanding why Harry was doing all of this research. It was clear to me that Margaret was in the race for lieutenant governor no matter what the numbers showed. But, trying to make plans four years away gave me a headache. I had a hard time taking the bid for lieutenant governor seriously because, in my mind, it was a miracle that we had made it through the Senate race.

I had a hard time figuring Margaret out, too. She wanted people to identify with her as a mother, yet she spent hardly any time with her two children. Mark Jr. and Tammy were beyond unruly. I found excuses to leave the office whenever they came in. Margaret also wanted people to identify with her as a Christian, yet most of her actions were totally un-Christian. I would have to agree, though, that Margaret had a sharp mind. She had no trouble keeping track of which people and which corporations had given her campaign money and how much each had given. She was a pro at playing the political game. She easily made winning deals. She had a gift for putting the best face on a bad situation and making people feel good, as if they had won—but Margaret was the only winner.

Many legislators complained that Margaret was combative with other senators in committee meetings and on the Senate floor. It seemed as if she looked for battles. If someone said something she did not like, she would scream back, be sarcastic, or embarrass the person any way she could. On one occasion a senator by the name of Timmons jokingly said that secretaries really have all of the power. Margaret totally lost it. She shrieked that Senator Timmons was a sexist pig who did not have the right to be a senator.

"I'll find some woman who will beat your ass in the next election!" she screamed at him. Luckily, there were no reporters around at the time or utter disaster would have befallen.

Margaret had no personal life at this time either, except for the computer salesman Dave Blair, who showed up from New Jersey every few weeks. She did not even have another senator or representative who was a good friend.

All of this behavior was in direct conflict with Margaret's new public image of being "close to Jesus." Fortunately for Margaret, the public did not notice because she had embedded herself within a Christian moral wall. Publicly she spoke against abortion or "baby killing," as she referred to it. Crime had to stop, she said, and she was adamant that the death penalty was the answer. In one speech she even said, "Strap them in the chair and send them to hell." The audience had cheered but the press had questioned her bluntness. Harry finally convinced Margaret that it was not a good political move for a Christian senator to talk about the death penalty in such a forthright manner. Margaret also advocated other ideas: Christian schools were the answer to the failing public education system; prayer in school would end the moral decay of society; and ending welfare payments would stop illegal drug use and teenage pregnancy.

Whether or not anyone agreed with Margaret's outspoken opinions, one thing was clear to me—her rhetoric did not match her behavior as a human being. What was most frightening about Margaret was her opinion of herself. She truly believed that she was this wonderful Christian, god-fearing woman fighting the evils of the world. Taking money for votes was a justifiable action that one had to do to fight evil one more day. She eased her conscience about her neglect of her children and her verbal abuse of others around her by saying it was the price one had to pay so that good would triumph and she could do God's work.

It was about a year after the Senate race that Harold Todds, a congressman from the second district, called and offered me a position as head of his staff. I jumped at the chance. No more of "the bitch." No more sneaky or disgusting tricks. I agreed that I would start working at Todds's office in two months. I would give a four-week notice and take a month's vacation before I started my new job.

When I went in to give Margaret my notice, she literally flipped out. One of the more eloquent names I was called was an "ungrateful son-of-a-bitch." I knew the next four weeks would be mentally and emotionally exhausting for me. Two weeks before my time was up, John Sanders, a senior staff member with Congressman Todd, called me. We set up an appointment for the following Monday at The Cornerstone, a local restaurant I liked. I assumed I was going to be filled in on the "privileged" information for my new position.

I arrived at The Cornerstone early and ordered a scotch. When Sanders arrived, I could tell he had bad news, for all of his body gestures radiated nervousness. As he wiped his glasses for about the fifth time since he had sat down, he squeaked out an apology that the Congressman, unfortunately, could not give me the job. He continued his prolific apology but never gave any logical reason why the job offer was negated. Finally, I was able to pry the information from him. I had all I could do to control the rage that welled up within me. I should have known. Margaret had hired a private investigator to dig into Todd's background and come up with some "dirt" that she could use as leverage. The investigator had found some indiscretion; what it was, Sanders would not say. However, it was important enough so that Margaret could use it to get what she wanted. She had had Harry call Todd and tell him that if he gave me the job, she would make sure the press got the information—anonymously, of course.

I purposely did not return to work for the next three days. No one from the office even called to question where I was. When I went in on Friday, mainly to get my paycheck, there was a letter in Margaret's handwriting on my desk. I opened it, expecting some sarcastic words to put me in my place. Instead, the letter praised the work I was doing and had done and stated that I would be getting a substantial raise. I saw this for what it was, though, just another form of Margaret's manipulation.

There were times when I realized just how much Margaret loved power. I had come to believe that all people enjoyed being in a position of power, but for Margaret power was different. Power to her was like heroin to an addict—she just could never get enough. The more she had, the more she wanted. Most of the time the employees in the office just saw her as "the bitch." But Margaret was a chameleon—the side presented to the public was that of an ordinary, ambitious politician, who was overtly Christian, but I saw the monster side, the side that consumed people in order to control their lives. Like the heroin addict, she would let nothing stand in the way of her addiction. If her children suffered, that was the price that had to be paid. If her husband died in the process of her satisfying her thirst for power, then he died. That's all there was to his death, except maybe the inconvenience of having a press conference. If I lost the opportunity for a better job, that was my problem, and Margaret would just say, "Why didn't he understand what I needed?" If she made a mockery of people's religion, that was the price they paid so that her need for power could be satisfied. In Margaret's mind, even Jesus loved power. According to her, Jesus sought to be the actual ruling king of the Jews, but he made a fatal mistake—he trusted a crowd that turned on him. Margaret saw the Apostles as stealthy men who capitalized on Jesus' mistake. That summed up the New Testament, according to Margaret.

Margaret's interpretations of events never ceased to amaze me, and because of my privileged knowledge of past events, I knew that in the race for Lt. Governor nothing would be sacred. Power had become her god. The need for it consumed her, and whoever got destroyed in the process really did not matter in the slightest.

What was even more frightening as I looked around at other politicians was that they were not much different. Some of them were more polite, some were even loyal to select supporters, but in the end, most were addicted to power. They said the right things publicly but, in truth, did what they had to do to stay in office. There were some exceptions, of course, real people fighting for a cause or just decent people who wanted to serve to do some good.

But, as I watched the political system, I saw these honest people losing more and more battles. They were being torn to pieces by the ogres like Margaret and corporate presidents, who also sought power endlessly. The Political Action Committees would find a "wanna be." They would put up the money for the campaign and create an image for their new star. Most likely the public would buy into the image and the "wanna be" would be elected as senator, congressman, or councilman.

The public would think they were being represented. In truth, though, the Political Action Committees would see their new star as simply an extended employee who protected their interests. The new senator or congressman was bought and paid for, and his or her vote in the legislature would be so predictable that I often wondered why newspapers bothered to print what legislation passed or failed. One could hardly call it news. The decision on how to vote had been made months earlier in corporate board rooms when the board members had decided which candidates were going to get their money. As Margaret would say at the end of some of her speeches, "God bless our political system!"

Chapter 6

The next three years went by quickly. Somehow, even though I had kept promising myself that I would leave Margaret's Senate office, leave the state of South Carolina, I found myself still immersed in her race for Lt. Governor. She had made it through the primary season with no opposition, but now that she was in the general election, a three-way race had developed. Margaret's main opponent was State Representative Elliot Shaw, a shrewd politician who had been the Speaker of the House of Representatives. His father was a manufacturer doing military contracts and had lots of money and connections. While his father made the money deals for the campaign, young Elliot, a tall, heavyset forty-four year old, played the part of a "good-old boy." During football season Elliot could be found at high school games around the state. He never missed the opportunity to shake hands with the family and friends of star players. Elliot's ambition in life was to have a big house and a fancy car and to be governor someday. His daddy had taken care of the first two, the house and the car, and was working on the third.

Margaret knew Elliot's weak point with the public—everything had been handed to him by his father. She loved to play upon this theme while speaking to crowds. She referred to him as "that little rich boy" or as the "silver shoe boy," which alluded to a fancy pair of boots Elliot had that were decorated with sterling silver stars and stripes. Margaret would stand before a crowd and in a voice of sincerity ask, "Can a little rich boy really understand how you feel after a hard day's work? Can he really understand how you feel about Jesus?" The crowds loved it.

Besides Elliot Shaw, there was an independent candidate in the race, Susan Darrel. She was an articulate speaker and well informed on the issues. Margaret hated appearing with her at stump rallies because Margaret's rhetoric sounded foolish next to Susan's detailed analysis of how previous economic laws had impacted the cost of government. At one stump rally the issue of crime had come up. Margaret's response was that we needed more jails to throw "them" into and give "them" the death penalty. "Them," of course, referred to black people. The words were selected carefully to appeal to racists without the press being able to print that such an appeal was being made. Susan, on the other hand, advocated the establishment of boot camps for delinquent teenagers. She cited studies which proved that the successful rehabilitation of young offenders through boot camps would reduce crime and, therefore, reduce the need to spend more tax dollars on jails.

Susan had grown up in Odessa, South Carolina. Her parents owned a local jewelry store, which did enough business to support the family in a moderate life style. Susan was an *A* student throughout high school and received a full scholastic scholarship to the University of South Carolina, where she studied business. She intended to return home and run her parents' jewelry store. Along the way, though, she became intrigued with law, so she went on to law school at a university in New England and graduated at the top of her class. After law school she worked for two years for a large firm in Greenville and then went home to Odessa to open her own office. She specialized in helping small businesses and was quite successful. Clients liked her keen mind, her attention to detail, and her genuine enthusiasm. Susan met her husband Stan when her parents retired and sold the jewelry store to him. Susan and Stan had a good marriage, and their two children could often be seen on the campaign trail with their mother.

Even though Susan had all of this going for her, she was not much more than an inconvenience to Margaret's goal of becoming lieutenant governor. Politics is, after all, about money, and Susan did not have much, at least not the kind of money it takes to buy television, radio, and newspaper ads statewide. She was a great candidate. She was articulate, had lots of good ideas, was committed to her principles, and had a family as close to perfect as one can get—but, she had no money. This meant she would be lucky if she got twenty percent of the vote on Election Day.

The good news for Margaret was that the polls showed that most of the votes Susan was going to get were coming from votes that, otherwise, would have been going to Elliot Shaw. If the trend continued, Susan Darrel's independent candidacy was going to make Margaret the next lieutenant governor.

Harry was now on a leave of absence from the Senate office, working full-time as Margaret's campaign manager. The campaign headquarters was located in a downtown storefront building. He had a staff of several people working under him. This left me operating the Senate office alone. It was a lot of extra work, but that was fine with me as long as I did not have to be intimately involved in the campaign. I did attend bi-weekly campaign strategy meetings, and I also met with Harry once a week.

As the campaign entered the last six weeks, Harry began to look so tired and worn out that I became concerned about his health. He had lost thirty pounds, and his normally ruddy coloring had turned wan. I met him at a neighborhood restaurant one night. When I asked him how he was doing, he began to complain about Margaret.

"That bitch has me working all day in the campaign office and I spend all my evenings delivering bag money. She doesn't trust anyone else, so I'm either on the plane flying or in my car driving somewhere in the state till two in the morning. And I've got the feeling that if we get caught up with, I'm going to be the guy holding the bag. Good pun, huh? Holding the bag? Get it?"

"Yeah, I get it. How much money has gone out?" I regretted the words as soon as they left my mouth. I knew it would be better if I did not know. "It's okay, Harry. I know that's confidential. Don't tell me."

But Harry spoke anyway, "Two hundred thousand, plus. Hell, it's been a nightmare just collecting it and keeping that kind of money off the books. Damn, Ren, it's crazy. I've heard that all of these so-called minority leaders are taking money from Shaw's people, too. We're doing all this, and I wonder who will get their vote in the end? But," Harry grinned, "I do believe we are paying the most. Wouldn't it be a kick in the pants if we're paying them off and Shaw's paying them off, and then the real black leaders, who won't take money, get them to vote for Susan Darrel and she wins!" Harry sat back in his chair. "What the hell do you think, Ren?"

The question made me nervous. It was as if he had read my mind.

Before I could answer, though, Harry said, "We have to watch our ass; our jobs are on the lines."

"Get some rest, Harry. You look beat."

Harry stared me. "Easy for you to say. Are you going to deliver the bag money for me tonight?"

The waitress came to the table at that moment. Harry wasn't very pleasant to her. "Can you just go away and not bother us for a few more minutes?" Harry said rather brusquely.

"I'm sorry, miss. Lynda? Is that your name?" I asked, reading her name off the identification tag pinned just below her left shoulder.

"Yes, sir, Lynda. Lynda Grayson," the waitress said.

I could tell that Harry had hurt her feelings, so I gave her my best smile and said, "We'll be ready to order in five minutes."

"I'm sorry," Lynda said. "I didn't mean to interrupt you. Some people get really upset if you don't get their order right away. I'll be back in a few minutes."

As soon as the waitress left, Harry started speaking again.

"Ren, don't worry about this election. We've got a sixteen-year-old girl who is going to show up at Skip Keen's door—you know, the news reporter—and tell him that Elliot got her pregnant and doesn't want to take responsibility."

"Come on, Harry. Do we have to do that kind of shit again?"

"Don't worry, Ren. The girl's been told she's working for some businessman named Don Page. Remember him? Elliot's father screwed him over pretty good in a business deal. If the girl ever comes clean with the truth, Don Page will take the hit. It's the double lie, Ren. Most people get caught lying because they lie just once. It takes two lies to make it work. Besides, you know Elliot's father is out there trying to figure out how to screw us over. We're just going to get them first."

This was too much. I changed the subject by pointing out a gorgeous girl who had just walked in. Lynda came back and took our order. The hamburgers and fries arrived within minutes, and Harry and I talked office gossip for the rest of the meal. Finally, I looked at my watch, pretended I was late for an appointment, and left.

Halfway back to my apartment, it finally registered with me who Don Page was. He owned an equipment company that drilled wells, Piedmont Drilling Equipment. He had been one of Margaret's big contributors for years. Why was Margaret putting him in the middle of some scandal? It made no sense to turn against someone who had helped us. It was yet another affirmation that Margaret would do anything for power. By the time I got back to my apartment, I had resolved once again to quit as soon as the election was over.

The phone rang as soon as I got in the door. It was the waitress, Lynda Grayson. I had left my credit card at the restaurant. Half an hour later I was back at the restaurant. The place wasn't very busy so I was able to thank Lynda personally.

"Thank you very much for calling. Lots of people wouldn't have bothered to even try to return the card," I said.

"Oh, you're more than welcome," she smiled. "I just looked your name up in the phone book. It wasn't really any trouble. I've lost my credit card before, more than once actually, so I know what a hassle it is to cancel it out and wait for a new one to come."

"You're right about that," I said.

"I'm sorry I got your friend so upset," Lynda said chagrined. "I haven't been working here that long, so people will have to bear with me."

"No, no. It wasn't your fault at all. Harry's been under a lot of pressure lately. He isn't usually rude like that at all."

Lynda was a very attractive woman. She must have been about thirty. She was petite, probably only five, five, and I doubted that she weighed more than a hundred and ten pounds. I was captivated by her smile. It was real. It radiated warmth and caring. I asked her if she wanted to get a cup of coffee before she went home, and she accepted without any hesitation. I knew the attraction between us was mutual.

Over coffee I found out that she was a widow. Her husband had died as the result of a car accident, but not before a small fortune in hospital bills had accumulated. He had been on a business trip and fallen asleep at the wheel. Since the accident had been his fault, the insurance company would not pay all of the expenses. She had lost her house but now shared a nice apartment with a roommate. She worked at the electric company during the day and waitressed three nights a week trying to pay off the debts. She wouldn't think about bankruptcy she said. It just wasn't the right thing to do.

I told her a little about my job, about Harry and Margaret. I didn't tell her about any of the underhanded stunts we had done. I knew I never would. Lynda was too good to have to be burdened with any of the "evils" that continuously haunted me. I often remembered that night as the beginning of a wonderful relationship. I saw Lynda as often as I could. Being with her always seemed a haven for me.

Two weeks before the general election, I received a call from campaign headquarters. An emergency strategy meeting was being called for 8:00 the next morning. I tried to think of excuses not to go, but in the end, I went. When I walked into the room, the first news I heard was that Harry had collapsed and was in the hospital. It became evident that there was a power struggle going on over who was going to take Harry's place as campaign manager. One of the workers suggested that I should take Harry's place because I had been around the longest. I declined, of course, saying I had my hands full with the operation of the Senate office and didn't need any more responsibilities. The arguing continued for a good half hour.

Then, Margaret arrived and settled the matter for all. She rose from her chair at the head of the table and in a low, yet authoritative, voice announced, "Jane Chappel will be the temporary campaign manager until Harry comes back." I could tell from the tone of Margaret's voice that no one had better question her decision. Jane's appointment made sense. She was one of our senior campaign workers and, actually, Harry's top assistant.

"Ren, will you please open the meeting with a prayer," Margaret ordered.

I opened the meeting with a prayer that Harry's health would improve. Praying seemed to make everyone in the room uncomfortable, everyone that is except Margaret, who went into her Jesus routine. That made me uncomfortable. The meeting was brief, and Margaret said she would bring Jane up to speed on everything.

After the meeting adjourned, Margaret asked me to have breakfast with her. I told her I had already eaten, hoping that would get me out of the invitation. Unfortunately, she gave me that look, the one that said she would not accept no for an answer. "Ren, we have to talk." So, off we went to breakfast.

After Margaret had eaten and I had had three cups of coffee, she began. "Ren, somebody has to do Harry's job, and you're the only one I trust."

"But, I thought you just appointed Jane to take Harry's place," I responded quizzically.

"Ren, I'm not talking about the campaign."

Suddenly I realized what she was talking about. My entire insides felt as if they had just dropped from a gigantic roller coaster.

"Ren, we only have one more delivery to make. I need you to do this for me."

Before I could say anything, Margaret was telling me where the bag money needed to go, who was getting it, and where I was picking the money up.

"When you are in Leesbury, you also need to stop to see a man named John Maxwell; he's a black funeral director. Word is he's not too fond of me. Cozy up to him, flatter him, do whatever you have to do, but try to get his support." Margaret looked at her watch. "Well, I've got an appointment. I'll get the check. Thanks, Ren. I'm depending on you for this." And then she left.

It was Monday morning; the delivery was not to take place until Thursday night. I had a lot to think about, a lot to worry about, between now and then.

I did not sleep at all Monday night. I spent Tuesday afternoon at a local bar. During the past year I had realized that my drinking had been getting worse, maybe even uncontrollable, so I had stopped going to bars completely. Lynda Grayson, the lady that I had been seeing for the last few weeks, was good for me. Drinking was not part of her lifestyle. Now here I was, sitting at a bar and realizing that I did not want to be there. But, it was my way of dealing with the bag money. I did not want to deliver the money, but I felt obligated to do so.

If I quit or if Margaret fired me, I knew she would make it impossible for me to get a job in the political arena in South Carolina, and that was the only field, besides the church, that I had any experience in. My salary was now over fifty thousand, and there was certainly no one who was going to pay me that kind of money as a neophyte in any other field. Besides, my relationship with Lynda was important to me. I didn't want to leave South Carolina or her. She was good, untainted. A quiver seeped through my whole body as I thought about all of the hoaxes and deceit Margaret had gotten away with.

I was also paranoid that, if I left, Margaret would use me as the scapegoat for all the past dirty tricks if they ever became a legal issue. Once you cross the line of illegal activities, it is difficult, nearly impossible, to return. Dirty tricks are like a bad addiction—they provide a momentary high and give you the sensation of being powerful. The next morning, though, you know who you are—a person who wins by destroying others. The truth drives you into such despair that another dirty trick needs to be done so that you can forget the debasement and feel the high again. One dirty trick leads to another and then another.

The public, or at least the majority of the public, saw Margaret as this righteous Christian woman, fighting to save them from immoral people—the murderers, the thieves, the abortionists. The list went on and on. She was saving them taxes too, at least the rich ones. People thought her a moral, ethical person, but under that thin veneer was the real person, a fiend who would destroy anyone who got in the way of her consuming need for more power. I knew that there was no book thick enough to contain the sinister way that she had plotted against her husband, her colleagues in the senate, and the public in general. Every lobbyist in South Carolina knew she could be bought. The only question was how much it would take.

Whenever an opponent confronted Margaret about her own record, she would lie or evade the issue. When environmentalists asked about her support of bills that destroyed the South Carolina environment, she hid behind the issue of jobs. Her standard defense was always "We need jobs for South Carolinians." When asked why she accepted so much money from corporations that were doing business with the state government, she hid behind her femininity. "In order for a woman to get elected," she said,   "she has to raise large sums of money, and these businesses are just trying to ensure that women get a fair chance." The fact that these corporations gave no money to women, unless they passed along state contracts to them, never entered Margaret's mind. She seemed to forget all the times that she had had Harry call to have the license of a contractor suspended for a few days so that he would be ineligible to bid on a job, allowing her contractor to slip in with the winning bid.

When questioned about dirty politics, her treatment of other senators that she did not like, and almost any other negative activity, her response would be a fervent, "I am a good Christian woman. How can you ask such a question? I know the press doesn't like Christians and they know that I am one. That's why they are always going after me!"

The truth of the matter was that we were constantly taking members of the press on fishing trips, buying them expensive meals, and getting family members appointed to state committees. Editors, especially, were treated like royalty. Some news people, though, would not accept anything, but they were in the minority. Once I remember sitting in a restaurant with Harry. A young reporter, just on the job for a few months, came in, and we asked him if he would like to sit with us. He ate with us, but when the bill came and Harry was going to pay it with office funds, the young reporter got really proud and boasted, "My paper would get upset if I jeopardized our neutrality by letting you buy me lunch. I'll pay for my own." So, we let him.

On the way back to the office, Harry and I had a good laugh. What the reporter didn't know was that Harry and I had been working with one of the board members of the newspaper, helping him to get a government loan for a car dealership that he and his brother wanted to start in a small city fifty miles outside of Columbia. In exchange, he was getting the editor to write good editorials about Margaret. Editors are a lot like cops. When they're honest and take their job seriously, they become the protectors of the people and deserve all the honor and respect they get. But, when they go bad, it's an ugly mess because they'll print or say anything if the price is right. And they usually sell out cheap.

Chapter 7

When Thursday afternoon came, I found myself driving toward Leesbury. I had the bag money. Earlier in the day I had carefully hidden it in the trunk of my car, but at the last minute I got a panic attack and decided to rent a car. I tried to reason everything out. If the police stopped me—which was very unlikely—and they found the money, I could always say that it must have been in the trunk when I rented the car. I even put my overnight bag in the back seat so that it would seem plausible that I had not even opened the trunk. Weeks later when I told Harry about renting the car, he laughed so hard that he choked on the coffee he was drinking. Months later when we were working alone in the office, he was still kidding me about the rental car for the bag money.

Bag money delivery had become routine for Harry, but it scared the hell out of me. I physically got sick to my stomach. As I headed toward Leesbury, I listened to some new tapes. I had bought them especially for the trip to take my mind off what I was doing, but it was not working. Finally, I tuned the radio to a talk station and listened to the political rhetoric from a local radio host whose name I can't even remember. All I remember was an endless string of rightwing callers, militantly arguing with the host. Two hours after I left Columbia, I drove across the city limits of Leesbury.

The map that I had been given to find where the drop was to take place did not seem to relate to where I was. Luckily I was an hour early. I stopped at a convenience store to get a cup of coffee and ask directions. I was only a couple of miles away from the street I needed to be on. I found Styles Street easily enough. The street was filled with one-story frame houses; I couldn't tell one from the other. I saw an elderly black man walking down the side of the street, so I pulled over and asked if he knew where Mr. Walters lived.

"Young man, it's the only two-story house on the street," he said concisely. Then he turned and walked on.

He was right. There was only one. I parked in front of the house rather than pulling into the driveway and went to the front door. As soon as I knocked, a young black man wearing headphones opened the door. A quick nod of his head told me to enter. There were several other men in a room to the left.

"I'm here to meet Mr. Walters," I said.

"Down the hallway to the back. His office is there."

I was about to say "thanks," but he had already turned and was heading back to the room with the men. At the end of the hallway, there was a door with light emanating through the etched glass window. I knocked and waited. To say that I was apprehensive was an understatement. How had Margaret talked me into this? I was about to knock again when the door opened. Before me stood a light skinned black man, rail thin, about five seven. He looked about fifty-five years old, but for the life of me, I could never figure out how old a black person was from his appearance anyway. As I stepped into the office, the man's suit, made of some silky material, reflected the light so brilliantly that I was blinded for a moment.

"Mr. Walters?" I asked tentatively.

"Yes."

"I'm from Senator Hall's office. I've got the delivery." At that moment I realized that I had forgotten the briefcase of money in the trunk of the car. I felt like an idiot.

"Excuse me, sir. I forgot my briefcase in the car. I'll be right back."

"No problem," he said. I could see a faint smile at the corners of his mouth. "Go right out this door here."

I excused myself and went to get the money. When I returned, Walters was still at the door, bidding me to come back in. The office had a dark mahogany desk, a four-drawer gray metal filing cabinet, and four simple cushioned chairs. The walls were bare. There were no family pictures, no licenses, no plaques or awards. No indication of who the occupant was. Walters motioned to a chair and I sat down. I knew he could sense my nervousness. The more I tried to control it, the more evident it became. I thought about beginning with some small talk. Maybe I could ask him what kind of business he was in. No, that might not be a good question considering the circumstances under which I was here.

Walters had opened the top drawer of the file cabinet. When he turned around, he had a bottle of whiskey and two clear plastic cups. When he glanced at me, I could see that he was amused by my nervousness. I knew he wanted to laugh, but he restrained himself.

"Do you want a drink?"

He didn't wait for an answer. He just poured some whiskey into the cup and handed it to me. I took the drink and began to sip it although I had an urge to down all of it in one gulp.

"I am impressed with your Senator Hall, Ren. She'll make a great lieutenant governor."

Panic surged through my body. He knew my name. How did he know my name? No one should have told him my name. I tried to think of something positive to say about Margaret, but nothing came to my mind. I knew I looked pathetic but I just couldn't think. Walters didn't seem to be bothered at all by my inarticulateness.

"My people should just go and vote for Senator Hall, but you know they have such great needs. A little extra money helps to buy shoes for the kids. Margaret, Senator Hall, is a smart lady, but she needs to stay away from that damn computer salesman. He's nothing but trouble. I got a call late one night a few months ago from Harry. Had to give a cop here in Leesbury five hundred dollars just so Margaret and her male friend could go on down the road. He was so drunk he couldn't even stand up."

I know my mouth dropped open. Harry hadn't told me about this. Was I going to be hit up for more money than was in the briefcase? The corner of my eye began to twitch, but Walters did not seem to notice.

"Luckily I had gone to school with the cop. He wanted a thousand at first." Walters smiled and let out a slight chuckle. "He still thinks I got $500, too, but really all I ever got was $250. Good pay for half an hour's work."

I still didn't know what to say to all of this. I was saved from making a response, though, when Walters said, "Is all that money in that little briefcase?"

I handed him the case, and he opened it.

"Looks good to me," he said.

I sat there for a good minute, but Walters didn't move. "Do I get a receipt for this?" I questioned. I had no more said the words than I realized what an idiotic question it was.

Walters burst out with a full laugh. "Yeah, sure," he said, shaking his head. He reached for the bottle of whiskey and put some more into my cup, still chuckling. "Here's your receipt," he said, raising his cup in a toast to me. "How's Harry doing? I heard he was sick."

"He's doing fine. He'll be out of the hospital in a few days."

"Well, tell him I was asking about him."

I could tell that was the cue for me to leave. I tipped my cup and let the whiskey slide down my throat. I needed the boost it would give me. I rose from my chair. Walters was already standing by the door, holding it open for me. When I was back inside the car, secure with the doors locked, I let out a deep breath. Margaret could deliver her own bag money from now on. I swore I would not do this again. I drove back to the main road at seventy miles an hour. I had an overwhelming urge to get away from Styles Street and my illicit deed. As I sat at the intersection to the highway waiting for the light to change, I knew I had better start driving carefully. Getting picked up after drinking that whiskey would be a messy scene. Driving much more sedately, I headed down the highway.

I was at least seven miles down the road when it hit me. I was supposed to see John Maxwell, the black funeral director, when I was in Leesbury. I contemplated not turning around, but how would I explain that I had been so scared about delivering the bag money that I had forgotten. Reluctantly, I reversed my direction. When I got to Leesburg again, I saw a restaurant and decided a cup of coffee was just what I needed. After ordering my coffee, I went to the men's room and splashed cold water on my face. Guilt had overtaken me. I looked at my reflection in the mirror. "Now you're a criminal," I said aloud to myself. What had happened to me? I detested people who took advantage of others who lacked the knowledge and funds to protect themselves. The reason I had become a priest was so that I could work among the poor and be of service to mankind. How had I gone from that lofty goal to carrying bag money? In the mirror I gazed at the reflection of a man I despised.

Chapter 8

I retrieved my coffee at the counter, as well as directions to Maxwell's funeral home. Fifteen minutes later I found myself before an auspicious building with twenty-foot high white columns. Chiseled on a sign of polished gray granite were the words Maxwell Funeral Home. The entire edifice was a symbol of professionalism. The modern brick building was immaculately landscaped with flowers and shrubs. On the left side of the building was a black canopy extending over a carpeted walkway. A shiny new hearse and two limousines were awaiting their next pilgrimage to the cemetery.

There were no lights on within the front rooms of the funeral home, and I almost drove by, assuming my tardiness had caused me to miss my appointment with Maxwell. As I was turning around, though, I saw lights toward the back of the building. I drove into the parking lot, got out of my car, and knocked on the back door. I dreaded this. Here I was doing exactly what Margaret wanted me to do—trying to get the black votes she couldn't buy.

"Who is it?" a man's voice asked.

"Ren Howell. I'm from Senator Hall's office. I'm here to see Mr. Maxwell."

A few seconds later the door opened, and an older gentleman, wearing a gray pin-stripe suit, ushered me in. He was tall and still quite muscular for his age. He looked me over carefully and then told me to go down the hall and take the first door on my right. I had the feeling that he was watching every step I took.

Maxwell was seated in a high back leather chair behind a large walnut desk. A plush oriental carpet covered the floor and expensive-looking paintings were on the walls. He was working at a computer but rose when I came into the room and shook my hand.

"Have a seat, Mr. Howell."

I started to give him the usual Senator Hall-needs-your-support speech, but he interrupted after the third sentence.

"I don't know why you think you need my support, Mr. Howell. Your candidate has bag money floating all over the city. You've bought every black vote you can, but a few of us are going to do what we want to do, not what you want us to do. Senator Hall sends someone in to buy the votes and our community ends up with a few dollars. But, what do we trade for those dollars? An opportunity that real representation would give us, a decent educational system, ownership of our own housing instead of those cubicles my people live in that you call government housing. We have no black business community. We trade millions away for a few dollars."

I wanted to tell him that there was more than a few dollars in that briefcase that I had just dropped off, but I knew I was in a no win situation. I also thought about denying the existence of any bag money but that seemed ridiculous. Maxwell knew too much. I thought the best bet might be to hit some neutral territory, so I decided to semi-agree with the man.

"Senator Hall needs to hear your point of view. I'll tell her what you said. Maybe I can get her to call you," I suggested.

There were a few moments of silence before Maxwell spoke again. "You look too smart to be involved with Margaret Hall," he said in a level tone. "You could do better for yourself. Don't you know her way of politics is going the way of the dinosaurs? Younger blacks know their vote is worth more than a few dollars. It is just a matter of time before Senator Hall and those like her are out of business."

Total silence floated in the room. I didn't know what to say. What could I say? To ease my discomfort, I said the only thing I could think of,

"Are you going to give me a tour? You have the most impressive funeral home I've ever seen."

A smile eased across Maxwell's face. I had finally said something that pleased him. He rose from his chair and with a sweep of his arm motioned me to follow him. The first room we entered contained perhaps fifteen caskets, made of every type of wood or metal imaginable. From there, we traversed a hallway into a small, yet beautiful, chapel.

"We don't use the chapel much," Maxwell said. "Most people use their own church."

Then we entered a large office area, attractively decorated in hunter green and walnut wood. The room contained three desks, at least twelve wooden filing cabinets, and two large couches upholstered in green tapestry. Definitely this was a regal environment for office workers. Farther down the hallway, opposite each other, were four large viewing rooms. They were ornate – velvet curtains, deep piled rugs, ceiling-high columns, and gold gilt trim. Sign-in books were placed atop carved walnut pedestals. Each time I told Maxwell how nice his funeral home was, his smile deepened.

Then, we turned around and went to the rear of the building into the embalming room. My attention was focused on only one thing—three bodies on stainless steel tables, two older men and a young woman.

"We have four guests tonight," Maxwell said.

"Four?" I questioned doubtfully. "I only see three."

Maxwell motioned me toward the side of a table at the far end of the room. When I reached him and looked down, I was in front of the lifeless body of a small, delicate baby. I instantly felt nauseous and bile rose in my throat. I ran out of the door of the embalming room. Maxwell followed and apologized, but I doubted his sincerity.

I knew it had been no accident when Maxwell said, "That's what your bag money causes. The death of little children. Blacks get a few dollars in bag money instead of the medical care they need."

I thought about saying sorry but it seemed so inadequate, and besides, it would not have changed anything.

Across from that room of death was a plain room with two easy chairs, a couch, a television, a refrigerator, and a coffeepot. Maxwell offered me a cup and I gratefully accepted. We chatted about the funeral business while we drank our coffee. Then, Maxwell gave me directions for a quicker way back to the interstate. I bid him good night and within ten minutes I was headed toward Columbia. All the way back, though, only two things were on my mind—Maxwell's comment that I looked too smart to be working for Margaret and the lifeless body of the baby.

Chapter 9

I went to the polls to cast my own vote around three o'clock on Election Day. I voted for every other position on the ballot and left lieutenant governor for last. I still had not made up my mind. I really wanted to vote for Susan Darrel, but I knew that if anyone found out, I'd be in big trouble. I also felt as if I owed Margaret my vote because I worked for her. Suddenly I looked down and I was punching the circle beside Susan Darrel's name. It was as if my subconscious had taken over, and I felt instantly jubilant. This was something I could do that Margaret could not control.

As soon as I walked out of the poll, I spotted Harry talking to some campaign workers. He had just gotten out of the hospital, and here he was already at it again. I instantly felt like a kid who has been caught doing something wrong. I even thought about going back into the building and out a side door, just so that I wouldn't have to talk to him. That might look suspicious, though, so I maneuvered my way over to Harry, saying hello to a few people on the way.

"Harry! Good to see you. How are you doing?"

"Great, Ren. Hope you did the right thing in there," he said as he smiled and put his arm on my shoulder.

What could I say? "Sure," popped out of my mouth.

Harry leaned toward me conspiratorially and whispered in my ear, "Another one for the bitch. Well, at least we'll be working tomorrow."

"Yeah, Harry. I'm glad to see you out of the hospital."

"I bet you are, Ren. Those late night trips can be a pain in the ass, can't they?"

I didn't want to be reminded about the bag money and my unpleasant experience with Maxwell, so I just told Harry that I was meeting someone and that I would see him later.

"See you at the victory party, Ren!" Harry gave me a thumbs up and then he went toward the poll. I went to my car.

The victory party did not happen that night. It was more like the next morning. All that night a couple hundred of Margaret's supporters waited in a large reception room of the Gerard Hotel, watching overhead television screens. The three candidates, Shaw, Darrel, and Margaret, were running close, and a clear victory prediction could not be made. Elliot Shaw's staff were at a ballroom at another Columbia hotel with hundreds of people doing the same thing we were. Susan Darrel's staff were at her campaign headquarters with about a hundred or so people watching the television sets there. As the results of the day's voting came in, the smell of victory was bounced from one candidate to another.

By late evening, though, Shaw and Margaret had pulled ahead of Darrel. Then, a little before midnight, the final results came in. Susan Darrel had done amazingly well for an independent candidate, receiving 28% of the vote. Elliot Shaw had gotten 35% of the vote, but Margaret had won with 37%. Later when Harry and I went over the numbers, we realized the minority vote we had bought and paid for with bag money comprised 68% of Margaret's votes.

I should have been happy, for I had everything to gain by this victory. I would now be the office manager for the Lt. Governor instead of just a senator. This meant more money and more power. Suddenly I admitted to myself that I had been wishing all along that Margaret would not win. That way I could end my misery of working for her.

Lynda Grayson, my girlfriend, came over and congratulated me. I tried to be pleasant and smiled. I was really attracted to Lynda, and she was the first woman I had ever gotten serious about. All I could think of was that if Lynda knew about the bag money and all of the scheming we had done to get Margaret elected, she probably would not be congratulating me. Lynda was the solid, dependable kind of woman a man wanted to marry and to be the mother of his kids.

I didn't like Margaret. I didn't want to work for her. Yet, there was another side of me, a darker side which I didn't like to admit to, a side that loved the clout of being the office manager, calling the shots, wielding political power at will. Every time I looked at this side of myself, I would shake my head and say, "You're sick, Ren." When I got in one of these moods, I would quickly find a drink and then another and another until the painful guilt went away.

Potentates

Chapter 10

The new trappings at the Lt. Governor's office were great. The responsibilities that used to be divided between Harry and me were now divided among a full staff. When I was overseeing the staff in the Senate office, I had been more of a glorified secretary. Now, I really was a manager. I even had my own secretary. Margaret had an appointment secretary, a driver, an office secretary, an advisor who studied the issues, and, of course, Harry, who, lacking any official title, began to call himself an operative.

Basically, Harry's job was to prepare for the next campaign at the taxpayers' expense. The other very important aspect of his job was to keep the money rolling in to the campaign treasury. And Harry was a master at it. The money gathered a lot quicker now because Margaret was seen as a viable candidate to be the next governor. A multitude of corporations wanted to make friends early. The other advantage we now had was that all the expenses of office personnel, phone, entertainment, etc., were at the taxpayers' expense. We no longer had to use any of the money we were collecting in donations.

Margaret took frequent vacations now although they were usually indirectly linked to some state business. That way the expenses could be paid for by the taxpayers. She spent the rest of her time speaking at Rotary clubs, Lion clubs, church conventions, and anywhere else where more than fifty people were gathered. Her other main function was to greet groups of visitors who came to tour the state capitol. She loved doing this because it meant votes for future elections. We had a photographer working almost full time doing publicity pictures.

Margaret had been Lt. Governor about twenty months when I received a call from a state policeman at eight o'clock in the morning. I had just walked into the office. Margaret's son Mark had been arrested. The officer who called said he could not give me any more details, but, off-the-record, he said that we needed to get Margaret's son a lawyer and quick. He didn't even give his name; he just said that Margaret had done him a favor when she was a senator. I dialed Harry on the phone and he came rushing into my office a few minutes later. We decided that Harry and James Taylor, Margaret's lawyer, would go over to the county jail and get the mess straightened out. About two hours later, I got a frantic call from Harry.

"Jesus Christ, Ren. They're going to charge the little prick with murder! You had better track Margaret down and get her back here. I'm trying to get the details now. I'll call you as soon as I know more."

Margaret was in Las Vegas, supposedly at some convention. I left messages on her cell phone, at her hotel, and at the convention center. I sat impatiently by the phone. It would be just like Margaret not to return my call just because she didn't feel like it. Thank goodness this time, after about two hours, she called.

"What is it, Ren? You know how I hate to be bothered when I'm away."

"Margaret, we've got a problem here. Mark Jr. is in jail. All we know so far is that he's being charged with murder. Harry and James Taylor are at the jail now."

"Well, can't they take care of things?"

I was dumbfounded. "Margaret, when this gets out…." I couldn't even finish. "Margaret, you need to be here to deal with this."

"Oh, all right. Book me a flight. I can be at the airport within two hours. That little bastard. Just like his father."

I didn't say anything except that I would see her soon. Shortly after I hung up the phone, Harry and Taylor came into my office and closed the door. Harry filled me in on what was going on.

"Mark Jr. robbed a convenience store on Dodd Street about 2:00 A.M. When the young female clerk wouldn't—or couldn't—open the safe, he shot her. By coincidence, an officer on patrol had stopped to get coffee. He saw Mark with the gun, so he called the robbery in. He saw Mark pull the trigger. When Mark saw the officer in the front parking lot, he ran out the back door. He only got a couple of blocks before two police cars cornered him and two officers wrestled him to the ground and got the gun away. The clerk identified Mark before they put her into the ambulance, but she died before she got to the hospital."

Harry did not look good. His face was ashen and I could almost see him tremble. "Harry, calm down. We can't afford to have you sick again. Margaret is on her way. Let her handle it. There's nothing else we can do right now other than tell Mark Jr. to keep his mouth shut. We'll figure things out when Margaret gets here."

I got Harry relaxed somewhat but then I had to deal with Taylor. He kept repeating, "I'm not a criminal lawyer! I do contracts. You need a criminal lawyer. I know nothing about murder trials."

"Fine. We'll take care of it," I tried to soothe him. I knew that Harry and I were never going to be able to make our next move with Taylor there. "Just get back to the jail and make sure Mark doesn't say anything until Margaret gets here. Check with your firm. See whom they would recommend as a criminal defense lawyer. Call me here as soon as you have a name." Taylor left to return to the jail.

"Harry, we need the best criminal lawyer we can get," I pronounced.

"Just a minute, Ren."

Harry left my office and returned a minute later with a bottle of whiskey and two glasses. He poured both of us a generous drink. Then, we began to plan out our next move. We had to have a press conference. It would be a nightmare, but it was necessary. Who would speak for Margaret? As the office manager, I would be the obvious choice, but Harry could tell that I was really uncomfortable with the idea. Harry, on the other hand, loved stuff like that, especially if television cameras were around. But, even he wasn't volunteering for this one.

Harry and I did agree on one thing, though, almost immediately. If Margaret was going to get re-elected as Lt. Governor, we had to insulate her from her son's horrendous crime. I suggested to Harry that Margaret might want to resign to take care of her son.

"God, Ren," he scoffed, shaking his head from side to side. "You really don't get it, do you? The bitch wants to be governor. Two minutes after getting into this office with us, she is going to be trying to figure out how she can use this tragedy to her advantage. She doesn't care about her son. She'll just be trying to figure out how she can get votes out of this mess, for crying out loud!"

I hated to admit it, but I knew Harry was right. Margaret had never shown much interest in her children. Why would she start now?

We finally decided that we would wait for Margaret and let her decide what she wanted to do. Also, someone had to get to the airport to pick her up. Just then, though, the phones started to ring. I mean all three lines coming into the office started to clang. Harry and I exchanged a glance—the press had found out. The secretary buzzed my office.

"Just tell them, 'No Comment,' and hang up politely," Harry instructed.

Harry and I quickly made a plan. Harry would fend off the press until five when the office closed, and I would pick up Margaret at the airport. There was no way we could come back to the office to meet. The press would be all over us. Instead, we decided to meet at Taylor's office at six o'clock. I called Taylor to let him know. We also sent Margaret's official car out on the road. The driver was instructed to keep driving around the Columbia area, not to stop for anyone. Harry would call him every couple of hours to check in. We knew that some of the reporters would think the car was going to pick up Margaret. This little evasive technique would keep them away from the airport and give us time to collaborate and strategize.

I really had no desire to meet Margaret at the airport, but the task had to be done. I had no idea what I was going to say to her. My gut instinct, as Harry had said, was that she was going to be more concerned about her political career than her son. What was I supposed to say? "Margaret, I'm sorry. I know this is going to ruin your political ambitions." I was still pondering what to say when Margaret walked through the arrival door.

I took one small suitcase from her. "Do you have any more luggage?" I asked.

"No, this is it. Someone else is taking care of the rest of it," she said.

I wondered who the "someone else" was, but I didn't really want to know, so I didn't ask.

The ride to Taylor's office was uncomfortable. A strained silence pervaded the car. I wanted to turn the radio on, but I was afraid we would hear one of those ill-informed breaking news stories—"Lt. Governor's son charged with murder." Margaret was the one who finally broke the silence.

"I'm hungry. Get me a burger some place."

There was a fast food restaurant just ahead, so I pulled into the drive-thru lane and ordered cheeseburgers and coffee. Margaret ate her food without hesitation. I didn't really have much of an appetite. We pulled into the private parking garage below Taylor's law firm. We were thirty minutes early so we sat in the car. I ate and Margaret began to talk.

"I'm not surprised Mark Jr. has done something like this. What should I have expected with Mark for a father? What a father figure to emulate! Mark could never do anything right. He was so naïve, so easily controlled. Mark never spent any quality time with Mark Jr. Now look at what it's gotten him."

Margaret spewed on like this for several minutes. It was unbelievable. Margaret was totally overlooking her own lack of commitment and attention to her son. Not once in all the years I had known her had she given her undivided attention to her children. She felt absolutely no responsibility for Mark Jr.'s behavior. Not once did she consider the impact of her conniving deals or her own despicable role in the death of her husband and the impact it had had on her children. She had no remorse for any of her actions.

At ten minutes of six we took the elevator up to the fourteenth floor to the law offices of McMartin, McMartin, and Taylor. We were instantly ushered into a conference room by an attractive legal aide who was working late on research. John McMartin, James Taylor, and Harry were already at the table. Both McMartin and Taylor were in their late forties. One look at their tailored three-piece suits and leather furniture told me their law firm was quite lucrative. An attractive brunette in her mid thirties, introduced as Joyce Stanton, was also at the table.

Taylor began the meeting by extolling the merits of the McMartin, McMartin, and Taylor law firm. He explained that McMartin Sr. was retired but had been a very successful trial attorney. I took note that he made no comment about McMartin Jr., who was sitting at the table with us. Taylor then recapped his dealings with the case for the day.

First, he had finally met with Mark Jr. and had told him to remain silent. Mark was not to say anything to the police until a lawyer was present with him.

Then McMartin spoke up. "Let me introduce Joyce Stanton. Although I have dealt with criminal matters, I have never handled a murder case. Joyce is an expert on criminal law. She has already tried three big murder cases and won every one. I'm sure we will all feel more comfortable if you retain her, Margaret, as the primary defense counsel for Mark Jr. She and I can meet with Mark Jr. the first thing in the morning."

"Is there any possibility that Mark will be found innocent," questioned Margaret.

This seemed an absurd question since a police officer had been an eyewitness to the crime. McMartin set aside her question, though, by saying he had to talk to Mark first. Stanton began using some legal jargon, suggesting that maybe she could find a way in which Mark's legal rights had been violated. She named a number of cases, which had no meaning to me, but it was obvious that she had prepared herself for the meeting. McMartin looked somewhat uncomfortable. I thought that it might be about what Stanton had said, but he soon made his concerns clear.

"Lt. Governor Hall, I don't mean to digress, but a case like this involving murder could run into tens of thousands of dollars. We want to commit our best legal services to you, but before we go any further, I need to know that that is what you want. If it is, the firm will be satisfied with a retainer of ten thousand dollars from you," he said. "We are truly sorry for the pain you must be going through right now." As McMartin said this, he leaned toward Margaret and put his hand on her arm. I knew it was meant to be a sympathetic gesture, to show that he was genuinely concerned, but it didn't work.

Margaret looked back at McMartin. She just stared at him for about twenty seconds and then rose from the table. "Thank you Mr. McMartin. Someone will call you in the morning." Margaret made no mention of the money. She nodded to us.

"Harry, Ren. Let's go."

No one spoke as we left the office and descended in the elevator to the parking garage. Harry had just turned to head to his own car when Margaret finally spoke.

"Harry, set up a press conference for one o'clock tomorrow afternoon."

"Do you want one of the lawyers present?" he asked.

"No. I'll handle the speaking myself."

"But, Margaret," I interrupted as I unlocked the car door, "you're under a lot of stress right now. Don't you think we should have a meeting in the morning and discuss our strategy? I know all of this is a shock for you. It's a shock for everyone." When I looked at her face, though, I saw a smirk begin to settle at the corners of her mouth.

"No, Ren. I know exactly how I want to handle this." With this statement Margaret bid Harry good night, opened the car door, and got in. A creepy foreboding began to engulf me. What was Margaret up to now?

The ride to Margaret's house seemed an eternity. I was glad when we arrived and she got out of the car. I felt like peeling out of the driveway, leaving a trail of rubber on the road, but I waited dutifully while Margaret turned on the lights in the house before I drove off.

I dialed Lynda Grayson's number. We had previously made a dinner date for eight o'clock. Earlier, after hearing the devastating news about Mark Jr., I had not known if I could keep it, but now I was ravenous for her company. I needed to be with someone normal, someone who did not spend every moment scheming to get ahead. Lynda was delighted that we would still be able to have dinner together. I was delighted too.

Lynda seemed to be the one untainted person in my life. We had been seeing each other two or three times a week now for almost two years. Lynda was nice, really nice. I didn't think she had ever had a corrupt thought in her life. She was easy to talk to and she was a good listener. I sometimes felt guilty that I didn't tell her anything about the underhanded, horrid things that I was involved in for Margaret, but I needed an escape from that side of my life. Lynda's innocence provided that escape.

Chapter 11

Margaret did not come into the office the next day until just before the press conference. By 12:30 there were television cameras and reporters in every inch of space in the press conference room. Margaret walked into the room and stood at the podium at the precise time the conference was to begin.

"If I may have your attention, please…. I have a statement to read," she began. In those few seconds, my mind was reeling with anxiety. What was Margaret going to say? Was she going to resign? Could she possibly try to say Mark was innocent? I didn't know what to expect.

"My son Mark has committed a terrible crime," Margaret continued. "He has killed a young woman in the youth of her life. I wish I could stand before you and say my son is innocent, but that is not the case. He is, indeed, guilty. The pain this is causing me, no one can fathom. I have come here today, before the people of this great state who have elected me Lt. Governor and to whom I owe a depth of allegiance, to avow that I will in no way obstruct justice. My son, no matter how dear he is to me, will have to face these charges just as any other person would who has committed such a despicable crime.

"I have been a good and loving mother. I have tried to guide him and give him every opportunity to be successful in life. Despite this, he has chosen his own road. It is not the road I would have chosen for him, but he is an adult, and he has made the decision." At this point, Margaret's voice quivered and she dabbed her eyes with a tissue. "In closing, I would like to say how greatly I appreciate the phone calls and notes I have received from so many people, offering me encouragement and sympathy at this time."

Margaret gave forth a sob and said, "I'm sorry, but I know you will understand that I cannot say any more at this time." With these words Margaret gave a half-hearted smile and a wave of her hand and turned from the podium.

Before Margaret took a step, though, a reporter yelled out a question. "What is the name of the lawyer you are going to hire to defend your son, Lt. Governor?"

"I am not going to hire a lawyer for my son," Margaret responded. "I think it is in Mark's best interest to plead guilty and ask the court for mercy."

Another reporter yelled out a question, and this one silenced the entire room. "Do you still believe in the death penalty for murder?"

I tried to move toward the podium to say there would be no more questions, but I could not get past the reporters who swamped the room. Harry, however, who was standing beside Margaret, grabbed the microphone and said, "There will be no more questions for today. Thank you for coming."

But Margaret took the mike from Harry's hand. "I'll answer the question," she said. Margaret slowly put the mike back into its holder. Every reporter in the room was waiting for her reply. Then she looked directly at the bright lights of the television cameras. Tears were seeping from her eyes.

"Yes, I do." And that was all she said. Margaret quickly left the room and went out the back exit, where her driver was waiting. No one else had caught on except maybe Harry. I knew that Margaret had purposefully answered the question about hiring a lawyer for her son so that the question about the death penalty would come up. She was playing politics. She was using this as an opportunity to affirm her position on the death penalty. I was incredulous. The bitch. She was going to use her own son—no, she was going to sacrifice her own son—just to fulfill her political ambitions.

Later that night, though, I began to understand just how Machiavellian Margaret really was. Harry was the one who filled me in. He told me that the prosecutor in the district where Mark had committed the crime was against the death penalty. Margaret had checked this out and knew that there was no real chance that Mark would get the death penalty. So, with this information, she was safe in holding to her position of being in favor of the death penalty.

The next morning Margaret returned to her previous schedule and took a trip to a three-day economic summit being held in Troy, New York. Margaret had not even bothered to visit Mark Jr. before she left. Since she had publicly refused to hire a lawyer, a public defense attorney was appointed, and because Mark was accused of a capital offense, there would be no bail. He would remain incarcerated until his trial.

Harry and I thought Margaret's trip had more to do with a rendezvous with Dave Blair, the computer salesman from New Jersey, than any economic business of the state. We knew the relationship had been going on since the death of Mark Sr., but for some reason, Margaret did not want to make the relationship public. Harry had suggested on more than one occasion that Margaret's political image would be helped if she were married. Margaret had been a master at playing the part of a poor widow, but that was beginning to wear thin with the public.

Chapter 12

The first few months after the arrest of Mark Jr. were a time of continual confusion for the office personnel. The official position of the Lt. Governor's office was that we had no comment regarding Mark. The reporters were constantly asking questions of the staff who worked in the office. Reporters would call them at their homes or accost them as they left the building. Skip Keen, the opportunistic reporter that I had come to loathe, even cornered a staff member in the ladies room. The harassment was done so persistently that some staff members forgot the official position and blurted out answers in frustration, just to be rid of the reporters. At times I even found myself doing what I was constantly telling the staff under my authority not to do—speculating on the outcome of Mark Jr.'s murder case.

On one occasion I agreed to do an interview about what it was like to be the office manager for the Lt. Governor. During the interview, the dreaded question was asked—did I think we would be in the Lt. Governor's office after the next election? As I began to answer, I found myself saying that the next election for the Lt. Governor would depend upon how Mark's trial turned out. I knew this was a huge blunder as soon as the words left my mouth. From that point on, I couldn't get the reporters to talk about anything else, and I had a stressful time saying nothing.

Beyond these occasional slips, though, we often leaked information to the press on purpose. Most of the time, this was done at Margaret's directive. Sometimes, however, Harry and I decided what information should be leaked, and we made sure the right people got it. We had a retired gentleman in the office named Ralph Madden, who worked part time taking care of constituent services. We used him as a conduit to pass the information. Harry would tell Ralph what needed to be leaked. Then, Ralph would call one of three reporters with whom he was friendly, one of them being Skip Keen, and relay the information. Ralph would always tell the reporter that he had to remain anonymous because he had gotten the information by eavesdropping on a private conversation between Harry and me. Within a day without fail, the "news" would appear on television and in the paper.

Several months passed with Harry and me playing this cat and mouse game, leaking to the press just what we wanted them to know. Margaret's image, despite her son's crime, was still solid. She was still the Christian woman, the friend of businesses, the job-getter for the people, an advocate of capital punishment. She was depicted as having the strength of the biblical Job in the face of all her troubles, and she was commended endlessly for not letting her personal problems interfere with her duties as Lt. Governor.

Finally, almost six months after his arrest, Mark Jr.'s trial was ready to begin. What we believed was going to happen was that the public defense lawyer and the prosecutor would cut a deal. Mark would plead guilty and get a sentence of life in prison. Before the deal could be struck, however, the prosecutor, Dale Ribbits, decided to play politics—he wanted Margaret to reverse her open opposition to the death penalty. Assured that he would force Margaret to recant her position, he asked for the death penalty for Mark.

Ribbits, who had been with the prosecutor's office since he graduated from law school, was a family man in his late thirties. He had big career aspirations but not the initiative or intelligence to match.

Unfortunately, what Ribbits saw as a political maneuver—one that he wasn't really serious about to begin with—soon took on a life of its own. Leaders in the Black and Hispanic communities pushed the idea. If the death penalty was going to be used against a young white upper middle class person, white officials would back down from supporting the death penalty in general, thus saving the lives of minorities who were on death row. Pro-death penalty activists saw Ribbits as their new hero. Ribbits, however, was not comfortable with what he considered his new notoriety, but he could not find an acceptable way to back down. He was under so much duress that he turned Mark's case over to an assistant in his office. Then, he had a press conference to announce that the case would not be given any special treatment, that the staff would handle it as they would any other.

At this point everything really backfired. Charles Daniels, Ribbits' gung-ho assistant, was very much in favor of the death penalty. Only two years out of law school, Daniels was truly surprised that his boss would give him such an important case. His boyhood dream had been to be a state legislator, so he saw this as an opportunity for a bright political future. He told friends,

"I've wanted three things since I was a boy: to be a state representative, a state senator, and a United States congressman. And if I can get that spoiled rich kid in the electric chair, I'll have all three. Hell, I might even skip the first two and go right to Congress."

The news media couldn't get enough of Charles Daniels, and Charles Daniels couldn't get enough of the news media. Within two weeks of appointing Charles Daniels, Dale Ribbits realized he had made a titanic mistake, but he could think of no way out of his conundrum.

There were problems on the defense side, too. The public defender, Scott Miller, who had intended to plead Mark Jr. guilty in exchange for a sentence of life in prison, now felt that the prosecutor's office had duped him. So, Miller called a press conference and said Mark was going to plead not guilty.

A reporter immediately asked the obvious question, "Are you saying he didn't do it?"

Miller was very uneasy and weighed his options carefully. "Yes, he didn't do it."

The public defender had now made the same mistake as Dale Ribbits. Both men, ambitious and overconfident, consumed with the politics of the situation, had tried to manipulate the system. And it had boomeranged. They had forgotten about the young girl who had actually been killed; instead, they were intent on their own careers and in being in the limelight.

Chapter 13

At the Lt. Governor's office the tension grew. The office personnel, the press, and the public all wanted to know what the Lt. Governor was going to do. Margaret, over the last few months, had tried—and succeeded—in distancing herself from the mess. She almost seemed unconcerned with what was happening. At least twice a week she would leave the office and simply say she would be unavailable. Harry and I often asked her if she wanted to leak some new information to the press or make a public statement. Margaret's only comment was "I've said what I have to say. Let's just drop it."

As if the situation with Mark Jr. was not bad enough, a new problem arose. Margaret's daughter Tammy, who had sought to distance herself from her mother and the mess involving her brother, had entered a summer term at a university in Texas immediately after her graduation from high school. After less than two months on campus, she had managed to get herself suspended.

Dealing with the matter landed in my lap. That meant a trip to Texas to talk with the administration. Harry and I were concerned that Tammy's suspension might become a political issue. Mark was already in jail for murder and now this. Margaret didn't need anymore problems with her bid for re-election just a year and a half away. I just knew that certain members of the press were going to call into question Margaret's ability to manage the state when she could not even manage her own children. If I couldn't resolve this matter, it might signal the political end for Margaret, as well as for Harry and myself.

When I arrived in Texas, I went immediately to the dean of students, Dr. Paul Hartley. Hartley was of medium height, slightly bald, and a bit stout. My first impression was that I would have no trouble flattering Hartley and cajoling him into dropping the suspension. I began by expressing my deepest regrets about the unfortunate situation. Two minutes later, however, I realized that I had totally underestimated the man. Tammy had slapped a female professor in the face and had been reported as openly hostile to the professor on a number of occasions. Her record also indicated several complaints of aggressive behavior toward her fellow classmates.

It quickly became apparent that there was no way that I was going to talk Hartley into reversing his decision about Tammy's suspension. He was willing to play ball, though. He was not over crazy about having the public know that he had suspended the daughter of the Lt. Governor of South Carolina, so he agreed to do away with the suspension if Tammy voluntarily agreed to leave the university. With this maneuver, Tammy's school record would not be affected.

I telephoned Margaret about the results of my meeting with the dean. We both agreed on one thing—Tammy should not return to South Carolina. I would take a couple of days and get Tammy settled in an apartment in Dallas. Then, Margaret would fly out and find another school for her daughter to attend.

Ten days later, after Margaret had returned from
Texas, she and I talked in her office. Tammy was going
to counseling to resolve her anger over her father's suicide. No mention was made, however, of any anger
Tammy might have toward her mother for all the years
of neglect. She was also enrolled in a Christian college
in Dallas and was continuing her education. Margaret
did not offer any more information, so I simply told her
that I was glad everything was working out. I was
somewhat nervous that the issue of Mark Sr.'s death
had come up, but I felt impotent to do anything about it.
I felt sorry for Tammy. I really wanted to tell her the
truth about her father's suicide, but that would mean I
would have to take responsibility for my part in his
death. My own self-preservation would not permit that.

We had just finished dealing with Tammy's situation when a call came to my office reporting that Mark
Jr. had been beaten and sexually assaulted in jail. Two
days later the incident was reported in all the newspapers and on the radio and television stations. Reporters
were everywhere. We couldn't even get out of the office
to have lunch. Margaret rented a suite at a hotel to
avoid the reporters who haunted her house.

We did everything as secretly as possible. Harry or I
went before the press on several occasions and said that
neither the Lt. Governor nor her staff knew any details
about the beating. We carefully avoided the word
"rape," however, when we talked to the press because
we knew that that word would sensationalize the situation even more. I tried to talk Margaret into going to
visit Mark in prison and then having a press conference
afterward, but she was firmly hostile to the idea. The
word *hostile* might actually have been too euphemistic

to describe Margaret's reaction. Every other word was a profanity as she vehemently refused to visit Mark at the jail.

I began to suspect that somehow even the phones were tapped. If anything in a conversation alluded to Mark, it was almost guaranteed to be in the newspaper the next day. We were literally under siege by the press. I thought it was time for Margaret to consider not running for re-election, but I knew she wouldn't listen to anyone who told her that.

Margaret went into her office only when she had some business that could not be done elsewhere. In the next three months she spent most of her time traveling out of state under the guise of economic development. She did this so often and so well that she actually got a number of corporations to develop subsidiary plants in South Carolina. In a few instances, she was even able to convince them to move their entire operation. This meant lots of jobs and new money. The combination made Margaret very popular.

Margaret had also been careful to let the Governor take some of the credit for her accomplishments. I couldn't believe it, but miraculously once again Margaret had turned tragedy into success. The citizenry was clearly behind her; she had won their support with her economic development. The news media could not ignore this economic prosperity. More and more attention was given to the money and jobs being generated, and fewer and fewer comments appeared about Mark Jr. To determine the effect of Margaret's refusal to get publicly involved in her son's murder case, Harry and I hired an independent company to conduct monthly polls. The underlying consensus showed that most men supported

Margaret's position to stay out of the politics of the case, but most women felt that she should intervene and help her son.

Potentates

Chapter 14

On a sweltering day in August, the murder trial of Mark Hall, Jr. finally began. The young prosecutor, Charles Daniels, was bent on getting the death penalty. His boss, Dale Ribbits, had tried his best to convince him to make a deal with the public defender—Mark would get life for pleading guilty. But, Daniels would not listen. As a matter of fact, Daniels threatened to resign and hold a huge press conference if Ribbits used his position of authority to force him to make the deal.

Scott Miller, the public defender, on the other hand, was convinced that he could get Mark off. According to him, someone else shot the clerk, and Mark just happened to be the next person in the store. Mark had seen the gun that the "real" armed robber had left behind and had picked it up. That is what the police officer taking his coffee break had seen. Furthermore, the prosecution was "going after" Mark just to get publicity because his mother was the Lt. Governor. Part of Miller's defense plan was to get as many Blacks and Hispanics on the jury as possible because they mistrusted the police and judicial system anyway.

The selection of the jury took two weeks. Scott Miller did all he could to get the jury he wanted, but the prosecutor objected to most of the jurors Miller favored (Blacks and Hispanics) because they displayed an intense distrust of law enforcement officers in the preliminary questioning. When the jury was finally picked, there were only two Black men and one Hispanic female. The rest of the jury was made up of seven white middle class males and two white middle class females.

Since the seating of the jury did not go his way, Scott Miller now perceived that his job was to convince one of the Black men or the Hispanic woman to create a hung jury. Over the next three weeks of the trial, Miller pursued this task so relentlessly that he finally alienated all of the other jurors.

In his closing statement, Miller argued, "Some of you will support the police and their tactics no matter what they do, but a few of you know how brutal and abusive of their power the police can be. With you few, the fate of Mark Hall, Jr. will be decided. Do you have the courage to stand up against a system you know has become corrupt?

" Let me leave you with this reminder. In a country called Germany, there were more than six million Jewish people ordered to death by a man named Hitler, but it was the police and the military who carried out the orders. Was the Holocaust, the slaughter of these millions of innocent men, women, and children, the responsibility of Hitler—or the police and soldiers who actually carried out his orders? Or does the responsibility lie with the citizens of Germany who would not say *no* to Hitler and his police?

" Here, today, the police have made a mistake, maybe even deliberately. You citizens, who have heard of police brutality and abuse too often to even think it is accidental, can put a stop to it now. All I need is one or two of you to have the guts and the decency to stand up against this corruption and say, 'No, Mark Hall, Jr. is not guilty.'"

Scott Miller was hoping that he could get a hung jury so that he could go back to the prosecutor and negotiate. He was also hoping that Dale Ribbits would then take the case away from Charles Daniels and do the negotiating himself. Miller had done his best in a difficult situation, but things did not go smoothly in the sequestered jury room.

The Black jurors questioned the fact that Mark had not taken the witness stand and declared his innocence. The Hispanic woman agreed, saying he "looked" guilty. The white jurors pointed out that the eye-witness, the police officer, had a spotless record with no complaints whatsoever against him. How they knew this was anyone's guess. After just two hours of deliberation, the jury came back with a verdict of guilty of murder in the first degree. Later, the death penalty was cited as the appropriate punishment. Still, no one really believed that Mark would be executed. There would be appeals or the governor would commute his sentence to life in prison.

At the Lt. Governor's office the secretaries spent most of their time answering phones and telling reporters that the Lt. Governor had no comment. Margaret tried to avoid the press for the first few days after the verdict was rendered. It became impossible to dodge them, though, so she decided to take a timely trip to Europe.

Harry and I were able to talk Margaret into having a press conference before she left. She would read a statement and answer a few questions. Then we would whisk her out of the building into a waiting car before she could be stampeded by the press. The fact that there was going to be a press conference was a news story in itself. From the time the press conference was announced until it actually transpired, we were under siege by reporters. There was an endless stream of them showing up at the office. We finally resorted to hiring additional armed security guards to keep them at bay.

When the day of the press conference came, Margaret seemed to have found new energy. The statement she read was simple, yet effective: "For months many people from the press have been pursuing me for interviews. I have not agreed to do any for two reasons. First, because I know no more about my son's legal case than is common knowledge and what appears in the morning paper. Secondly, such an interview would be very painful for me. As you can imagine, these have been difficult days for me. I have always said that everyone should be equal under the law. It would be hypocritical of me to interfere with due process, especially for personal reasons."

When Margaret spoke her last words and paused, the questions began.

"Why didn't you hire a lawyer for your son?" one called out. And the questions continued to be fired. "Will you try to get his sentence reduced to life?' "Do you feel the death sentence was the right decision?" "Will you run again for Lt. Governor?"

"Please," Margaret seemed to plead, "let me answer one question at a time. The answer to the first question of why I didn't hire a lawyer for my son is that I felt that if he was guilty, he should plead guilty and ask the court for mercy. What was the next question?"

A reporter spoke up. "Lt. Governor, you have always been pro-death penalty. How do you feel about the death penalty now?"

Margaret took a deep breath, making sure it was audible to all, "In the midst of this tragedy, doubts do enter my mind, but I still hold to my position—the death penalty is a deterrent to murder. And I must also consider the family of the victim, Cindy Tobaz. They have lost a daughter."

Another reporter yelled out from the back of the room, "If the death penalty is such a wonderful deterrent, why didn't it keep your son from murdering Miss Tobaz? Maybe he thought he could get away with it because he was the son of the Lt. Governor."

Then, a reporter asked if Margaret thought the death penalty was the right decision in this case. Margaret responded quickly, "If he had pleaded guilty and asked for mercy, a judge might have made a different decision than the jury did."

At this point Margaret moved away from the microphone and I stepped in. "That will be enough questions for today. Thank you for coming." Margaret was already following Harry to the waiting car. Reporters began bombarding me with questions, but I ignored them. The unanswered question that stuck in my mind, though, was, "Does the Lt. Governor intend to run for re-election?"

Potentates

Chapter 15

About two months after Mark Jr.'s trial, the reporters, for the most part, went away. The office personnel were able to get back to their normal duties. The backlog of work seemed endless, but within a month the office was running smoothly again. Margaret's trip to Europe had gone well. She was receiving praise—even from opponents—for the new business she had brought to the state.

Margaret made a formal announcement that she would seek re-election as lieutenant governor. As she expected, there was very little negative press, for how could the media condemn a lieutenant governor who had brought so much prosperity to the state? Margaret was back on the campaign trail, visiting churches and civic groups, such as the Rotary and the Lions Club, and cutting ribbons for the grand opening of new businesses.

In one African American church, after Margaret delivered a speech, one elderly lady got up and asked how Margaret could let her son be executed. Margaret's response was flawless. "Those of us who believe in the death penalty also believe in fairness. If my son had gone free because he was my son, the son of the Lt. Governor, shouldn't the fifteen black men on death row also go free? I am sure they have mothers who love them, too."

The other church members, although uncomfortable, could see the justice in Margaret's words. From that time on, whenever she was among African Americans and was asked about Mark Jr., she answered the same way. And it worked. Margaret got their support.

Margaret had a prepared answer for any question regarding Mark Jr. She had spent hours orchestrating and recording them in her mind. There was an answer for African Americans and an answer for Hispanic Americans. There was an answer for an all-male group and an answer for an all-female group. For women, Margaret would say, "A mother loves her son, no matter what. The situation I find myself in is more painful than you can imagine." For white males, Margaret would say, "Even though this situation is painful, I have always believed that if a person does a crime, he must pay for it." Her answer was always appropriate and tuned explicitly for the group she was addressing.

And her facial expression never changed. She always seemed pained, yet resolved, about the situation. Margaret's delivery was so flawless I was sure she had trained herself before a mirror. The bottom line, however, was that whatever she was doing worked well because she was getting a good reception everywhere she went.

During all of this, Harry had been bringing in "campaign" money. He had been speaking to people, mainly corporate big shots, who would contribute cash for the promise of favors to come. One safe was so full we had to buy another. I, myself, was directing a letter campaign to raise money, which legally I wasn't supposed to be doing because I was an employee of the state, not one of Margaret's re-election campaign staff. The "legal" money was coming in so fast that we had to open new accounts because we were over what the federal government would insure on a single account.

The re-election campaign was going so well that we were all nervous that we had overlooked some angle. Personally, I was looking forward to the day that the campaign work would be officially moved to a separate campaign headquarters. Then, I would be out of the process. At that time Harry would take a leave of absence from the office and run the campaign and that was fine with me. I had one more week to wait till this would happen, and that would not be a day too soon as far as I was concerned.

The race for lieutenant governor had not attracted any opposition in the primary, but in the general election a young lawyer named Miles Harper announced his candidacy. Harper was five years out of law school and had no money. He was a very articulate speaker, however, who was well versed on the issues. One afternoon when I was having lunch with Harry, I mentioned that I thought Harper had a lot going for himself.

"In politics," said Harry, looking at me with firm eye contact, "being an eloquent speaker, knowing the issues, and being honest will only get you a cup of coffee, and that's if you have a buck to go with it. The money we have collected has scared off all the seasoned candidates. In the state of South Carolina, there are plenty of millionaires, but none of them wants to spend his millions getting rid of Margaret. Ren, the bitch is in again, no sweat. All we have to do is convince her that you and I are the ones that keep getting her elected. Who knows? Maybe she'll even be governor. Look, I do my job and stay away from her as much as I can. I can't stand to listen to her complain. We don't get any thanks but we make pretty good bucks. Ren, the world is all screwed up. We're just here playing our little part. Besides, the train's moving so fast we couldn't get off even if we wanted to."

I looked up at Harry. "What the hell does that mean?"

Harry's eyes darted to a good-looking girl entering the café and then back to me. "Just philosophy according to Harry."

I had noticed a few days ago that most of the money was gone from the safe. I needed to ask Harry about it, but, at the same time, I really did not want to know what he had done with it. "Harry, you have the money that was in the safe, don't you?"

"You know, Ren, Margaret, you, and I are the only ones with the combination to those safes. You know Margaret is not going to dirty her hands. I didn't say anything to you because I know you don't want to know any more about the bag money than you have to. You know what? Buying votes in a statewide election is hard work. I spend most of my time on a plane or in a car, carrying money to somebody. That Ken guy Margaret hired as my assistant isn't worth shit, and I don't trust him. Half the time I wind up doing his job as well as my own."

"Harry," I said, "you need to be careful you don't get sick again. You want me to talk to Ken or keep an eye on him?"

"Yeah, talk to him. Maybe you can get his ass moving. But, keep in mind we only have him do legit stuff."

"Harry, you don't need to tell me that. I'll check on him tomorrow and let you know what happens." Then, an idea occurred to me. "Harry, have you ever considered that the problem might not be with Ken? Maybe there just isn't enough legit work to do."

Harry laughed but it was a troubled laugh. I could tell that he was uncomfortable with what I had said. Harry had changed after he had been sick. He went out and did all of this crap to win an election, but he never liked to admit that any of it could be classified as illegal. I remembered one time, when Harry and I were having a beer in a bar, I told him that my conscience often bothered me. I asked him if he was ever troubled with what we did. I will never forget his response, and I have spent much time mulling it over. He said, "Ren, the man at the animal shelter spends all day convincing people that the strays are cute little puppies and will make good pets. Some people wind up taking one home. Every person that goes into that shelter sees him as a good man who takes care of homeless dogs. But— and this is the important part—after the last person has left for the day, he locks the door. Then, this same man, who has been telling all those people how nice the puppies are, takes some of them out of their cages and brings them to a box. He puts those puppies into that box and turns on the gas. Ren, we all have a dark side. The difference between you and me is that I acknowledge mine, but you are in denial about yours. Besides, I'm like every other damn political operative—I can't afford to have a conscience."

The months passed and once again election night came. Margaret won by a landslide. The television commentators speculated that she was going to be the next governor, but nobody could figure out what that would mean. Would she pardon her son if she were governor? Would the people elect her knowing that she had that power? One commentator summed up Margaret's political future this way: "Lt. Governor Margaret Hall would definitely be South Carolina's next governor if her son had not committed murder. She has a knack for surviving sticky situations, but this may be too sticky even for Lt. Governor Hall."

I pondered this statement at great length. Was Margaret so smart? Or was Harry just good at buying votes? We had bought another election. We would have lost to a weak opponent if we had not purchased thousands of votes. An empty feeling hit my stomach and I felt a sharp pain. My involvement in this process of buying votes with bag money and selling favors sucked the very life out of me. I quickly went to the back of the reception hall where a bar was set up and got a double whiskey. The liquor made my stomach burn, but it felt better than that empty feeling.

A few minutes later, I looked over and saw Lynda Grayson come through a side door. I immediately put on a happy face. I had never told her how we won elections. She saw me as a smart, shrewd operative that was going places. The truth was I knew I was neither smart nor shrewd. The truth was I had dark, abhorrent secrets that only I and the demon I wrestled with knew about. Some days the demon was sure he had my soul in hell, but the struggle went on. And, although there were fewer and fewer, there *were* days when I was sure I would escape and have a new life.

Chapter 16

If the news commentators had no idea what Margaret was going to do next, she sure did. On the Wednesday after Election Day, everyone took the day off except the secretary. As soon as Harry and I got to work Thursday morning, Margaret summoned us into her office. Without batting an eye, she announced that we were to start preparing for the governor's race. She did not ask our opinion; she just told us that the governor's race was our next assignment. I laughed but Margaret's stare quieted me almost immediately. She was serious.

She was going too far this time. People were not going to elect someone as governor who had a son on death row. Maybe she had gotten some sympathy votes in the last election, but that was bound to wear out. Even though I was thinking that this was ridiculous, I heard my mouth say, "That's great. We're in the governor's race."

Harry was talking before I even finished. "Well, we're going to the top."

We both knew there was no sense in trying to argue with Margaret. When we left her office and the door was securely shut, Harry put his arm on my shoulder. We walked side by side down the hall, and Harry whispered into my ear, "The woman is nuts, F-ing nuts."

That was Harry's style—too much of a cultured gentleman to use the word aloud but not enough of one not to think it. Harry and I parted when we came to my office. We agreed to have lunch the next day. He said that he had something important to talk to me about. I was curious but not curious enough to invite him into my office at the moment. I was still reeling from the shock of Margaret's announcement. I had been expecting that she would run for governor, but I had never expected her to start the campaign process this soon.

I had to get as much work done as I could because I was leaving the office a bit early to meet my girlfriend, Lynda. We had been seeing each other for four years now. During the first two years we had seen each other steadily once or twice a week. During the last two years, I had seen her much more often. I was very serious about the relationship. I knew I wanted to marry Lynda, but she had never pressured me about it. Lynda had long ago stopped working her second job at the restaurant. Tonight we were going out to dinner and then to a comedy club. I was hoping that if I arrived early enough, before her roommate got home, I might entice her into the bedroom. There was a good chance of that because I had never even seen her roommate in all the time we had been dating.

I finished some paper work and did an interview with a young man just out of college. He had majored in government and wanted a job involving politics. Then I made several calls that my secretary had put on a "must do" list. I was done with my work and on my way out the door by two o'clock.

When I left the office, I stopped at the mall. I went directly to Martin's Jewelry. Margaret's announcement had shocked me, but all day my mind kept thinking about Lynda. I realized how important she was to me. She had such a calming effect on my life. In a split second, I made the decision to ask her to marry me. I would to buy the ring and have it with me when I asked her tonight.

I entered Martin's and began to look at the rings in the case. The sales clerk, a young woman, asked if she could help.

"I'm getting married. I want to get a ring, not too small but not too gaudy either."

"Here, what about these? Is there a special cut or setting that you have in mind? What size is the lucky lady's finger? Did you want white gold or the traditional?"

I realized I didn't know anything about buying an engagement ring. I needed some help before making such an expensive purchase. I remembered that Harry had helped a man named Raymond with some legal problems. Raymond owned a pawn shop that specialized in jewelry. He also made regular donations with the word *thanks* written in the notation part at the bottom of the check. I could probably get his opinion. It would be better to be safe than sorry. It was getting late and I still needed to go home to shower and change clothes before I picked up Lynda.

I was home only a few minutes when the doorbell rang. I opened the door and saw a heavyset man with a crop of black hair. He had on an inexpensive suit, noticeably worn at the cuffs and collar, and carried a briefcase in his right hand.

"My name is Lt. Wrank," he said, flashing me his badge. "May I come in?"

I instantly thought he was here to arrest me. The police must have found out about every horrible thing Harry and I had done for Margaret. I should have had the foresight to have bail money. What would I do now? My heart was pounding and my stomach was doing flips. I even think I forgot to breathe. Finally, my panicked mind heard Lt. Wrank speaking.

"If you just let me in, this will only take a few minutes."

I opened the door fully and led him into the living room. He sat in one of my two overstuffed chairs and put the briefcase on the hassock in front of him. His hands started to fidget as if he were nervous.

Why was he nervous? I tried to calm myself.

"Can I get you something to drink?" I asked.

"No, I'm in a bit of a hurry. Need to get back to the station. Let me get right to the point. I'm here about a woman that you've been seeing. Lynda Grayson. We've been investigating her for months. We believe she's involved in a drug ring with a man named Sammy Regan. Actually, she lives with him."

"No!" I blurted out. "You're mistaken. That's not possible. I've been dating her for years. I'm going to ask her to marry me."

Lt. Wrank held up his hand to stop me. "Mr. Howell, I know this is a shock to you. But, believe me, we are not mistaken. I have some pictures to show you. We have taken these during our surveillance of Ms. Grayson."

He opened his briefcase and pulled out a large manila envelope. He slid out a number of photos and handed them to me. I began to flip through them. The first few were just pictures of Lynda's car. But then there were pictures of a man putting a small box into the trunk of her car.

"That man is Sammy Regan. That box contains drugs."

"So what," I said. "This doesn't mean Lynda knows anything about it! I've never even seen this man. You said Lynda lives with him. I've been to her apartment a number of times. I've never seen him there."

"Have you ever spent the night there?" Wrank asked.

I was silent for a minute. "Well, no. Lynda didn't want to inconvenience her roommate, so if we spent the night together, she always stayed here."

"I'm sorry I'm upsetting you, Mr. Howell, but I'm sure about what I'm saying. There is no doubt whatever that she's involved. These things happen. Someone moves a package to make a little extra money. They only intend to do it once, but they like the money. And it's easy, so they do it again and then again. Then, they *are* involved."

All I could do was sit there and shake my head no.

Lt. Wrank pulled a legal looking warrant from his briefcase. "This is the court paper allowing us to tap her phone. I've heard her with my own ears. She's involved all right." He slid the paper back into the case.

"This isn't happening," I moaned, still in shock.

"Mr. Howell, we know that you don't have anything to do with the drug ring. The reason I'm here, quite frankly, is that the people above me don't want Lt. Governor Hall to get upset at us. She always votes for the funds that come to our anti-drug unit. All we want you to do is get out of the way. When we snap a surveillance photo, you keep showing up. I don't blame you. Ms. Grayson is a good-looking lady. But, if we turn over all of the evidence we have so far, it will be seen by a lot of people. Eventually some of these people will start asking questions—questions about you. And if they ask about you, that could cause problems for the

Lt. Governor. Remember when you borrowed her car for the afternoon about four months ago? There were drugs in the trunk then."

"Oh, my God! Drugs? I didn't know," I stammered.

"We know the only reason you used her car was because yours was in the shop. We checked. But if the newspapers get wind of this, they are going to have a field day. You know you're in a high profile position. We don't want to embarrass the Lt. Governor or cause her undue problems. So, we're trying to handle this. You need to help us out, Mr. Howell."

I looked at the lieutenant. "I don't have anything to do with drugs. What do you need me to do?"

I was having mixed emotions. I still couldn't believe Lynda was involved in something like this. But, I was deeply relieved that this policeman was not here to arrest me. My panic had been unfounded. He knew nothing about what I had done for Margaret. Then, I almost felt kind of proud that I was the outstanding citizen, the one who was on the right side of the law. I wasn't involved in any drug deals.

"This is what we need you to do, Mr. Howell," the lieutenant said. "Do not take any more calls from Lynda Grayson. Don't see her. Don't communicate with her or with any of her family or friends. They're probably not involved in this, but we don't know for sure. No contact at all, okay, not for any reason. Can you promise me this?"

"You want me to just drop her? Not even give her some excuse for not seeing her any more?"

"Yes, Mr. Howell. No contact. Don't talk to her about anything. Can you do that? Can you promise me that you won't see her or answer her calls?"

"Yes," I finally said with great hesitancy.

"Good, then. We should be able to keep you out of this mess. We don't want to give the media a chance to make any trouble for the Lt. Governor, now, do we?"

The lieutenant searched through some papers in his briefcase. He took out two and handed me one of them.

"Mr. Howell, I need you to sign this."

I read the paper.

"I, Reginald Howell, here do swear under oath that I have never been involved in distributing illegal narcotics. I further agree to assist law enforcement officers in any way that I can to arrest and convict such persons who have been knowingly distributing illegal narcotics."

I looked up at Wrang. He had a pen in his hand and offered it to me.

"This is just a formality, you understand," he said.

I nodded. I took the pen, set the paper on the coffee table, and signed my name.

"Thank you, Mr. Howell. I knew you'd cooperate. You're a good person. The Lt. Governor, she's first class. Does a great job helping law enforcement."

I just nodded again and handed him back the pen.

"Oh, one more thing and I'll be on my way."

He handed me the other piece of paper and I read.

"Dear Lynda,

I have been seeing another woman. I am in love with her and want to marry her. I am sorry to end our relationship this way, but I did not want to take a chance that you would make me feel guilty and talk me out of it. Please do not call me or come to see me. That would only be painful for both of us."

I looked up at the lieutenant questioningly.

"We have to end your relationship with Ms. Grayson without tipping her off that you know about the drug business. We don't want to compromise our investigation. This letter will accomplish that objective."

He handed me the pen again but I didn't take it.

"You need to get on with your life, Mr. Howell. You don't want to be involved with anything to do with illegal drugs now, do you? The consequences are too unpleasant. Sign the paper please."

I took the pen and signed.

He put the signed paper and the pen back into his briefcase. "You did the right thing," he said, getting up from his chair. "You don't mind if I trouble you for a glass of water, do you?"

"Sure. No problem," I said. I went to the kitchen, poured a glass of cold water from the refrigerator, and gave it to him. He emptied it in a few swallows. "More?" I asked.

"No thanks. That was good. I've got to get back to the station."

I walked him to the door. He extended his hand and I shook it.

"Don't worry. You did the right thing," he said again.

"Thank you, Lt. Wrang," I said as he left.

I felt stupid for having said "thank you." My mind was still racing with everything that had happened. I was glad he was gone. How could I not have known that Lynda was dealing drugs? I needed a drink but I didn't have any liquor in the apartment. A bar. I hadn't spent my nights drinking in a bar for over two years—the two years that I had become so serious about Lynda.

An hour later, though, I was sitting in a bar, drinking too much and talking to a strange woman. It was as if the last four years had never existed. Lynda was gone, and with her my hopes and dreams of a normal life had evaporated. The desolation of my old life came rushing back at me. It was a life of drinking and loneliness, of greed and deception.

The next morning I woke up late and with a tremendous hangover. By the time I got myself together and into the office, it was eleven o'clock. I made the calls from the list on my desk, skipping all the ones who had called just once in favor of those who had called repeatedly. When I had finished the last call, my secretary buzzed me and said Harry was ready to go to lunch. Harry. I had totally forgotten about lunch with Harry since I was wrapped up in my own misery.

Suddenly I was curious about this important conversation that Harry wanted to have. Harry was a fast-food junkie, so as I left my office, I was already preparing an argument for my choice of restaurants. My arguments quickly evaporated when I got to the lobby, though, because Harry suggested we go to my favorite restaurant before I had a chance to say anything. On the way to The Hound, Harry and I chatted about office politics—who was doing a good job, who was getting slack.

When we sat down in the restaurant booth, however, Harry began to get really fidgety, so much so that he was beginning to make me nervous. I was beginning to wonder if that bitch, Margaret, had sent Harry to fire me or to ask for my resignation. Harry placed his order, but before I ordered, he changed his order. Then, he got up to make a phone call, even though I knew he had his cell phone with him. A few minutes after he returned, he got up again to go to the men's room. That was it; I had had enough.

"Harry, sit down. If you've got something to tell me, just tell me."

Harry looked at me for a second and then his eyes fell to the table. "I think you are going to be shocked," he said.

I glared at him but he did not look back.

"Is it that bad?" I asked.

"Yeah. I don't know how else to say this. Margaret likes you."

That was it? Margaret likes me. My mouth was open, but I couldn't even muster enough sense to close it. What in hell did Harry mean 'Margaret likes me?' I responded with a half-lie, "I like her too."

"No," Harry said. "I mean she really likes you."

This was ridiculous. No, it was insane. What was I supposed to say?

I outright lied this time. Sarcastically I said, "Well, I really like her too, Harry."

"No, Ren," Harry blurted. "I am trying to tell you that she's in love with you. You know she needs to be married. It would help her public image."

"Harry, are you crazy? She may need to be married, but not to me. Why doesn't she marry that Blair guy she used to be so friendly with?"

"He wanted to get married. But he wanted Margaret to quit politics and go live in New Jersey. I don't have to tell you what her answer was to that. Listen, Ren. Just take her out on a date. Just one date. That will satisfy her."

"Damn it, Harry. You're crazy. You want me to take Margaret out on a date? Harry, we call her "the Bitch," remember?"

"The boss is always the bad guy, Ren. It's the competition. When they're women, we call them bitches just because we don't know what else to do. Our male ego sometimes gets the best of us. I'm sure Margaret's really nice on a personal level."

I was really angry. "Then why don't you go out with her?"

"Ren, you know I'm a happily married man. Take her out. Your girlfriend won't find out."

"I don't have a girlfriend anymore, Harry!" Then, suddenly, I was telling Harry the whole disgusting story about the previous afternoon. I had told myself that I would not talk about the betrayal, that I would not even think about Lynda again, but deep down inside I was hurting terribly.

When I finished my sad story, Harry simply said, "See, Ren, that makes it easier. Just take Margaret out on one date."

Talking about Lynda had worn me out. I had no fight left in me. "Okay, Harry, one date. That's it. I'll ask Margaret to lunch."

Harry should have quit then, but he didn't. He kept commenting about what a good-looking woman Margaret still was and what an important position she held. The whole conversation was bizarre. Harry was trying to give me a pitch—me, the expert at conning. Admittedly I saw Margaret as an attractive woman, but I didn't really see her as human. She lacked that sincere compassion, which I so admired in those I idolized as my heroes. I knew there weren't many Mother Theresa's in the world, but Margaret totally lacked the ability to see a situation from the other person's point of view. She had no understanding of how a person may have arrived at a painful place in his life and be unable to find his way out. Margaret's base of operations was herself. If she couldn't gain, there was no sense in proceeding. I wondered for a moment if I could ever change her into a loving person.

God, I was going insane. I needed a reality check. How could I even consider such thinking? My thoughts moved on. Maybe she acted the part of a bitch because that was the only way society would allow her to have a position of power. If she acted any other way, she would have been dismissed and sent home to bake cookies for her husband and children.

Suddenly, Harry snapped me out of my reverie. "Ren, it's time to get back to the office." I realized that Harry had been talking to me for the last couple of minutes, but I had not heard one word he had said.

Chapter 17

When I got back to the office, I asked my secretary to buzz the Lt. Governor's office. I asked Margaret's secretary to have her to stop by my office when she came in. I decided to ask Margaret to lunch when she was on my turf. In all the time I had worked for Margaret, she had never come into my office. I had always been summoned to hers. If we were going to have a "date," my male ego insisted that I set the terms. I still could not believe Harry had talked me into this. A date with Margaret? It seemed ludicrous.

Ten minutes later, I had talked myself into calling off the lunch with Margaret. I scurried around and found a letter from Senator Pressley. I could tell Margaret that that was the reason why I needed to speak with her.

It was almost five in the afternoon. I was making my last phone call, promising more favors. My shoes were off, my feet were up on my desk, and my suit coat and tie lay on the arm of a nearby chair. Suddenly the door opened and there stood Margaret. I swung my feet from atop my desk and popped up from my chair. Before I could say anything, though, Margaret smiled and whispered, "Go ahead. Finish up. I'll just sit here and wait."

She sat in the corner, looking not at all as she did in her big leather chair in her office but rather like a submissive female who had come looking for a job or some political favor.

I had been thrown off guard my Margaret's unannounced arrival. My secretary never let anyone into my office without buzzing me first. I guess she considered Margaret her "big" boss. And, I had to admit, Margaret looked good from where I was sitting.

As soon as I hung up the phone, Margaret began talking in a low, soothing voice. "You have a nice office, Ren. How come you've never invited me here before?" The pleasant look on her face shocked me. She was no longer the Margaret I knew, all business and domineering. She looked passive and vulnerable sitting in that chair in the corner of the room.

I totally forgot about Senator Pressley's letter. I ignored Margaret's question and asked if she would like to have lunch with me Friday afternoon. Her response caught me totally off guard. "I'd be glad to if you allow me to cook dinner for you tomorrow night at my house."

I couldn't quite picture Margaret cooking dinner, but somehow I found myself agreeing to the arrangement. Maybe I was making a big mistake. I didn't know what to say next so I asked about her daughter.

"Tammy is doing fine. She called a few days ago to say she had made the dean's list. She said her therapy was helpful, too. She sounded happy. She asked about Mark, and I told her that his appeal had been turned down. I wish that I had had more time to talk to her. I feel so guilty, Ren. You have done so much to help us, and I don't even think I have taken the time to thank you properly. I really appreciated your going to Texas and straightening out that school mess. You are such a good man, Ren."

This couldn't be Margaret, I thought in disbelief. This woman radiated warmth and concern for others. I didn't know what to say, so I kept it simple.

"Thank you, Margaret." In my mind I thought, "I don't know if I'm good. I was just doing my job, trying to keep the negative publicity out of the papers."

A silence enveloped us then. "Oops," I said. "I'm late for an appointment. Let me walk you back to your office and get on my way." I felt silly as soon as the words left my mouth. Why would I walk her back to her office? But, she surprised me again.

"That's really gentlemanly of you."

After leaving Margaret at her office, I headed for a bar where political types hang out. I exchanged civil greetings with a few of the state representatives and senators and some other office managers. Then, I found a table in the back and sat alone. I drank ginger ale. I wanted a double scotch, but I needed my wits to think clearly. Yet, I wanted everyone to think I was drinking, being sociable. So, I drank ginger ale on ice. No one could tell it from a mixed drink. When you are involved in politics, you are expected to drink. If you don't drink, people look at you with suspicion.

As I sat there by myself, I began to mull over what had happened in my office. Was I wrong about Margaret? Was she really a different person than I had thought she was all these years? What was love anyway? Had I stayed working for Margaret so long, lying to myself, saying I was doing it for the money when really all along I had another motive? Maybe I was just feeling vulnerable because I was still angry about Lynda. Why hadn't I asked Lynda to marry me years ago?

Suddenly, my thoughts were interrupted my some men who I recognized worked for the Governor.

"Hey, Ren. May we join you? Hate to see you all by yourself back here."

"Sure. Have a chair."

Five minutes later I felt my hospitality being violated by a barrage of questions about Mark Jr. They asked the same question fifty different ways—what was the Lt. Governor going to do about her son? Each time I gave them the same answer—nothing. Then, almost as if they were half-warning, half-threatening me, they said, "You know, Ren, the Governor is not going to pardon him unless the Lt. Governor publicly asks him to."

"Come on, both of you. Enough. The Lt. Governor is not going to ask special favors for her son," I said. "Let's change the subject."

We talked about football and twenty minutes later I left. I hated conversations about Mark Jr., and when I use the word hate, I mean hate in the fullness of its meaning. The thought of Mark in jail made me physically sick. The thought of him getting executed was beyond my ability to imagine.

So many times after the death of his father I had considered becoming a "big brother" to him, a surrogate father. But, instead of doing what was right, I chose to do what most people do—nothing. The price of doing nothing is always expensive. There was not a day that passed that I did not torment myself about how things could have been different. My relief from this pain on past evenings was exactly the same as it was going to be this evening. I would go home and watch mindless television shows, and if my mind wandered back to reality, I would turn up the volume.

The next evening I arrived at Margaret's house at eight o'clock. I rang the doorbell, and a few seconds later she opened the door.

"Come on in, Ren. Let me have your coat. Would you like a tour of the house?"

"Sure," I said. I really didn't care but I felt awkward. Margaret walked me through the living room, dining room, kitchen, and bath downstairs. There was also a nice patio area in back of the house, which could be seen from the sliding glass doors in the kitchen. Upstairs there were three bedrooms and a bath

In one of the bedrooms was the largest glass aquarium I had ever seen in a home. Inside was a huge snake, probably some type of boa. Margaret must have seen my apprehensive look because she said, "Oh, don't mind Big Ronnie. He's harmless. Mark Jr. got the snake years ago, and then he lost interest in him. I've become quite fond of you, haven't I, big guy?" she said, placing her hand on the glass. "It's quite empty around here now with the kids gone. Well, that's it," she said as we walked back downstairs.

"Why don't you sit in the living room while I finish up in the kitchen. Here's the remote for the television. Dinner will be ready in a few minutes."

A rerun of the Andy Griffith show was on, so I left the channel there. About ten minutes passed before Margaret came back.

"So, you're a Mayberry fan, too," she said.

I told her that I was. As we sat down to dinner, we continued our conversation about our favorite characters and episodes. I have to admit dinner was great. We had roast beef, baked potatoes, salad, and apple pie for dessert. I complimented Margaret and meant it. She jokingly replied, "I probably have all kinds of talents you don't know about."

Sometime during dinner we came up with the idea of taking a ride to look at Christmas lights. We rode around for over an hour although it seemed as if we were gone only a few minutes. We drove through brightly lighted neighborhoods where almost every house was decorated for Christmas. As we came out of one neighborhood, there was a quaint little church with a manger scene set up on the lawn. People were outside serving hot chocolate and beckoning cars to stop. We parked and visited with the church members while we drank their hot chocolate. I don't think they ever recognized Margaret as their Lt. Governor.

The evening was serene, full of geniality. Once Margaret and I were back in the car, she reached down and held my hand. I hadn't held hands since I was a teenager. Lynda and I had never held hands. It felt good. When we came to a traffic light, I didn't want to let go of Margaret's hand, but my car was a straight drive and needed to be shifted. As soon as we were through the light, though, I took her hand again. Somehow, driving down the street holding Margaret's hand, seemed even more intimate than having sex.

When we got back to Margaret's house, she did not invite me in as I had expected her to. We made arrangements for lunch the next day. Then she said good night, gave me a light kiss on my cheek, and got out of the car. I waited for Margaret to enter her house, and then I backed the car out of the driveway.

I was humming and I knew I was smiling. The evening had been totally enjoyable. But then nagging questions kept bombarding my brain. What was I doing? Why was Margaret interested in me now? Where was this relationship going? Why hadn't Margaret invited me in after our drive? Was she just taking the development of the relationship slow? This was crazy.

On the way back from looking at the Christmas lights, I had been figuring out how I would turn Margaret down if she invited me in. Now, because she hadn't invited me in, I felt let down. Women always confused me. I knew I should run in the opposite direction. I knew I should distance myself from Margaret and never think about it twice. But I couldn't. Life can be difficult enough under normal circumstances, but when you no longer know why you do what you do, the confusion can become catastrophic.

Chapter 18

Christmas came and went and so did New Years, and both were spent with Margaret. By the time spring came, I was madly in love with Margaret. Although we had not gone to bed together, our relationship seemed so intimate. We had candle-lit dinners. We snuggled on the couch watching television. We found excuses to see each other in the office several times a day to sneak a kiss.

In mid-September after a ten-month relationship, I asked Margaret to marry me. She agreed immediately. I was thinking about setting the wedding date for the following December, but when Margaret accepted the engagement ring, she hugged me tightly and said, "Can we have the ceremony in June? I always wanted to be a June bride."

I also had been thinking of a small wedding in a small chapel, maybe even that small church where Margaret and I had had hot chocolate on our first evening together. But, Margaret had different ideas about that, too. Her guest list kept growing and growing. .

Margaret and I had agreed that we would split the cost of the wedding. It didn't take me long to realize what a mistake that was when I found myself writing out a check for ten thousand dollars. And before the wedding was over, I would be writing out two more checks—one for another ten thousand and one for five thousand. Every time I would broach the subject, Margaret would tell me about people who had spent a hundred thousand dollars on their children's weddings and how cheap ours was in comparison.

Margaret often reminded me that as lieutenant governor she couldn't slight people by not inviting them or be cheap just to save a few dollars. She didn't want any negative publicity from the media. Somehow it seemed easier to write out the check than argue with her. Marrying a lieutenant governor was an expensive ordeal.

I also had a suspicion—but didn't know for sure—that Margaret had been taking money from the safe in the office. This money had never seen any bookkeeping process, so it was difficult to know for sure. Harry and Margaret had some way of keeping track of it, but I had never involved myself. As far as I was concerned, the money was dirty via its acquisition. I knew this process wasn't exclusive to Margaret, that the majority of politicians dealt with crooked money, but the less I knew about it, the better I felt. The question I had now was whether or not the money was being used for the wedding, which seemed to get more elaborate as each week passed. I finally dismissed the worry, though. I figured it was better to have Margaret use her unrecorded office money than to spend any more of my own. I convinced myself that I was so much in love I shouldn't care what Margaret or Harry spent that money on—they could buy votes or buy a wedding. It was all the same to me. But, the truth was that dirty money being put into my wedding bothered me terribly.

The growing list of wedding guests looked like the *Who's Who* in politics. Our wedding was becoming a public spectacle. It made me feel extremely uneasy. Deep down inside, I questioned the whole relationship. How could Margaret be such a different person than the "bitch" I had grown to detest? But whenever Margaret walked into the room, put her arms around me, and kissed me, I would suddenly forget all of my objections.

I realized I didn't have the courage to speak up about anything concerning the wedding. Two days before the wedding Margaret hit me with another bombshell. It should have opened my eyes, but it didn't.

"Ren, dear," Margaret cooed, "you don't mind if I keep my own last name, do you? I don't want to lose any name recognition with the voters. You understand, don't you?"

Her request sounded logical, especially in the field of politics. So, I said, "Sure. I understand," but a part of me felt resentful that I wasn't more important than her political career.

Margaret's daughter, Tammy, flew in from Texas the night before the wedding. I met her at the airport and couldn't believe how different she was. Her wild hair was neatly trimmed at shoulder length. The loud, seductive outfit she typically wore—a token of her rebelliousness—was replaced by tasteful black linen pants and a modest short-sleeved blue knit sweater. She had an air of confidence and stood straight instead of slumped as I remembered she used to. The young lady that now stood before me, giving me a genuine smile and hug, was nothing like the sulking, spoiled brat that had been suspended from school in Texas.

Margaret was still busy finalizing wedding details, so Tammy and I had a quiet evening to ourselves to visit. Tammy listened carefully as I told her about the wedding. She reached the same conclusion I had—the wedding had become nothing more than a political advertisement for Margaret. Tammy didn't say it with resentment toward her mother, though. She was genuinely concerned about me.

"With Mother you know politics is going to come first. Ren, are you sure you can be married to someone like that?" she questioned.

I didn't answer her. The truth was that I had asked myself that same question a lot lately and I didn't like the answers I got. I wasn't really up to anymore introspection right then, so, instead, I asked Tammy about the school she was now attending.

She talked excitedly. In her first two years at the school, she admitted that she was a mess. She hardly ever went to classes and actually only earned three credits. Finally, her therapy sessions had clicked. She had begun to understand herself and to come to terms with her neglected childhood. Now, she was doing great at the Christian college and loved her classes, especially her psychology class. Much of what she was learning was helping her to deal with everything that had happened in her life. Her enthusiasm buoyed my spirits. I just sat there and let her talk, enjoying her youthful ardor.

Then, without warning, she looked at me and asked, "Have you been to see Mark?"

"No," I said, "Your mother doesn't want to talk about it. And I didn't want to interfere in a family matter." The second the words came out of my mouth, I felt inept.

"But you're just like family, Ren. And tomorrow you will be family," she said. "Besides, Mark needs someone like you. I don't resent my mother as much as I used to. I'm trying to tolerate who she is, what she is. And I know she'll never change. I didn't come home any earlier because I knew we'd squabble if we saw each other too much. And I'll be flying back to Texas tomorrow evening right after the wedding. I don't want to miss my classes on Monday."

"You're probably right," I said. I was still amazed at how much Tammy had changed since I had last seen her. She was so much more mature. The resentment about her failed childhood no longer consumed her. Instead, she was focused on the future and how she was going to live her life. Shortly after eleven, I gave her a hug, said good night, and headed back to my apartment. I knew I wasn't as enthusiastic about the next day as I should be.

At three o'clock in the afternoon on the second Saturday in June, I found myself standing at the altar of First Baptist Church, the largest church in Columbia, waiting for my bride to come down the aisle. In a few minutes the official part of the wedding was over. Then it was back down the aisle to the waiting limousine, which took us to the reception. In the limousine I tried to be the loving husband, telling Margaret how much I was looking forward to our wedding night. We would spend the night at Margaret's house before leaving Sunday on our honeymoon. This would be the first time I had actually spent the night at Margaret's house, and we would spend it together as husband and wife.

As we entered the reception hall and I saw the throng of people, I automatically put on my political face. I did this whenever I was at a political event, working the crowd. It was as if my mind or my soul left my body, and by rote I became the deal maker. When I had my face on, I was the master of political operatives. It was a game. I could work people, make promises, and get their money. Hell, I could suck dollars out of a turnip farmer. The whole experience made me high. I loved the power I had over them. But, when the event was over, I would crash, hating myself for what I had done.

I didn't want to put the face on today. I wanted today to be different. But I couldn't help myself. It was the only way I knew how to face a crowd. So, the day of my wedding became like any other—I worked. Every guest there was there to be hustled, and I gave it everything I had. If I didn't raise a half million for Margaret's campaign chest that day, I didn't raise a dime. I saw Harry was working the crowd, too, as hard as I was, and so were some of our other campaign workers, trying to become pros like Harry and me.

Later, when I fell exhausted into bed at Margaret's house, I realized my wedding had just been a big fundraiser for Margaret's campaign for governor. The office safes had been spent from freely over the last couple of months, but after today both would be full again. Cash as a wedding gift was never illegal. A few more events like the wedding and there would be enough money to buy every vote in South Carolina, at least the ones that were readily for sale. I didn't like what had happened, but it is hard to complain about the music when you are the main fiddle player.

I looked at Margaret lying next to me in bed. She was fast asleep. My expectations for the evening were gone. I was not upset about Margaret going to sleep because I was too drained from the day's activity to make love anyway. It would have been a burden. That had to be the most ludicrous thought ever—the idea of making love on your wedding night as a burden. Panic roiled up inside me. What had I done? Why had I married Margaret?

Weary as I was, I couldn't sleep. I got up, went into the living room, turned on the television, and watched mindless sitcoms. I never really watched a complete show, just surfed the channels randomly. I guess my physical actions bespoke my mental turmoil. I didn't really want to focus on anything right now.

I awoke on the couch several hours later. The television was still playing from the night before. In the bedroom, Margaret was still sleeping. I thought about waking her, getting her to take a shower with me, and then making love before we had to catch a cab to the airport for our two-week honeymoon in Europe. Instead, I opted to shower alone and let Margaret sleep.

When I got out of the shower, I felt more refreshed and I read until Margaret woke up. We ate a light breakfast of toast, cantaloupe, and coffee in silence. Then, Margaret disappeared into the bathroom for almost two hours.

We wound up having to rush to get to the airport, and Margaret's chauffeur drove like hell, zipping in and out of lanes. As soon as he dropped us off, we trotted to the departure gate. Thank goodness I had had the foresight to send our luggage to the airport the day before. We were the last people to board the plane.

Although we had not purchased first-class seats, we were seated in first class as a courtesy to Margaret's position as Lt. Governor. After we were settled in our seats, Margaret took my hand and apologized for ruining our wedding night by falling asleep. I smiled and gracefully accepted her apology, not letting on that I was not really disappointed about the night before anyway. Margaret made promises about what would happen when we got to Europe, but when we reached London, both of us were suffering from jet lag so we agreed to spend the next morning in bed together.

I must admit the wait was well worth it. We spent a few days in London and then flew to Rome, Paris, and Geneva. The honeymoon seemed much too hectic, for everywhere we went Margaret had some corporate president or politician she needed to spend a few hours with. I had not paid any attention to the honeymoon plans before, but I now realized that all of the "city hopping" in Europe correlated with Margaret's political agenda.

At first I tagged along to her meetings, but then I just stayed in the hotel suite. People could say what they wanted about Margaret politically, but no one could deny that she was a master at economic development. She brought plants and money to South Carolina. The people of South Carolina appreciated her good work, but I would have appreciated a bride at my side during my honeymoon.

Chapter 19

When we returned from our honeymoon—it would be more appropriate to say our business trip—Margaret continued to be very busy. Some days I hardly saw her at all. I had given up my apartment and moved into her house. It still seemed like Margaret's house, not our house.

I was curious about how much money had come in since the wedding. I wanted to check the safe but I did not want anyone to see me. I wanted to wait for an opportunity when both Margaret and Harry were out of town. It finally came. Margaret was in California and Harry was in North Carolina. When I opened it, I saw what I expected—lots and lots of cash. I was suddenly startled by the voice of Dennis Holmes, an aid who worked in the office clipping news articles about Margaret. I had not heard him come in.

"Oh, it's you, Mr. Howell. I thought we were being robbed. I just came back to the office for a bit to finish up some work. I didn't know you were still here."

"Everything is fine, Dennis. I'm just finishing up some work, too."

I closed the safe, locked it, and walked with him back to his work station. I checked the work he was doing and complimented him on a fine job. Then, I went back to my own office. I didn't feel like going home. I just sat in my office, thinking. I had never seen so much cash in the safe before. I grabbed a calculator and quickly added the amount of legitimate money Margaret would need to run for governor. By my calculations, it would take a minimum of five million. Television spots were expensive and we would need a full schedule of ads. We were two years away from Election Day, but I knew we needed to start raising legitimate funds that were on the books. I had checked today and we had slightly over seven hundred thousand dollars in the bank. That was a long way from five million.

Over the years we had helped a lot of businessmen. Most of them would need help in the future. And there were always constituency groups out there that wanted a new environmental law, higher wages, or some kind of consumer legislation. The very fact that these groups existed made it possible for politicians to raise money. No businessman is going to give up dollars unless he feels threatened, and we always assisted them in feeling threatened.

The second way we had of raising funds was getting the government to open the treasury to businessmen. This happened in various ways. For years, one way had been to create research projects since technical advancement was a priority. A company, favored because it had been generous in its campaign contributions, could be given a government grant to work on an idea it had. If the idea did not work out, the business didn't lose anything because the government had paid for the project. Most of the time there wasn't even a legitimate reason for the project. It was just another way to get money so that somebody's college kid could play with a chemistry set during the summer. On the rare occasion that something actually resulted from one of these projects, the business made out big time because the government had paid for the research.

Politicians liked projects like this because they usually got a ten percent return on "their" money. Everyone affected by the grant showed his thankfulness: the original company that got the grant, the construction company that built the building, the car dealership that sold the automobile, and the owner of every other imaginable purchase, including office supplies. We "advised" the businesses getting the grants which contractors to use or where to purchase the materials. Of course, we already had an arrangement made with these contractors and company managers. Once the order was made, the ten percent was in the mail. Once in a while someone wouldn't pay. We would call and tell them we needed their help. If they did not respond, we would cross them off the list and find a new contractor or company that would cooperate.

Sometimes these contracts would end up inflated by one hundred percent because so many politicians at different levels had their hands out. The same contractor that was paying us might also be taking care of a few state senators or representatives, local officials, or even the governor. If there was federal money involved, even United States congressmen and senators had to be taken care of. Sometimes this meant just sending the maximum donation allowed by law, but in most cases the businessman was expected to get some of his friends to send in the maximum donation too.

All of Margaret's trips to Europe were paying off with big dividends. Checks arrived monthly from European businessmen whom Margaret had helped, and every time a new corporation was formed and construction of a building was begun, our contractors were used. There was also MAE (the Management Association for Europe) which was comprised of a group of European entrepreneurs. MAE paid Margaret in stock for sitting on its board. Within ten years she would own the majority of the stock. Meanwhile, these businessmen would continue putting assets, mostly real estate, into the corporation. This was merely a legal way to repay her personally for favors she had done for them. Margaret would take a few trips to Washington and have her office personnel set up United States corporation status for MAE members so that they could get government money. Gratitude might be shown in the form of a small office complex, which increased the assets of MAE and, likewise, the worth of Margaret's stock.

My present job, while Margaret and Harry were away, was to gather the names of five hundred businessmen who would donate ten thousand dollars apiece to Margaret's campaign for governor. I sat at my computer till two in the morning and came up with 350 names. The following evening I did the same thing. These would be the seven hundred we would begin with. Out of these seven hundred names, we would be able to get the five million we needed for the campaign. These people would receive personal phone calls and visits. They would be wined and dined, flattered and cajoled, until they were sold on Margaret being the next governor of the state. We would do whatever it would take to get their support and their legitimate money. On the third night, I made a computer list of all of the other people who had contributed to Margaret's campaigns in the past. Each would get a letter, maybe many letters, and phone calls asking them for their financial support.

That evening the idea of Margaret being governor became real to me.

Chapter 20

The next matter Harry and I had to concentrate on was what the issues of the governor's campaign would be. The problem with most issues is that they have as many people on one side as they do on the other. Take abortion for example. If you take a stand one way or the other, you will most likely lose as many votes as you gain. People can be stirred up more easily to protect their own interests than they can be to crusade for some moral issue. We needed an issue for Margaret's campaign but not a divisive one. We needed an issue that an overwhelming majority of people could support.

As I thought about Margaret's career, the exact issue we needed became clear to me—economic development. For the next few evenings I worked late in my office developing a bill that Margaret would have introduced into the Senate. The bill would create an Employment Commission Office (hereafter to be known as ECO). The bill would allow the commission to make loans to businesses by selling bonds to the public. These bonds would be guaranteed by the state's credit rating. In a practical sense, several businesses would be involved in each issuance of bonds. This would be an excellent tool for new businesses, which had no credit rating, to get money and for established businesses to borrow funds at an extremely low interest rate.

I had no trouble convincing Margaret and Harry about the merit of the ECO bill. They were delighted. Several months later, when the bill was voted on in the Senate, there was very little opposition. Most senators were afraid that they would be labeled anti-jobs if they voted against the bill. The main opponent of the bill was Senator Sam Wylie. He was sure the businesses would fail, the bonds would become worthless, and the taxpayers would have to pick up the tab. For most senators, that scenario was too far in the future. For now, they wanted to go home to their districts and say they had done something positive about the economy and the need for jobs.

Within a few months, the ECO bill had also made its way through the House of Representatives. A week later the Governor signed it. He knew that if he didn't, we would tear him apart in the next election for vetoing the "jobs bill," which it had been dubbed by its many supporters. The Governor did what he had to do, and signed the bill into law. But he knew what we did—the passage of the bill gave Margaret new credibility among the voters. They saw her as efficient, productive, and able to get the job done. Margaret had been seen in the past as a champion of economic growth, but this bill established her reputation statewide as the person who could make the growth happen.

As soon as the Governor had signed the bill, Harry moved quickly to make sure the commissioners appointed were of our choosing. This was going to be difficult because we had no inherent right to select them. There would be seven commissioners, three chosen by the Governor and four by the Senate. Harry immediately began to manipulate the choosing of the commissioners by the Senate.

He met with a "friend" named Adam Jenks, who was also the mutual friend of Senator Clarke, who was to head the Senate committee that would choose the four commissioners. Harry slipped several thousand dollars to Jenks. In return, Jenks gave Senator Clarke a five-thousand-dollar campaign contribution and, of course, kept a couple thousand for himself. Later, he called the senator and suggested the names of four people that his "constituents" thought should be appointed as commissioners. These people were, of course, the ones that Harry had told Jenks we wanted appointed. Jenks also promised Senator Clarke another campaign contribution if the candidates were successfully appointed. Needless to say, this was money, which we would be glad to pay.

Once our candidates were nominated, we worked on the senators to vote them in. Again, Adam Jenks was worth his weight in gold. If a senator did not appear to support our candidate, money would be offered in a discreet way. Jenks might say, "I could get Mr. Jones and Mrs. Smith to give money to your campaign, but it's going to be tough if you don't vote their man onto the commission. After all, they are really close friends." The biggest worry for most senators is coming up with campaign money, so within a few weeks, having spent $160,000, we had successfully lined up our four candidates and gotten Senate approval.

The three commissioners that the Governor would appoint were another matter. Harry went to see some "friends" of Margaret's campaign who were also mutual friends with the Governor. The term "friend" simply indicated that the person had donated a substantial amount of money to both Margaret's campaign and the Governor's campaign. These people had no ideology other than what was good for them personally. Harry convinced them that if they would convince the Governor to appoint the candidates we were secretly supporting, we would make sure that they, or their relatives, would get the first loans from the Economic Commission Office.

Each friend or group of friends approached the Governor with a single candidate from his locality. In this way, the Governor's operatives would not know that he was under siege. The friends, of course, suggested to the Governor that donations would be made to his campaign. The Governor would have no reason to doubt this because all of these people had contributed to his campaign in the past. One of the Governor's friends put it to him clearly—the more money he got in business loans, the more money he could contribute to the Governor's campaign. Harry and Margaret kept me out of all direct negotiations, but Harry filled me in when we had lunch together every few days.

Several weeks of Harry's stealthy maneuvering went by. One afternoon when I came into the office after running a number of errands, my secretary told me to go to Margaret's office. When I entered, both Margaret and Harry were sitting there, all smiles.

"Well, Ren," Harry gloated. "We did it. The Governor just appointed two of our candidates."

"We own six of the commissioners. Six out of seven isn't bad at all," Margaret beamed. "Harry, you're the best. Governor's mansion, here I come!"

"Fantastic!" I said. "Money can accomplish anything."

Within a few weeks Harry had gotten the commissioners to pick his choice of executive director. His name was Sherlock Workman, known as Sky because he was always saying, "The sky's the limit!" He was tall and handsome and quite articulate. Sky was also an out and out crook, but since he wore a suit and had an MBA, no one called what he did underhanded.

The first loans made by the ECO, as promised, went to the businessmen who had gotten the Governor to appoint our candidates. The total amount of the loans made to hold up our end of the deal was fifty-two million dollars. This must have set a new record for the most bribe money paid to appoint six commissioners.

With all of our "debts" paid off, the loans then went to businessmen who were willing to donate substantial sums of money to Margaret's gubernatorial campaign. A million-dollar loan could be had for ten percent or $100,000. Then, ten percent of the $100,000 went to Sky for "managing" the Economic Commission Office for us. The phrase, "No checks. Cash please," became a joke among Margaret, Harry, and Sky.

Margaret made her formal announcement of her intention to seek the governor's seat immediately after the first loans were done. When the media asked Governor Allen his opinion, he just nodded and said, "Lt. Governor Hall has done a lot for the economy of the state of South Carolina. However, I think a year from now the people of this fine state will still elect me as their governor." Then, he gave one of those foot-wide smiles he was famous for. Governor Allen didn't know it, but he was playing right into our hands. Margaret's success with economic issues is what would win her the governor's race. And Governor Allen had just admitted publicly that Margaret was good.

The second sale of bonds for the ECO was for sixty million dollars. About five million of the sixty million in loans went to friends or relatives of the commissioners. We showed our appreciation by not charging the ten percent campaign contribution. The remaining fifty-five million in loans brought in campaign contributions of 5.5 million. Sky received his ten percent, or $550,000. I was a bit surprised when Margaret also gave Harry ten percent because I had not been privy to this arrangement before now. Harry had been the mastermind behind accomplishing all of this, though, and had worked almost day and night, non-stop, for months. He had earned every penny as far as I was concerned. Now, in addition to the legitimate money we would raise, this also left 4.4 million dollars in the "hidden" campaign fund.

Margaret purchased an old store building in Columbia. To keep it out of her name, she incorporated. As far as the public knew, the building was owned by Security Funds Corporation. We used the second floor as "getaway" office space for meetings, which we wanted to keep private from the news media and the public. Harry would also meet "donators" there when he was going to receive a sizable amount of cash. The downstairs was turned into a pawnshop, ostensibly owned by a Nevada-based corporation, which, in turn, was also owned by Margaret. Harry had three safes put in: one in the back room, one for the pawnshop, and one for the cash campaign money. Finally, Harry even "hid" the entryway to the second floor in what appeared to be a storage closet so that his coming and going would be more private.

The pawnshop was the best looking one in the city. The manager pretended to be the owner and everyone thought he was. The real reason for the pawnshop was to launder the ECO money that we received. This was done by making out receipts and sales slips for merchandise that really didn't exist. After that, it was just a matter of depositing the money into the bank. As more ECO money came in, all that was needed was another pawnshop. The only hindrance was that Harry was already working day and night. During the day he did his work at the Lt. Governor's office, and at night, he juggled the books at the pawnshop.

Again, I found myself deeply depressed. When I had thought up the idea about the Employment Commission Office, I had seen it as a redemption. I thought that if Margaret, Harry, and I did something good, maybe we could justify the evil we had done. But it was useless. Everything good I tried to do turned negative. The dilemma I faced was that I could not rebuke Margaret, since she was my wife. Nor could I rebuke Harry because he was just doing what Margaret asked.

I knew I was the weak one. Margaret and Harry had complimented me frequently on thinking up the idea of the ECO. And I had accepted their compliments, never letting them know the truth—that I had never wanted the ECO to be just another scheme to fill the safes with millions of dollars.

I wanted to say something, but, deep down, what I wanted more was for Margaret to love me, to make love to me. Since our honeymoon, Margaret had always been amicable to me, but now we had almost no intimacy. During the honeymoon we had made love almost every day. Now, I was lucky if Margaret and I made love once or twice a month. I didn't complain about the ECO funds because the passion with which Margaret made love after a sizeable sum of money came in staggered the imagination. I secretly hated the money yet waited impotently for the same money to arrive so that once again Margaret would make love to me. Some women become sexually aroused by a candle-lit dinner, some by a gentle massaging of the neck. Margaret became uncontrollably aroused by green one-hundred-dollar bills.

I had tried to relieve the pain in my soul by creating the ECO, but now that, too, was a monster out of control. As I sat in my office one evening, the biblical verse, "The love of money is the root of all evil," kept throbbing in my mind. I finally left the office and went to a bar to have a few drinks. There was no sense rushing home. The house wasn't mine; it was Margaret's. I didn't have a home. Besides, Margaret was not home very often anyway.

Chapter 21

We were prepared to fight Governor Allen for every vote. Months of work had gone into finding every piece of dirt we could. Actually, the Governor's record was neither good nor bad. For the past eight years he had just been there. He had not even vetoed one bill. The best dirt we could come up with was that he had a mistress. The only problem with using this information to create a scandal was that everyone in South Carolina already knew about the woman. If anyone was upset about the mistress, they had long ago gotten over it. The only thing some people were upset with was that it was not fitting for a South Carolina governor to have a "damn Yankee" for a mistress. "Damn Yankee" was the expression used to refer to someone from the North who had become a permanent resident of South Carolina. Yankee was the term used for Northerners that brought in tourist dollars. There was a common joke in South Carolina and, I expect, in all Southern states. A South Carolinian would ask a Northerner, "What's the difference between a Yankee and a damn Yankee?" Of course, the northerner would have no idea. The Carolinian would then gleefully say, "A Yankee is one that comes and visits. A damn Yankee is one that stays."

Margaret made it through the primary with no opposition, not because other politicians believed they couldn't beat Margaret, but because they thought it would be impossible to beat an incumbent governor in the general election. Everyone in our office also knew that we were taking a tremendous risk giving up the lieutenant governor's seat to run a race for governor. It would be a race that was almost impossible to win under normal circumstances, but with Mark Jr. in jail, sentenced to death for murder, what chance did Margaret have?

Deep down in my heart, I knew that Margaret would come up with something to ensure her victory, but somehow I could not get myself to feel good about winning. I wasn't just upset about the vote buying. Somehow I had more or less adjusted to that. Besides, I knew the Governor would be out buying votes too. I wasn't even really upset about the bribes. I had grown accustomed to them, too.

Politics was about money. Money bought votes. It bought television ads that vandalized your opponent and television ads that made you look good. Money bought newspaper ads, radio ads, and billboards. Money bought influence with groups of people and the outright purchase of votes. I had played the game long enough to know that there were lots of good candidates out there, but if they had no money, they always lost. The public buys what it sees on television, and television costs big bucks. Without money there was no television. So, without money you were out of the game.

After every major election a small group of concerned voters would start to talk about campaign reform. The idea would get some press, but it would fade before the next election. And each time the campaign cycle rolled around again, the amount needed to make a serious run for office increased, creating a need for even more money than before. Politics was like a high stakes poker game. If you were going to play, you had to ante up. But, anteing up did not guarantee that you were going to win. One thing the money did guarantee, though, was that the campaign was going to get nasty because the amount of money that was out there to be gotten—a staggering amount—raised the stakes. The money to be gotten created a need to win—at any cost.

Margaret and I barely saw one another during the last six months before the election. She was on the campaign trail, crisscrossing the state, gathering votes. I had become a celebrity through my marriage to Margaret, and my own schedule was filled with speaking engagements. Giving these speeches, I began to see how far removed the constituents were from their elected officials.

People, at least the ones I spoke to, saw the election process in terms of issues and, much of the time, in terms of intellectual issues. For politicians, however, the election process is tactical—make "friends" with affluent people and then carry out their agenda since they are the ones with the money to support your campaign. This, in turn, will make it easier to make more friends with more money, allowing the politician to advance to yet a higher position.

Every time the politician rises to the next level of power, he says, "I'll do what I want when I get elected to the next office, but for now I must compromise and be content." Maybe the politician's aspirations for a higher office come true. He might be the Governor, the Speaker of the House, the Senate *Pro Tempore*, or the chairman of some Senate committee. Having arrived at his goal, though, he sits in his big leather office chair, only to realize that he has no power—the power is in the hands of the men that paid for him to win. Realizing this, he also realizes he is only a pawn in a game, a pawn who can easily be replaced.

The politician takes his comfort from his pseudo-power: the big office, his staff that answers only to him, the reporters who think only he has the answers, his picture in the paper or on television, and, if he gets lucky, the limousine that takes him every place. Some even derive a feeling of power from thinking that their obituary will read well. The politician is so filled with love for his pseudo-power that he dares not ask if he should retire because the answer may reveal more than he cares to know about himself. He is like a boxer who cannot quit but who knows that if he keeps taking hits to the head, he will become brain dead. Yet, he cannot stop. There has to be one more fight. For the politician, it is not the brain that dies but the soul, rendering the spirit non-functioning. I couldn't speak for Margaret or Harry, but I could feel my own soul slipping away.

Chapter 22

The State of South Carolina was ready for Margaret. The crowds were huge. They wanted to hear the word *jobs* and Margaret said the word *jobs* because that's what she needed to say to get elected.

Harry and I were in a state of panic about the Governor, though. His campaign seemed dormant and we could not figure out why. Was he so sure he was going to win that he didn't even think he needed to campaign? Or, did he have some trick that he intended to pull off at the last minute? Harry and I met every couple of days to speculate about what was happening, but both of us were at a loss as to what the opposition was up to.

As we moved into the last three weeks of campaigning, we both came to the conclusion that there was going to be a last minute surprise. I feared that somehow the Governor's workers had found out about the corruption in the Employment Commission Office, and they were going to leak it to the media. Harry thought that they were going to leak a story accusing Margaret of buying votes wholesale. The tension was about to kill me.

We were both wrong. Two weeks before the election the South Carolina Department of Corrections announced that the execution date for Mark Jr. had been set for the day preceding the election. The Governor had played his trump card. When he was asked if he was going to commute the sentence to life imprisonment, he responded, "This is a difficult situation for me. We are talking about the son of my political opponent. If it were someone else, I would say he is dying for the crime he committed, but, in this case, I will always wonder if it is happening because of the politics. So, if the Lt. Governor asks me to commute her son's sentence to life in prison, I will do it so that the people of this great state will not have to agonize over this anymore."

When I first heard this on the five o'clock news, my feelings were conflicted. Part of me was angry and disappointed because, if Margaret did ask Governor Allen to commute Mark's sentence, people would see her as a hypocrite. It would be the end of her political career, and all of our hard work would have been in vain. But then I realized I was delighted Mark Jr. would live and my guilt would be eased. I assumed Margaret would immediately take the Governor at his word and ask for Mark's sentence to be commuted.

The next person being interviewed, however, was Margaret. She was in front of a hotel in Charleston, and Harry was standing near her. Margaret's response left me ice cold. "I have repeatedly told the people of South Carolina that it would be unfair for me to interfere in this case. We can not have two standards for justice, one for the children of elected officials and another for ordinary people. The Governor must make the decision. As a mother, my prayers are with my son. As Lt. Governor, I must obey the law like any other citizen. My son's life is in the hands of the Governor."

Neither Margaret nor Harry had said anything about this press interview to me. How long had they known that this is what Governor Allen had been planning?

I sat in my office feeling despair. The Governor had intended to entrap Margaret, but she had called his bluff. The polls were close with Margaret leading by two percent. If she asked the Governor to commute Mark's death sentence, she would certainly lose the election. But, I thought, this was her son we were talking about. Shouldn't—or rather wouldn't—a parent do anything she could to save her own child?

Margaret had a fundraising dinner that night and a campaign luncheon the next day. I called Margaret at her hotel, but she wasn't in her room. I left a message for her to call me at the office as soon as she came in. I also tried Harry, but all I got was his voice mail. I waited but no return call came from either Margaret or Harry. I must have dozed because when I awoke it was seven o'clock. I tried Margaret again but she still wasn't in.

On my way home, I stopped at the pet store. I had to get some mice for Margaret's snake, Big Ronnie. I didn't look forward to this task because the owner of the shop, Mr. Blackston, kept hounding me to convince Margaret to sell him the snake. Big Ronnie was the off-spring of a boa named Cain that Mr. Blackston had had as a pet. Four years ago his house had been totally de-stroyed by fire, and Cain had either been incinerated or escaped. Either way, Blackston had been trying to buy Big Ronnie ever since. He had first tried to purchase it from Mark Jr., who had bought the snake when it was just a baby. Mark had refused to sell and now Margaret refused to sell. I bought six mice from Blackston and deposited them into the mice cage at home. I never fed

Big Ronnie. Margaret enjoyed doing that herself and I didn't mind at all.

I sat by the phone all evening, but Margaret still didn't call. I fell asleep in the chair and was stiff when I awoke the next morning. I got into the office around 9:30. My secretary said Margaret had called and she and Harry would be back by four and wanted to meet with me that afternoon. I wondered why Margaret hadn't bothered to call me at the house?

Time seemed not to pass at all. I was constantly looking at my watch as I tried to do some work. I was hoping that Margaret would come in early before the meeting to see me. It had been almost two weeks since I had last seen her, and I was anxious to talk to her about Mark Jr. I was really praying that she would ask the Governor to stay Mark's execution. She would forfeit the governorship, but that was all right with me. We could move on and have a new life. I told myself that I had had enough of politics anyway.

At four o'clock I went into the conference room to wait. Margaret and Harry arrived at 4:10. Margaret barely said hello to me before we started to go through the list of mundane campaign issues—who was giving money, who hadn't given money, television time schedules, how the debate had gone, what the polls said, and so on and so on. After two hours there still had been no mention of Mark Jr. It became obvious to me that neither Margaret nor Harry was going to bring up the subject.

At six o'clock Margaret stood up and announced, "Well, that's it. I have a speaking engagement at 7:30." As she went out the door, I went after her.

"Margaret, let's get a bite to eat before you have to speak."

"Okay, as long as it's on the way. I realize we haven't had much time together in the last few weeks."

As we rode to the restaurant, Margaret assured me that things would be better after the election. I wanted to talk to her about Mark Jr., but I didn't want to do it in the car because I knew the driver could hear what we were saying.

We stopped at The Iron Grill and went into one of their semi-private alcoves at the back. As soon as we ordered our food, I broached the subject. "Margaret, about the Governor's ultimatum? I wish you would reconsider your decision and ask him to stay the execution. We are partly responsible for everything that has happened in Mark Jr.'s life."

"Ren, let's not talk about this while we are having dinner together for the first time in a long while."

"But, Margaret, we are talking about Mark Jr.'s life. This isn't just any kid. This is your son!" I knew I was raising my voice, but I couldn't believe her cavalier attitude.

"Ren, I mean it. I don't want to talk about this." Margaret promptly changed the subject. She told me how much she loved me and intimated how good she was going to make me feel the next time we were in bed together. I was soon absorbed in the much-needed attention Margaret was lavishing on me, and I forgot about Mark Jr.

As dinner ended, Margaret said, "Ren, come with me while I speak. After all, I won't get to see you again for a while. I have speaking engagements in Greenville, Spartanburg, and Rock Hill. I'll be going non-stop for three days."

I knew nothing could happen after Margaret's speech because she would be too busy wooing contributors, so I turned down the invitation to accompany her. I hated those public events anyway. I felt like a wallflower. The only way I knew how to cope with crowds was to put on my other face and become the deal maker. I wasn't in the mood for that this evening. I was in the mood to take my wife home to bed, but that wasn't going to happen.

Instead, I left the restaurant in a taxi and went back to the office. I got into my car and went home alone to an empty house. In the last couple of months, since Margaret had been gone so much, it had become more of a home for me. We had talked about buying another house, but we could never decide on the price range. We had plenty of money to buy whatever we wanted, but we were afraid of buying something too elaborate and drawing negative criticism before the election. So, we lived in an eighteen hundred square-foot brick house in a middle class neighborhood. The house was nicely furnished. We could afford what we wanted, but Margaret always haggled with shopkeepers to get the best price she could. Haggling and making deals was in her blood.

Chapter 23

_____

At the office the next day, the phones rang non-stop. Reporters wanted to know if Margaret had changed her mind about asking the Governor to intervene in Mark Jr.'s sentence. The secretary always gave the same statement, which she read from a sheet Harry had written up. "The Lt. Governor stands by her commitment to leave the decision up to the Governor. She cannot interfere with justice or ask for special favors just because she is the Lt. Governor."

Ever since the Governor's announcement, the office had been deluged with calls from the press. I knew that for the next few days until the election the halls would be throbbing with reporters. I thought about moving in with Harry at his office above the pawnshop, but I finally decided that was a bad idea. We didn't want to call any attention to his private office, so instead, a week before the election, I rented a suite of rooms at a hotel in Myrtle Beach, using a fictitious name, of course. I called Margaret, and she promised to join me there as soon as she returned from Rock Hill. I had two direct phone lines installed by the end of the day.

Harry was having even worse problems than I was. The campaign office was completely under siege. At least at the State House office we had plenty of security guards, and although we never asked the guards to remove a reporter, their very presence kept a semblance of control. At the campaign office, however, there were no guards. Reporters would push their way past the front desk into the main office area, demanding to speak to whoever was in charge. As a last resort, Harry had ordered all the doors locked and only employees or known campaign volunteers were allowed in. This left at least twenty reporters hovering outside the doors, and each one of them wanted a story. And, after waiting for hours, the reporters were not in a good mood. Every time someone came or went, the person was inundated with questions.

I suggested to Harry that he relocate the office personnel and take refuge with me in Myrtle Beach. At least this way he would be available to help Margaret and me make any last minute political decisions. Harry did not like the idea but finally agreed. At the last minute, thank God, two young, yet very capable, college students, who were doing an internship with our campaign, agreed to keep the office open and functioning. Harry left them with a skeleton staff so that it would not be immediately obvious that he had fled. The rest of the volunteers were relocated to a branch campaign office less than an hour away in Florence.

That night Harry packed up all the confidential papers from his campaign office and put them into the trunk of his car. There were only two boxes since most of the "our eyes only" papers were at Harry's private office above the pawnshop. He also installed a deadbolt on his office door even though there was nothing left at the headquarters of any value.

The next morning Harry met the two students at a coffee shop and gave them their instructions—keep the office entrance locked, answer the phones, and walk in front of the windows frequently so that the reporters would think that normal campaign activity was still going on inside. Harry had had a large television set up in the office a month before. With that and a couple hundred dollars that he gave them for pizza and miscellaneous, they were all set for the next few days.

Within a few hours Harry was installed in the suite of rooms at the hotel where we—Margaret, Harry, and I—would wait out the execution of Mark Jr. I did not know about Harry and Margaret, but I still believed that the Governor would commute the death sentence at the last minute. Since the interview, Governor Allen had held his silence on the matter. When questioned by reporters, his only reply was that Mark Jr.'s fate was in the hands of the Lt. Governor.

During the last six months, the campaign for governor had taken on a bitter tone. The Governor and Margaret could barely stand to be in the same room together. Governor Allen constantly accused Margaret of lacking leadership and "playing to" the voters. Margaret accused the Governor of running the state under a "good-old-boy" system. And, in the middle of this political power struggle was a young man on death row.

It was now just three days until the execution deadline. I spoke to Margaret on the phone that afternoon.

"Everything has been going great," Margaret said. "I've got strong support in the Greenville area, but I'll be glad when all this is over. I need a vacation."

"Margaret," I suggested, "why don't you stop and see Mark Jr. before you come to the hotel."

"Christ, Ren, how many times have I told you to leave it alone!"

"But, Margaret, he's your son. He must feel totally alone."

"It's enough! I don't want to hear anymore," she hissed.

I couldn't just leave it alone. "Margaret, do you want me to go to see Mark for you?" I offered even though I dreaded the thought. I was stunned at how irate she became at my suggestion.

"Stay out of my damn business, Ren!" she screamed, and the sound of the phone being slammed down reverberated in my ear. I was married to Margaret. I thought it was my business.

Margaret called me back an hour later and apologized, saying she realized I was only trying to help. She told me she knew the Governor was bluffing, that he would never execute Mark. Besides, there were lawyers working on getting a federal judge to postpone the execution.

Margaret's calm voice put me at ease again. She also sounded quite pleased with all the crowds she had spoken to. No one had given her a hard time. Only the news reporters were unruly, almost physically attacking her, trying to get comments. She was going to continue campaigning right up until the end because she did not want to appear as if she was hiding out or afraid to face people.

Harry and I had dinner delivered to our suite. Before I had to leave for a speaking engagement in Conway, I wanted to discuss our strategy about what we would do after the execution deadline. Harry and I came up with two scenarios, one in case the Governor commuted the sentence to life in prison and the second in case the federal judge stayed the execution. We never even considered the third possibility—that Mark would actually be executed.

I'm not sure why we did not consider that third possibility. Harry may have sensed that I was uncomfortable talking about the execution or maybe Margaret had told him to keep me busy and "chilled out" about it. Another possibility was that neither of us could face the idea of Mark Jr. being executed. Both Harry and I had watched him grow up. Even if he had been a pain in the neck and a royal brat the few times he had come to the office to see Margaret, we did not want him dead.

If the Governor commuted the death penalty to life-in-prison, our strategy was to have Margaret deliver a statement saying that as a mother she appreciated the Governor's action and she would certainly sleep better knowing her son was no longer on death row. If the judge stayed the execution, we would remain silent, trying to make it through Election Day without responding.

Harry and I had not had time to talk personally in weeks. Sure, we had had lunch together several times, but there was always so much business to take care of. And speeches! I was so tired of going to all of those socials and making campaign speeches for Margaret. In those three days in the hotel suite as Harry and I just talked, I sensed a different Harry, one who wanted to escape all the deceit and tragedy we were enmeshed in. Harry wanted to start a little business of his own someplace. He wanted to quit but didn't know how. After all, Harry knew what had happened to me years ago when I had tried to leave Margaret's employment.

I had been picking up several different newspapers to read each day. They were full of stories about Mark and speculation about what would happen to him. One gruesome story detailed the effects of electrocution on the body—how the body is burned from the inside out, how the person's eyes pop, and how the hands go up in the air if they are not strapped down securely. The next day's stories were about preachers visiting Mark Jr. and what his last meal would be. There was even an article about what Mark's body would look like after execution. The reporters were hungry and they were having a feeding frenzy. The stories got crazier and crazier. Nothing was off limits. The following day I threw the newspaper into the trash without reading it. It would be weeks before I read a newspaper again.

Chapter 24

The execution had been set for 12:01 A.M., November 5, a Monday. When I awoke Sunday morning, I found Margaret in bed with me. She had come in early in the morning and had not disturbed me because she knew it was almost impossible for me to go back to sleep once I had awakened. Margaret seemed so distant in our marriage most of the time, and then she would do something endearing like this. It was hard to figure out our relationship.

After I had taken a shower, I went into the kitchenette and started some coffee. While it was brewing, I looked out the window to check the weather. I couldn't believe it. A television mobile unit was pulling up out front. I knew that it would be just a matter of hours before the place would be swarming with reporters.

I woke up Margaret and then Harry and told them the press had found us. Mentally I could not take any more badgering by the press, and Margaret didn't need it either. I made a quick decision. I called Chris Rodgers, the president of Zannel Corporation, one of our big campaign contributors, and asked if we could use their small corporate jet. He had allowed us to do this in the past when the jet was not being used; of course, we always returned the favor with political benefits. Chris said the pilot would be waiting for us at their hanger at the airport. Then, I called a hotel in Atlantic City and reserved a two-bedroom suite. When I looked out the window again, there was a second mobile unit. Within a short time the press would figure out which rooms we were in.

We took only the most confidential of papers with us. I called the front desk and made arrangements for the suite not to be disturbed by anyone. The three of us left through the delivery entrance. Margaret was wearing one of my suits, which was much too large for her, and had a hat pulled down low over her forehead. At least if anyone saw us, we would appear to be three men, and people would assume Margaret was still in the hotel. Within minutes the three of us were in Harry's van, heading for the airport.

I knew we stood a chance of being hounded by reporters at the airport, too, but our luck held and there were none. My tension eased the minute we got on the plane. Margaret wanted to stay in South Carolina, but Harry and I convinced her that if reporters couldn't get in touch with her, demanding a statement, the Governor could not use it against her, and South Carolinians would still support her in the election. What the reporters could not print, people could not read. Harry would cancel her final speaking engagements from the hotel room in Atlantic City. Within half an hour the plane had clearance and we were on our way.

When we landed, we paid the pilot a substantial "bonus" to keep the jet and himself on standby, ready for the return trip the next day. He was given specific orders to check in with us every three hours. We gave him an extra thousand to gamble with—and to keep his mouth shut. We did not want him calling reporters with details of Margaret's whereabouts. We even kept a low profile by taking a taxi to the hotel instead of the usual limousine.

I paid for the hotel suite for one night. My plan was that the Governor would commute the sentence at midnight, and we would fly home the next day. Margaret would not be available to make any statements, and by the time reporters got to her on Election Day, it would be too late to print anything that mattered.

As soon as we got to the suite, Harry said he wanted to go down to the casino. He quickly showered, changed his clothes, and left. Margaret and I went down to the casino soon afterwards. I played the slot machines while Margaret watched. I tried to coax her into trying her luck, but she said that she didn't like to play anything she couldn't control.

The day seemed to pass in slow motion compared to what we were used to. We went shopping, played more slot machines, and then went back to the suite, but the day still lingered. It was hard to relax when we were so used to never-ending activity. To alleviate the boredom, I made reservations for us to see a stage show that night.

I kept reassuring myself that the Governor would commute the sentence at midnight. Margaret was acting as if nothing was happening. A few times I thought about trying to talk to her about Mark Jr. I wanted to reassure her that everything would work out, but after the last time, I knew if I said anything, we would end up in an argument. It was easier to keep my mouth shut than to say anything.

That evening we went to two shows, one featuring a well-known comedian and the other a magician. We went back to our suite about 12:30. Margaret went right to bed and was asleep within minutes. I wanted to watch the news on television, but I was afraid to turn it on, afraid that Margaret might have been wrong about the Governor. I opted, instead, to go back down to the casino.

I gambled for the next three hours and drank Scotch. I very seldom drank these days, and when I did, it was usually beer. This morning, though, it seemed like the time to drink hard liquor. At three in the morning, I made my way back to the suite. I knew I was quite tipsy. When I opened the door, Margaret and Harry were sitting on the couch. Harry looked drained and his shoulders were slumped. As soon as I shut the door, he blurted out, "They executed him, Ren."

I went into a rage. "I knew they were going to do it! I knew they were going to do it! We should have given the Governor what he wanted. Damn it! Damn it! We shouldn't have played games. We should have given the Governor what he wanted."

Harry walked over to me and grabbed my arm. In a voice just above a whisper he said, "Watch what you're saying. Think about Margaret."

A new reality hit me. Margaret. What must she be feeling? I sat beside her on the couch. She wasn't crying, just sitting there quietly. I was afraid she was in shock, so I pulled her gently toward me, trying to convey all I felt in the hug I gave her. I must have held her like that for five minutes. Then she whispered in my ear, "I love you."

"I love you, too," I said.

"The bath has a Jacuzzi," Margaret said. "Why don't you go into it for a while and relax. I'll get it ready."

A few minutes later Margaret came back, kissed me lightly on the lips, and said the tub was ready. I thanked her and went into the bathroom. The hot, bubbly water did feel good. Gradually, some of the tension began to ebb from my body. But, I also felt enmity inside. The booze was wearing off, and the reality of Mark's death was becoming more and more clear.

I suddenly found myself praying. I hadn't prayed intensely in years, not since I had left the priesthood, but now the words just sprang forward. I needed to pray. I begged God to have mercy on me and on Margaret. I prayed for forgiveness. I prayed for Mark Jr. I must have prayed for half an hour. I felt drained but I felt full, full of God's love and forgiveness. I wanted to find Margaret and share this with her.

Even though more than an hour had passed, Margaret and Harry were still talking politics. "Margaret, I've been thinking about Mark Jr.," I interrupted. The icy look on Margaret's face told me that I should not continue, but I really wanted to discuss my new-found revelations with her. "I think we should pray," I said.

Harry's facial expression was that of a man about to be tortured. I knew he thought he was going to have to suffer through one of Margaret's endless prayers, which he knew by heart because he had heard them so many times before. I thought the prayer angle would be fool-proof, but Margaret's response left me speechless.

"Ren, I'm sorry that you are having such a hard time with Mark Jr.'s death, but I have an election to win."

I was speechless. I went to the built-in bar, filled a glass with gin, and went into the bedroom to watch television.

Chapter 25

On the flight back to South Carolina, all Margaret and Harry talked about was by how many votes she would win the election. They talked eagerly about what it was going to be like when Margaret was governor. I was still upset about Margaret's callousness toward Mark Jr.'s death. But, maybe it was just her way of handling the tragic situation. I was sure that she was hurting deeply inside and her tough front was for appearance's sake.

I sat quietly by myself, thinking that Margaret would come to me sooner or later to discuss the issue of funeral arrangements. She didn't. Finally about ten minutes before we were going to land, I interrupted Margaret and Harry's conversation and asked her what arrangements she wanted to make for Mark's body.

"Oh, Ren, can you just take care of that. I'm going to be so busy with the election today," Margaret said pleadingly.

I was taken back a bit. How could Margaret not be concerned? All I could think about was Mark's body. I needed to get it away from the prison and to a funeral home.

From the Florence airport we drove immediately back to the hotel suite that we had vacated so quickly the day before. The reporters were gone. I guess they had finally figured out our evasive maneuver and left. Harry made some calls to our people who were doing the exit polls. He smiled wide as he reported.

"It's early, not even eleven o'clock, but so far we're winning big, especially in minority precincts. Well, we bought the votes, didn't we!"

The bag money had paid off. All of the wheeling and dealing had paid off. Margaret was in the lead.

I went into the bedroom, called a funeral home just outside of Columbia, and made arrangements for Mark Jr.'s body to be picked up. The director said that he could attend to it immediately. I emphasized a dozen times that this had to be done quietly and discreetly.

Margaret, speaking in the background, said, "Tell them to give him the best. Don't worry about the money," she said. After I hung up, she smiled, "Don't act so glum. Everything is fine now. Sympathy gets votes you know."

I didn't answer. I didn't care about the votes. I didn't care about the election. Sure, Mark would have the best now. But, in my mind I kept thinking that Margaret should have given him the best when he was still alive.

Less than two hours later I was standing in Boyd's Funeral Home. Mr. Dennis Boyd, the proprietor, was not even five feet tall and was very thin. From the back, one could easily mistake him for a ten-year-old. Looking at his face, I guessed he was in his late forties. He wore an expensive black suit and was the epitome of politeness. He pointed to a body bag on a table. I knew Mark was inside. Then, Dennis Boyd picked up a footstool and carried it over to the table. Almost in slow motion, he stepped up onto the stool, reached out, and unzipped the bag.

"This isn't going to be pleasant," he said softly.

I glanced at Mark's body and quickly looked away, but the image with every gruesome detail was still there.

Boyd put his hand on my arm and guided me to a room full of caskets. He was speaking to me, but I was aware of only fragments of what he said. I knew he was trying to be sympathetic and said Mark's death was a tragedy, and he also said something about voting for Margaret earlier that day.

Mr. Boyd explained in detail the features of the various caskets, but all I could picture in my mind was Mark zippered up inside the body bag.

"Could you give me some idea what the Governor would feel comfortable spending? I'm sure we can arrange a nice funeral."

I looked up at the funeral director, shocked. He had referred to Margaret as the Governor, not the Lt. Governor. I guess he misconstrued my puzzlement because he said, "Were the caskets I showed you more than what you wanted to spend?'

"Oh, no. Money is not the problem, Mr. Boyd."

This immediately put a smile back on his face.

"I like the mahogany one with the blue lining. How much did you say it was?"

I had the impression that Mr. Boyd was a bit irritated that I wasn't paying better attention. We finally came to an agreement about all of the details. The funeral costs came to a little over ten thousand dollars. I wrote out a check and reminded him that everything should be discreet. There would be no wake, no calling hours, no announcement to the media, just a simple memorial service for family only. I knew this was for Margaret's benefit, not Mark's. In her mind, she had worked hard to win the governorship. She didn't want anything or anyone messing it up for her at the last minute, including her dead son.

On my way back into Florence, I stopped at a hotel lounge and had a drink. I was the only person there except for the bartender. The television was on and a commentator was giving the exit polls. Margaret was winning by a comfortable margin. I practically gulped down my first scotch, but I slowly nursed the second. The election commentators kept rehashing all of the economic development that Margaret had accomplished for South Carolina. "Great strides forward" is how they referred to it. And, of course, they said what a great idea the Employment Commission Office was. Margaret was "a friend of business" and "a friend of the working man." The commentators didn't say a damn thing about the bag money, though. Nor the bribes. Nor the kickbacks.

I knew that I was wallowing in my own misery and guilt. I didn't want to leave the solitude of the lounge, but if I stayed there, I would get drunk. It would be better to get back to the hotel.

When I let myself into the suite, it was close to four. Margaret and Harry were sitting in the living room.

"Hi, we're glad you're here. Harry and I have decided that I will only stay for a few minutes at the victory celebration party tonight. It wouldn't look good for me to stay too long. I'll go in and thank all of my supporters, but then Harry will take over and I'll leave. He'll tell the press that I'm elated about my victory but that I'm grieving for my son. He'll insist that the band start playing and that everyone there go on with the celebration. He'll tell them that despite my personal loss I will be ready to take the oath of office in January. I should get everyone's respect and sympathy for this maneuver. What do you think, Ren?"

I opened my mouth to ask her what personal loss she was referring to, but I didn't say the words. I couldn't tell Margaret what I felt. How empty I felt. She seemed to have absolutely no comprehension of sympathy or empathy for someone else. There was no trace of the Margaret I had married. So, I just agreed and said what she wanted to hear. "Sure. Sounds good. Should get you votes in the next election."

"Well, that's settled then," said Margaret with satisfaction. "I want to go to California right after the funeral. There's a manufacturing company there that makes some unusual gadget that goes into military aircraft. I've been trying to get the chairman to open a subsidiary plant here in South Carolina. I want to see him in person, try a little friendly persuasion to get him to make the commitment. I'd like to start off my term as Governor with a bang. They've agreed to send a private plane to pick us up. I want you to come, Ren. You need the rest. You look so tired."

I found myself agreeing although I wasn't sure why. That was a lie. I did know why. No one disagreed with Margaret and escaped unscathed.

"Oh yes," Margaret added, "Tammy called and said she was coming to the funeral service. Will you please pick her up at the airport tomorrow, Ren? Harry and I will be busy dealing with some money matters."

"Sure, no problem," I replied.

I shook my head. Margaret wasn't even officially governor yet, and here she was already planning to use the office to hustle more money. It would be pointless to say anything, so I played the role of the good husband and said nothing. I was looking forward to seeing Tammy, though, despite the tragic circumstances.

Margaret got up from the couch, went into the bedroom, and closed the door.

"Did the funeral arrangements go okay?" asked Harry.

I could tell from Harry's tone that he really wasn't concerned. All of my restraint caved in and emotion poured from me. "Damn it; he's dead, Harry! He's frigging dead. Don't you get it?"

"I'm sorry, Ren. I was just asking. Calm down before you give yourself a heart attack."

Before I could answer, Harry switched on the television. He surfed through the channels, looking for news on the election, but it was still too early for anything official. The only thing being reported was exit polls. Margaret came out of the bedroom. Harry got up, flicked off the television, and said, "I'm going to check on the campaign workers and the local percents. I'll be back about seven." Then he hustled out the door, leaving me alone with Margaret.

I was sitting on the couch. My first urge was to jump up and scream at Margaret, to tell her how disgusted I felt about the election, about Mark Jr.'s needless death. But then, I felt her hands massaging my neck and shoulders.

"Can I order you anything from room service?" she asked.

My anger dissolved immediately. Maybe Margaret really did care. And I surprised myself by saying, "Sure, order me a drink."

I watched Margaret pick up the phone for room service. The vision of Mark Jr. lying on the stainless steel
table in the funeral home flashed into my head again,
but I resolved to put it out of my mind until the day of
the funeral. However, in a not-so-latent recess of my
brain, popping up unexpectedly like a jack-in-the-box,
was the unavoidable question—why had I allowed
Mark Jr. to be executed?

Potentates

Chapter 26

One drink led to another and after the third Margaret led me to the hot tub and after that to bed, where we had sex for the first time in months.

Around 6:30 we ate dinner, delivered by room service. The meal was pleasant, and I enjoyed this quiet, intimate time with Margaret because it had been a rare occurrence during the last year.

At 7:15 Harry knocked on the door and entered. The intimacy evaporated in a blink as Margaret went into political mode, firing question after question at Harry. I listened for a few minutes and then sought sanctuary in the bedroom, where I finished watching an old John Wayne movie. I thought it would be nice to be John Wayne. He was always the hero who saved the day and got the girl.

When I returned to the living room, Margaret was watching the news on the television, switching from one channel to the next. Harry was on the phone making a rapid succession of calls. Suddenly he stopped. When he pivoted around, there was a broad smile on his face.

"You both had better get ready. Governor Allen is going to concede at ten. We'll want to get back to Columbia and downtown to the Plaza so that Margaret can thank all of her supporters and staff." As he spoke, Harry raised his left arm in a victory salute. I smiled but not very enthusiastically. This victory had cost way too much as far as I was concerned.

As Margaret and I got dressed in the bedroom, neither one of us spoke. The feeling of concern and love Margaret had shown me a few hours ago was now non-existent. She had reverted to the self-absorbed political queen she was.

We drove to the plaza in Harry's SUV. He had long ago given up the minivan for what he called the "more masculine aura of adventure." Margaret had elected to sit in the back so that she could concentrate. I sat up front with Harry. I didn't want to hear anything else about the election, so I asked Harry about the new CD player that he had just had installed. In the visor mirror I could see Margaret studying a piece of paper. I assumed it was her victory speech but I didn't ask.

When we arrived at the Plaza shortly after ten, there was not a parking place to be found, and there were news media representatives galore. Harry quickly dialed a number on his cell phone, and within a minute a campaign volunteer, whose name turned out to be Jimmy, came out through the glass doors of the hotel lobby and up to the SUV. The three of us got out and Harry tossed the young man the keys to the vehicle. Harry told Jimmy to park just a few blocks away and to wait for his call. As soon as Harry called him, he was to immediately go to the left side entrance near the rear of the hotel. It was unlikely that there would be any reporters back there, so we should be able to get back into the SUV and back to the hotel unnoticed.

We inched our way through the media. Margaret repeatedly told reporters that she would make a statement later. Inside the Plaza, a campaign worker guided us to a small meeting room. As we passed the main ballroom, we could see that it was packed with people. I wondered whether the majority were just ghoulish spectators wanting to see what Margaret looked like after the execution of her son or whether they really were supporters. To a politician, though, it doesn't really matter. A crowd is a crowd. You get them any way you can.

In the conference room Harry ran through the series of events that would happen within the next thirty minutes. It would begin with Margaret's introduction, the announcement of Governor Allen's concession, Margaret's acknowledgement of me, and so on and so on.

The agenda played out just as Harry had planned. Margaret could have gotten an Oscar for her performance—just the right amount of grief over the death of her son and just the right amount of happiness about her gubernatorial victory. Her victory speech was dignified; the crowd applauded profusely. Within less than an hour Margaret and I were back in the SUV, and Jimmy was driving us back to Florence. Harry had stayed at the Plaza, as planned. He would speak to the reporters, thank our supporters, and keep the party going.

Margaret talked to Jimmy about politics all the way back to Florence. It was obvious that the young man idolized Margaret, and he was thrilled when Margaret invited him up to our suite for a drink before he headed back to the Plaza to return Harry's SUV. I took the bottle of scotch that Margaret and I had been enjoying earlier and went into the bedroom. I started to watch the late night show but fell fast asleep before seeing much of it.

The next morning we moved to a hotel in Columbia because we were afraid that the press would catch on to where we were. Margaret's avoidance of the press was simply a stall tactic. She knew their prime interest was still the execution of Mark Jr. Harry had had someone check Margaret's house, and, sure enough, the press were still camped out there. We knew that at any moment someone at the hotel might give us away—a clerk, a maid, another guest who happened to identify us. Then the media would be hounding us for comments. By the time the funeral was over and she returned from California, Margaret knew things would have settled down a little. Then she would address the press.

Tammy was arriving on a one o'clock flight. On the way to the airport, I grabbed a cheeseburger and fries at a "greasy spoon." As I parked in the airport lot, I suddenly got indigestion. I didn't know what I was going to say to Tammy. How did I explain why Mark Jr. had to be executed? Why was I the one picking her up anyway? At a time like this, shouldn't her mother be doing it?

I needed a drink. I slid into a bar at the airport and ordered a double scotch. It didn't take me long to down it. I heard the announcement that Tammy's flight was disembarking. I was almost at the gate but made a detour into the bathroom. When I came back out, I saw Tammy standing in the waiting area. She was dabbing the tears watering her eyes with a tissue. As I headed toward her, she saw me. With no inhibitions, Tammy ran to me, threw her arms around my neck, and gave me a hug.

"I thought you had forgotten me," she said with a teary smile.

Suddenly, a flash almost blinded us. Then another and another. The press had found us.

"Not now please!" I thundered to the reporters. With one hand I grabbed Tammy's arm, and with the other I grabbed her backpack and small suitcase. At a canter we headed to the main terminal, down the escalator, and out to the parking deck. The press were right behind us. We literally hopped into my car and raced down the ramp to the exit tollbooth. I handed the lady in the booth the exact change and showed her a twenty-dollar bill.

"It's all yours if you stall them," I said, nodding to the approaching press vehicles behind me.

"You got it," she said and the twenty disappeared into her pocket.

I merged into the highway traffic, and looking in my rearview mirror saw the media still backed up at the tollbooth. I thought we were free and clear, but then I noticed a dark blue van with a large antenna following way too closely. Then I caught a glimpse of a video camera. I called Harry on his cell and quickly told him the situation. Within five minutes a state trooper car with its lights flashing forced the van to pull over. Good old Harry. There was no denying it. He sure had the contacts.

When we were free of the press again, both Tammy and I gave a sigh of relief. Tammy even let out a little laugh.

"Well, what do you know! My mother's political connections have finally come in handy," she smiled. I knew exactly what she meant.

"Can we stop and get something to eat?" she asked. "I'm starved. I just haven't felt like eating until now."

We went to a truck stop where she ordered a club sandwich and a glass of milk. Then, what I dreaded happened—she began to ask the unanswerable questions. Why didn't her mother ask the Governor for a pardon? Did her mother just think the Governor was trying to trick her? Why hadn't her mother hired a lawyer for Mark? Had her mother run for governor so that she could pardon Mark? These were the same questions I had been asking myself. There was no way that I could answer her, though, because I didn't know the answers myself.

"Did you know that I visited my brother in prison?" she asked.

My mouth fell open. "I had no idea," I said.

"I did. Three times actually. Every time I saw him he swore he was innocent. He kept asking why Mom wasn't helping him."

This information left me in shock. Again, guilt that I hadn't even visited made me almost physically sick. By instinct, though, I reverted back to my days as a priest and said, "I prayed for his soul." I felt foolish after saying the words, but actually they seemed to make Tammy feel better.

The waitress brought Tammy's sandwich and poured more coffee in my cup. As Tammy ate in silence, I pondered Margaret's insistence on being thought of as a Christian woman. I really had not thought about it any more deeply than that it was ridiculous for Margaret to pretend such a thing. I knew that she didn't really give a hoot about God. But now I fully understood. She knew that her religious comments made people feel better. She was invading the very sanctity of their souls. Margaret did anything it took to manipulate people, anything to get power.

Tammy finished eating and we started back to the hotel. She was quiet for a while and then she said, "I don't know why you married my mother, but I'm glad you did. I feel closer to you than I ever have to her. I've confided in you today more than I have confided in my mother my entire life. And I know you were concerned about my brother. I hate to say it, but truthfully I don't think my mother really cared whether or not my brother was executed. I don't hate her, though. I just...well, I guess I just pity her."

Again I didn't know what to say. Anything I could think of sounded too trite. I thought of saying that Margaret really did care for her and her brother, but both Tammy and I knew that such a statement could very well be absurd.

Just before we reached the hotel, Tammy asked if we could go to the funeral home. That was the last place I wanted to go, so I started to make up excuses. "Your mother might not like that idea. Besides, we've been gone so long, your mother might think something has happened to us."

Tammy's response was automatic. She picked up my cell phone and dialed Margaret's private cell number.

"Mother, this is Tammy. I'd like to go to the funeral home before I go to the hotel. Is that okay with you?" She passed the phone to me. "She wants to speak to you."

"Hello, Margaret. It's Ren."

"Ren, I don't know why on earth Tammy wants to go to the funeral home today. I just have too much to do. I hate to impose but do you mind terribly taking her?" Margaret was using that sweet little voice she had perfected when she needed someone to do something for her.

"Sure," I found myself reluctantly agreeing and disconnected.

"Thanks, Ren."

"Okay, but if we get there and there are reporters, we drive by," I said.

"All right," Tammy said after a moment of hesitation.

Chapter 27

There were no news media vans, no reporters. Mr.
Boyd had been true to his word and not told anyone. If
he had told even one person, I knew the place would
have been swarming with television cameras.

"It will be better if we park in the back," I said to
Tammy. "Less likelihood of anyone seeing us."

I drove to the back door and parked. I really didn't
want to do this. I wanted Mark Jr. out of my mind, but
here I was bringing his sister to see his body. I knocked
on the back door. No one came so I knocked again,
harder this time. Still no one came. There was one car
besides mine in the parking lot, an older red Toyota.
Definitely not a funeral car. I pounded on the door, and
this time it was opened by a young man.

"Hi, I'm Ren Howell. Is Mr. Boyd here?" I asked.

"No, but I can call him and let you speak to him if
you want."

"Thank you. That would be great."

I went back to my car and got Tammy. The young
man escorted us to a small reception room, containing a
couch, two chairs, a few boxes of tissue, and a phone.
He picked up the phone and dialed.

"Dad, a Ren Howell is here and wants to speak with
you."

The young man listened a minute and then handed
the phone to me. I barely got out the word hello before

Mr. Boyd interrupted and said he would be there within ten minutes.

When I hung up the phone, the young man extended his hand. "I'm Dennis Boyd II," he said, shaking first my hand and then Tammy's. I could tell that his father had trained him well so that he would one day take over the business. "Can I get you something to drink—coffee or a soda?"

"I'll have some coffee," I said.

"Nothing for me but thank you," replied Tammy.

Within a couple of minutes, Dennis returned with the coffee. With each sip I took, I kept hoping Tammy would change her mind.

As promised, less than ten minutes after the phone call, Mr. Boyd himself arrived. As he shook our hands, he said, "What can I do to help?"

"If it isn't too much trouble, Tammy would like to see her brother," I said.

"Mr. Howell, will you come with me for a moment?" Then he looked at Tammy and said, "We'll be right back. My son will stay with you until we return."

I followed Mr. Boyd into his office. He motioned me to be seated and then he closed the door. He sat in his elevated chair behind his desk. "Mr. Howell," he began in a very serious tone, "execution does not leave the body in very good shape. I thought we were going to have a closed casket? I don't think it's a very good idea for this young lady to see the body. She needs to remember him as she last saw him."

"Oh, I agree with you, Mr. Boyd, but she was quite insistent. Let me talk to her again." Boyd had given me just the excuse I was looking for to get out of the place. I returned to Tammy and relayed Mr. Boyd's concerns.

"Tammy, I only saw Mark Jr. for a second but I wish I hadn't," I pleaded.

Tears appeared in her eyes, but with resolution Tammy just repeated, "I need to see my brother. I really need to see my brother."

I returned to Boyd's office and told him she would not be dissuaded.

"Are you sure, Mr. Howell?"

"I'm not, but she is."

I followed Mr. Boyd back to the small reception room where Tammy waited expectantly. He tried to talk her out of viewing her brother's body, as I had, but she remained adamant.

"All right then," he said and led us down the hall, past his office, and into a room that resembled a small chapel. The walls were pale yellow and the woodwork a rich mahogany. The casket rested on a dais, surrounded by five flower arrangements. It was simple, yet very tasteful. I put my arm around Tammy, trying to comfort her. Mr. Boyd opened the lid of the coffin.

The sight was grotesque. Mark's arms were twisted and his fingers looked as if they were broken. His face was frozen in fear, and one side had a huge burn that was still evident despite Mr. Boyd's efforts to conceal it. I do believe that if Margaret had been there at that moment, I would have strangled her.

Tammy began to collapse but I caught her. Mr. Boyd quickly closed the lid and the two of us helped Tammy to a chair. Boyd called for his son to bring a glass of water.

Twenty minutes later I had Tammy back in the car. Mr. Boyd bid us good-bye. As I left the parking lot, I looked in my rear view mirror and saw Mr. Boyd shaking his head from side to side.

Tammy didn't speak a word. She just sat there as if she were in a trance. About a mile from the hotel, she uttered the exact words that I had been thinking. "How could my mother have let this happen to him?"

Chapter 28

Harry had already reserved a separate room for Tammy at the hotel. I had the plastic key card in my jacket pocket. I had envisioned Tammy having a visit with her mother in our suite before she went to her own room, but I decided now that I should just get her into her room so that she could rest. I helped her out of the car, and I kept my arm around her as we went through the lobby and up the elevator.

I opened the door to her room and asked Tammy if she would like to lie down for a while. She nodded yes, so I gingerly helped her to the bed. She lay in a fetal position, knees drawn up almost to her chin, and a steady flow of tears seeped from her eyes. I did what I could to soothe her. Ten minutes later she agreed to try to sleep, so I left, telling her I would return in a couple of hours.

When I walked into our suite, Margaret was on the phone conducting business. When she hung up, I thought she would ask about Tammy, but she didn't. I began to tell her everything that had happened anyway. I wasn't really surprised when Margaret didn't appear interested in the least. When she interrupted me to say that she had to make another call, I gave up and went into the bedroom and turned on the television.

Two hours and two drinks later, I went back to Tammy's room. I knocked on the door and then let myself in with the key card. Tammy was still on the bed but she was awake and she wasn't crying.

"Ren, why did this happen? How could my mother let Mark die?"

I sat on the edge of the bed and gave Tammy a hug, a hug that related my concern for her and my frustration about her brother's death. "I don't have the answers, Tammy. I wish I did," I sighed.

I tried to change the subject by asking her about school. She talked about it for a while. School was great and she had made the dean's list again. She had decided to declare her major in psychology. I told her that psychology had also been a favorite of mine in seminary. One topic led to another. Tammy was interested in the "looking glass" theory, which basically promotes the idea that a person becomes what those closest to him think of him. If people see the person as a loser, he becomes a loser. If they see him as successful, he becomes successful.

"Remember when you came to Texas and talked with the dean when I got into trouble. Do you remember what you told me?"

Actually I didn't, but Tammy reminded me.

"You told me that I couldn't use my rotten childhood as an excuse for my behavior. You told me that I couldn't live the rest of my life blaming my mother for not being a mother. The only person who would get hurt would be me. You told me I had to live for myself, discover my own potentials, and never give up. Well, I've finally done that. I am doing that. Ren, you were the first person who ever acted truly concerned about me. It took a while, but now when I look in the mirror, I don't see a kid who is just a bother, just an inconvenience. I've learned that I don't have to act up just to be noticed. I see a young woman with great potential, and I assure you I am going to be successful one day."

Tammy looked at me to see my reaction before she continued. "But not like my mother. I know you married her. I still can't figure out why, but I'm glad you did. For me, that is. But I swear before God that I will never be like my mother."

This time she leaned over and gave me a reassuring hug.

"I just wish that you had had the opportunity to encourage my brother like that," Tammy said.

I wished I had too. "Well, we had better go see your mother now," I said.

"Okay, I'll get ready," she said, picking up her knapsack and going into the bathroom.

While I waited for Tammy, I picked up the remote and started surfing channels. I made a point of skipping over any news channels. Twenty minutes later Tammy emerged from the bathroom in a conservative navy blue sheath. Her hair was fastened on both sides with gold colored barrettes, which matched the simple gold chain she wore around her neck. She did a little twirl and asked how she looked.

"Very nice," I said, really meaning it.

"God, sometimes I can't believe how I used to dress. When I look at some of my old pictures, I can't believe I went out in public dressed like that," she said with a slight shake of her head.

When we entered her mother's suite, Margaret went to Tammy immediately and gave her a quick hug. I thought things might go all right until Margaret opened her mouth.

"In the name of Jesus, let us pray," she said, taking Tammy's hand and leading her to the sofa. I knew what was coming so I made an excuse to Margaret and Tammy and went into the bathroom. Through the door I could hear Margaret say, "Oh, God, help Tammy, my daughter, get through these terrible times. Help her to accept Jesus...." I recognized the words. This was the "prayer" Margaret used with people every time she wanted to avoid a political issue or talking about a problem. The only part of the prayer that changed was the person's name. Margaret's message was always "I'm a Christian so I'm better than you, and if you would just get 'right,' your life would be better. But, you are so bad, and since I am superior to you, don't you dare question me."

Margaret especially loved to use this "prayer" when she fired someone. She would give the person a long list of his failures and tell him that his services were no longer needed. But, then she would say how much everyone liked him and wished him the best of luck. Margaret would then reach out, grasp the person's hand, and say, "Now let us pray." Then she would go into her "prayer." The ending was always the same—she would say a fervent "amen," make eye contact with the person, and then say, "You may leave the room now." When Margaret finished, the person would inevitably be sitting there in shock.

When I heard Margaret say, "Please forgive my daughter for her transgressions...," I was incredulous. Couldn't Margaret see the transformation in Tammy? Couldn't she appreciate the beautiful and intelligent young lady she had become? I wanted to erupt in anger. I wanted to scream at Margaret that it was enough, but instead I calmed myself and stayed out of the way. I had been reading a magazine article about women's golf when I finally heard Margaret say a loud, "Amen."

The living room was encased in silence when I reentered. Tammy's eyes were wide. She was just staring at her mother, who was sitting on the sofa with her eyes closed and a very satisfied smile on her face.

"Tammy," I said, "why don't you tell your mother about your classes and how well school is going."

Tammy took my cue and started to tell her mother about her classes and a new friend she had made. It didn't take long for Margaret to become bored. She turned to me and smiled, "Ren, why don't you take Tammy out to dinner. I can't go. I've got too many calls to make, and besides, I'm afraid the reporters will be all over us if they see me. I want to avoid them for as long as I can."

"I'd like that, Ren. It will get me out of the room," Tammy said.

I immediately sensed that what Tammy really meant was that she wanted to get away from her mother. "Sounds good to me," I said. "I'll knock on your door in about thirty minutes, okay?"

"Great," Tammy replied. "I'll be ready."

Thirty minutes later we were in the car. I decided to take Tammy to Mintal's in Lexington. It was a nice place, sitting right beside the river, and it had great prime rib. I gave the hostess a tip, and she seated us in a secluded section by a window, which overlooked the river. We both ordered the prime rib, baked potato, and salad. I was hoping to avoid any further talk about Mark Jr., but it was not to be.

"Why didn't my mother talk to me about my brother?" she asked.

I hedged a bit and tried to make up an excuse. "Maybe she is so upset she can't even talk about the situation," I said.

"No," Tammy replied. "I think it's something else. It seems as if she doesn't even care. I'd call her every week, and each time I tried to get her to visit Mark in jail. She refused to go. How could she not want to even see him?"

"I don't know. She got angry every time I suggested it, too," I said with a shrug of my shoulders. "Sometimes a person just can't handle a situation. Your mother has been through a lot."

I had to change the subject because I couldn't explain any of it. So, I said, "The river is beautiful this time of the year, isn't it?"

"Yes, it is. I like Texas but I miss home," she said.

Then we talked about her studies some more until our food came. During dinner our conversation turned to the innocuous subject of food, the difference between Southern cooking and Texan cooking. Avoiding the subjects of Margaret and Mark Jr., dinner passed quite pleasantly. On the way back to the hotel, Tammy asked me to swing by a drugstore so that she could buy a pair of panty hose.

At the hotel I walked Tammy to her room. She gave me a peck on the cheek and said she would see everybody in the morning. When I opened the door to our suite, no one was there. About an hour later Margaret and Harry arrived together.

"Oh, Ren, Harry and I just drove by the Governor's mansion. It won't be long before we will be living there. Then I decided I was hungry so we stopped to get something to eat," Margaret said in a cheerful tone.

That's odd I thought to myself. She couldn't go to dinner with her daughter or her husband but she could go with Harry. But, then, she and Harry were co-conspirators in a lot of things I wasn't privy to. Margaret must have sensed what I was thinking because she defensively added, "Don't worry. Harry got us a private dining room so that we wouldn't be stampeded by reporters. Oh, the mansion is just great. You're going to love it, Ren."

"I've seen it before," I replied rather sullenly.

"Yes, but that was different. Now it's our mansion, Ren," she said. "I've got so much to do before we leave for California. You don't mind if Harry and I talk some more, do you?"

"No, of course not. I'm tired. I'll just get ready for bed," I said. "I want to get up early and check with the funeral home to make sure everything's okay."

Chapter 29

I woke up shortly after seven the next morning. I made coffee, read the newspaper, and watched the morning show on television, waiting impatiently for nine o'clock to arrive so that I could call Mr. Boyd. When nine finally came, I dialed. Mr. Boyd answered on the second ring.

"Good morning," I said, obviously not feeling it. "This is Mr. Howell. I just wanted to make sure that everything was in place, that there weren't any problems."

"Relax, Mr. Howell. Everything is arranged," he said assuredly, "and ready for one o'clock."

"Did you get a minister without any problems?" I asked.

"Of course, Mr. Howell," he replied. "Rev. Brown from Bethel Church will do the service. I explained the situation and he is very discreet. There will be no problems with the media."

"Thank you very much, Mr. Boyd," I said. "We'll see you shortly before one then." I hung up the phone, feeling a little bit better.

I went to tell Margaret that everything was all set at the funeral home. She was already on the other phone, doing business, so I had to wait a few minutes for her to finish up.

"Everything seems to be going smoothly as far as Mr. Boyd is concerned," I said to Margaret.

"Oh, that's good," she replied. "Ren, I have more business that I have to attend to. Do you mind taking Tammy to breakfast? Actually, I already spoke to her and she said that would be fine. She'll be ready at 9:30."

I was beginning to feel angry again with Margaret. Couldn't she even take time to be with her daughter on this morning of all mornings? But, I knew it wouldn't do any good to say anything. I just shook my head and said, "No problem."

Tammy was quiet at breakfast. She ate hardly anything and she didn't say anything about Mark. I think she just took solace in being with someone. After breakfast, she said that she just wanted to go back to her room to lie down until the funeral service.

At her room door I said, "I'll be back at 12:15. If you need anything, just call me."

"I will," she replied. "And, Ren ... thanks for everything." I gave her a hug and left.

Margaret was on the phone dealing with another political situation when I got back. As soon as she hung up, the phone rang again. This time it was Harry with bad news. He had just had a call from one of his moles. The press knew where we were and would probably be at the hotel within half an hour.

"Just help me get these papers packed up. They're essential," commanded Margaret. "We can send someone back for the rest later. Ren, call Tammy's room and tell her to pack quickly."

Before the thirty minutes were up, the three of us were at the back door of the hotel. Harry was waiting.

We agreed that the best thing to do was to split up. Margaret would go with Harry. Tammy would ride with me. We would all meet at the funeral home at one o'clock. Tammy had both her suitcase and backpack with her, so I threw them into the back seat of my car. As we left the cover of the parking garage, I looked for news vans but saw nothing. I thought that we had been awfully lucky to out-maneuver them.

There was no sense in getting to the funeral home early. That would only upset Tammy more. Tammy said that if we stopped at a truck stop she could finish getting ready. At the restaurant we both ordered coffee. Tammy used my cell phone to call the airlines and confirm her 4:00 flight back to Texas.

"The morning news had reported thunderstorms around the Dallas area," Tammy said, "so I was worried that the flight might be delayed. But, it's going to leave on time. I really want to get back to Texas. This place doesn't feel like home anymore. No offense to you, Ren."

"No offense taken," I said, and she smiled for the first time that morning.

Potentates

Chapter 30

Tammy and I arrived at the funeral home at 12:45. Margaret and Harry were not there yet. Mr. Boyd himself met us and gave Tammy a small package of tissues. At 12:55 Margaret and Harry made their appearance, and right on their heels was a tall, middle-aged man, wearing a clerical collar. Mr. Boyd introduced him as Rev. Brown. I shook his hand and his grip was firm and reassuring. When Mr. Boyd introduced Rev. Brown to Margaret, her response startled and even embarrassed me. She gave him one of her political smiles, totally inappropriate for the present occasion, and said, "I hope I got your vote in the governor's election." Rev. Brown lifted his eyebrows but didn't reply. I immediately liked the man.

Mr. Boyd led us all into the small chapel. The closed casket, containing Mark's body, rested at the front before the walnut railing of the altar. Rev. Brown asked us to bow our heads and began the invocation. He read the traditional scripture, the 23rd Psalm. As I heard him say, "The Lord is my shepherd, I shall not want," my eyes misted and I truly hoped that Mark Jr. was at peace. Rev. Brown gave a brief eulogy. Mark, he said, was a young man who had died too soon. I was not sure whether Rev. Brown knew that Mark had been executed or if he was just avoiding the subject. Tammy was seated next to me. I could hear her muffled crying, her head bowed to her chest. I put my arm around her. It was a gesture to comfort her and to let her know that I shared her anguish.

Then Rev. Brown asked, "Does anyone have anything they would like to say?" The words surprised me because I did not know that this would be a part of the service. I saw Margaret glance at Harry as if to say, "Do something." I thought that maybe I should stand up and say something, but then Tammy stood up.

"My brother was a good person. He just didn't get the love he needed. I should have done better. We all should have done better." Tammy turned and looked at Margaret. "And, Mother, you especially, should have done better." Then she sat back down. Her shoulders quivered and she began to cry softly again.

I silently applauded Tammy for standing up to her mother, for saying what I had always thought. But I was afraid of Margaret's reaction to her daughter's words. I didn't have long to wait, though.

Within a few seconds, Margaret stood up. "My daughter is right. I should have done more...."

For a moment I thought Margaret was actually sincere, that she was going to admit to her neglect of her children because of her ambition, her quest for power. But, when I heard Margaret say, "Rev. Brown, I'd like to pray," any hope that I had of that shattered. Margaret began her "I am a good Christian" prayer. Five minutes later, as Margaret continued to expound her "Christian" qualities, Rev. Brown gave a sigh of aggravation. He realized that he had just lost control of the service.

I looked at Mr. Boyd for assistance, but he had his head bowed, obviously avoiding the situation. Margaret continued to pray non-stop for almost another five

minutes. I wondered why man used God to so consist-
ently explain his misdeeds.

When Margaret finished, a smile at the corners of
her mouth, Rev. Brown made a parting comment about
the Lord being with us. I thought to myself that I didn't
know if God was on this journey we were on—it felt
more like Satan.

All of us were ushered into the same funeral car for
the ride to the cemetery, except Rev. Brown, who drove
his own car. At the gravesite, Rev. Brown said, "Let us
gather around." The words were obviously meant for a
large number of mourners, not this small group consist-
ing of only Margaret, Tammy, Harry, and me and, of
course, Mr. Boyd, who was standing respectfully a few
feet to the side. I could tell from the look on his face
that Rev. Brown knew his words sounded a bit foolish,
but he continued anyway with a short prayer. The prayer was lost on me. I was too busy speculating on what
would happen next with Margaret. Whatever happened,
I knew I lacked the courage to leave. I would be there,
caught in the undertow.

Chapter 31

The four of us rode back to the funeral home in total silence. I kept hoping that Margaret would say something comforting to Tammy, but I could sense the void that existed between the two of them. I knew instinctively that Tammy felt it was hopeless to challenge her mother. Despite her terrible and neglected childhood, Tammy had turned into a truly good and caring person. Away from here at school in Texas, Tammy seemed to thrive; she was happy, self-assured, and outspoken. Contact with Margaret, though, eroded that happiness and self-confidence. Tammy had also confided to me her fear that if she incurred her mother's wrath, her monthly allowance could end. She needed this money to survive while she completed college. The less contact there was between Tammy and her mother, the better off Tammy would be. Sadly enough, I also knew that Margaret would feel nothing but relief in not having to bother with her daughter anymore.

Back at the funeral home Margaret asked, "Ren, will you get Tammy to the airport? I have some important papers that I have to go over with Harry before we leave for California. I'll meet you at the hanger at six o'clock. Here are the directions," she said, handing me a slip of paper.

I didn't like the idea and started to object, "Margaret, don't you think…."

"Please, Ren, don't argue. Just do this," she said firmly. She walked over to Tammy and put her arms around her shoulders. The gesture was a pseudo-hug. Their bodies didn't even meet. Mother and daughter didn't even look at each other.

Almost as an afterthought, Margaret called out to Tammy, "Do well in school. If you need anything, just call me. I'll talk to you when I can." But the words were carried away on the breeze because Margaret had already turned to go as she was speaking. Tammy smiled a little when she heard that I was bringing her to the airport.

At the terminal she checked in at the counter. We still had time so we went to a café not far from her departure gate. I had coffee and she had a soda. Fifteen minutes later, her flight was called.

"Are you going to be all right?" I asked with concern.

She gave me a bear hug. "I'll be okay. I've learned to be tough. The question is whether you'll be all right."

I just nodded yes. Before Tammy went through the boarding door, she turned around again. In a very sober tone she said to me, "Ren, you be careful. Make sure my mother doesn't stress you out too much. I won't be home again, ever. But call me anytime when you need to talk, and come visit when you've had enough of Mother."

With that said, she smiled and walked away. I watched the plane until it had taxied out onto the runway. With Tammy's departure, I felt an inexplicable loneliness.

Margaret had said that she would take care of getting our things packed and the luggage to the airport. I still had almost two hours to waste before I needed to be at the hanger. Obviously, the easiest way to spend it was in a bar. I nursed two drinks, not enough to inhibit my driving but enough to dull the nagging premonition attached to Tammy's warning. I still had an hour to wait.

I decided I might as well get to the hanger early and make sure that there were no last minute glitches. When I pulled in, Harry's car was already there. I parked behind the hanger so as not to be in anyone's way. As I walked up to the hanger door, I heard voices. I almost tripped over my undone shoelace, so I stooped to tie it. I was listening to Harry and Margaret. At first I thought it was just campaign talk. Then, Margaret said something I will never forget.

"Ren is having a harder time with Mark Jr.'s death than I am. I have to confess something, Harry. Right after Mark murdered that girl, I knew I had to do something to get through the mess that little bastard got himself into. I went to a hypnotist and had him implant into my mind that Mark wasn't really my son. That way when I was asked questions about him I wouldn't be over-emotional. It worked. I knew people thought of him as my son, but I didn't have any feelings toward him. I had to go back a dozen times before the hypnotism finally worked." Margaret's voice sounded elated.

"Sitting here right now, all I feel is that some kid died in the electric chair. But, the whole matter doesn't get any deeper than that. And it's over now, anyway. You're the only one who knows this, Harry, and I don't want anyone else to know—ever. Including Ren. What do you think, Harry? Am I smart or what?"

"You did what you had to do, Margaret, to get through a bad situation. That's what it's all about. Actually, I think the way you acted about this has made people admire you more. You showed them you can handle a tough situation and stay levelheaded. You won votes from all this."

"Yes, I did, didn't I?" said Margaret.

Then Harry continued, "I'm not worried about the situation with Mark. That's behind us. But, we might have a new problem. Janson called and he's hitting us up for more money."

"Who's that?" Margaret queried.

"The man we hired to impersonate that police lieutenant to break up Ren and Lynda. Remember? He reminded me that he had to pay the photographer who rigged up those pictures a lot more money than he had planned on. Something about it taking a lot more monkeying with than usual. You know, trying to make one picture out of two. He says he's in a jam and needs five thousand."

"What do you think? Should we give it to him or will he keep trying to get more?" asked Margaret.

"I think we should pay him. He did a hell of a job. We'll have other jobs for him and we can deduct it from his pay."

"Okay, do it," Margaret said, "but tell him if he tries to weasel any more money out of us, we'll have a real lieutenant visit him."

I felt as if someone had just punched me in the gut and I was unable to breathe. I just stood outside the hanger, staring at the door. What a fool I was! I had been deluding myself about Margaret. She had no feelings. How could she have done this to me? To scheme like that to break up my relationship with Lynda—the woman I loved, the woman I had been going to marry. And for what? I knew the answer. I was a pawn in her political games. She had wanted a husband to make her appear more settled and she had chosen me. I was nothing more than a way to get votes.

Deep down inside, I knew that I was angrier with myself than with Margaret. I had known what Margaret was like, for God's sake, after working for her for all these years. I knew first hand how deep her deception could go. How could I have been so gullible? How could I have gone along with this charade? I hadn't even given Lynda a chance to explain. I had swallowed the detective's story hook, line, and sinker. I had fallen into the trap with no questions asked. Margaret was a conniving bitch. I felt like strangling her, but I was so emotionally drained that I couldn't even move.

First, I had to calm down. I didn't want to say something in anger that I would regret later on. Maybe, though, I deserved what I got for being such an idiot.

I emitted a sigh of resignation. Somehow I got my emotions under control. Within my soul, despite how angry I felt, I knew I wouldn't do anything. Margaret left nothing but devastation in her wake. And what about Mark Jr.? How could she just dismiss her own son like that? He had been no more than a kid. I thought mothers were supposed to fight to the death to protect their young. The steps that Margaret had taken to reject her son were incredulous. No one would believe me if I told them what she had done.

Then, my thoughts drifted to Harry? Was he as evil as Margaret? I had trusted him. I had thought he was my friend. How could he equate the death of a human being with votes? Everything that was happening was unbelievable, totally unbelievable. But I knew how dangerous Margaret could be, and the best thing for me to do right now was not to let on that I knew anything. It was now a matter of my own survival.

I walked the last steps to the hanger door and called out, "Hello, I'm here."

"There you are, Ren," Margaret said. "I wondered where you were. The plane is fueled and the pilot is ready. Are you feeling all right? You look a little pale."

No, I thought. I'm not. But before I said anything, Margaret continued, "You can rest on the plane. Okay."

Margaret was happy. That was it. That was part of what was silently eating at me. She should be grieving. She should be almost unable to function because of her grief. But, she was happy. Cheerfulness emanated from her. This was wrong, I thought, very wrong.

Harry looked strained from the day's activities. If he didn't watch out, he would wind up having another heart attack. But, this time I didn't feel as badly for Harry as I had before. The old adage, "You reap what you sow," popped into my mind. I applied it to Harry with a sense of satisfaction, but then I pushed the thought aside because the idea that it could apply to me too began to seep into my consciousness. Harry escorted Margaret and me to the corporate jet. When Margaret had ascended the steps, he put his arm on my shoulder, "Ren, get some rest and enjoy California. Don't worry about anything." Then, he turned and headed for his SUV.

After I got settled in the plane, I had the fleeting thought that maybe the plane would crash and this whole mess would end. There were some problems in the tower and we had to wait about forty-five minutes for clearance to take off.

Just before we began to taxi down the runway, there was a pounding on the side of the plane. The flight attendant opened the door and Harry hopped in. He had a mile-wide grin on his face. "I stopped at the lounge at the terminal. They had Miles Lennel, the political talk show host, on television. Let me be the first to bear the good news. Lennel said, and I quote, 'Governor Hall, with her savvy business sense and her ability to deliver jobs will definitely be a presidential candidate in a few years.'"

With a quick wave of his hand, Harry disappeared out the door. The attendant closed it tightly, and within seconds we were taxiing down the runway and lifting off.

As we flew over the city, Margaret leaned close to me. "Look out the window, Ren. See that great state of South Carolina? It's all mine. But this isn't the end. I'm going to have more. I'm going to be President of the whole country some day, and you'll be a very famous man because you'll be the husband of the President." Margaret leaned her head on my shoulder. "You'll see. It will all be worth what we've gone through."

I pretended to close my eyes so I could get some sleep. I was wide-awake, though, thinking. Power. Margaret never got enough. She always needed more. She loved power. Why did I stay if I was so sickened by what she did? I knew the answer but I had been too scared to say it to myself. I was addicted to the power as much as Margaret was. We needed each other because we made each other more powerful. Why had I married her? She didn't love me—she didn't love anyone. Again, I knew the answer—power, just for the power.

My mind immediately went to the snake that Margaret kept in a large aquarium in the spare bedroom across from the master suite. On the other side of that room was a cage with an ample supply of mice. Margaret's weekly ritual was to take two of the mice with red marks on their backs and feed them to the snake. The snake quickly devoured them. Margaret would then walk back to the mouse cage and put some food into it. She would enjoy watching the mice scramble for the food for a few minutes and then decide which two would be the future sacrifice. When she had made up her mind, she would pick the two up and draw a line on their backs with a red magic marker. The mice would scamper away when Margaret reached in her hand, but she always got the ones she wanted. These were the mice that would be devoured by the snake at its next feeding. When I asked her why she did this, she replied, "It's the power, the power to choose who will die. I know that I am in control. I love that feeling." As I lay back in the plane seat, I felt very uncomfortable. I wondered if the red mark had already been placed on my back.

Micro and Macro Power Warriors

By
Amos

Micro and Macro Power Warriors

Chapter 1
Power Games

———————

Power is commonly defined as the ability to act with some kind of authority. When referring to man, the quest for power most commonly comes down to a struggle. In our government, power gets divided among the President, Congress, and the courts. Since the President decides who will be in the Cabinet, he controls the segment of the government that we refer to as the departments, such as the Department of Energy and the Department of Defense. Each department is headed by a Secretary, who goes to Cabinet meetings and helps the President to create policies. Each department also has an Undersecretary, who actually runs the day-to-day operations. Then, Congress has the power to make laws, and the courts have the power to enforce the laws and to decide if the laws are constitutional.

All of these people, individually and as groups, have power. Each segment is trying, in some way, to reach out and usurp or curb the power of some other segment. We often hear the legislative branch accuse the courts of overstepping their boundaries and of legislating laws. Then, we hear the judges from our courts complaining that the legislature is making laws that are unconstitutional. And within the Cabinet, policies are created that are not called laws but (in government speech) "codes." Just as we do with laws, we have to comply with these codes or face the alternative, which is usually a fine or jail. In other countries these power conflicts sometimes still result in special elections, assassinations, civil wars, and even genocide.

In the corporate world the power structure consists of a board of directors and an executive staff, headed by a CEO (Chief Executive Officer). Sometimes, although not always, this corporate system becomes more streamlined than the government's so that the common goal of making a profit can be realized. The need for profit, however, does not eliminate power struggles. The fight over power can lead to coups, character assassination, and sabotage within the corporation.

One might say, "Well, so goes the world of politics and business." The problem, though, is that we carry these power issues over into other parts of our lives. Power struggles are found at home between spouses, siblings, and parents and their children. Power struggles are found in competitive activities and social groups such as PTO's and civic clubs.

Power struggles can even be found in churches, where one would expect to be free from such behavior. Arguments, based on power struggles, often break out and divide congregations. The following expressions are frequently heard: "It's the pastor's responsibility." "No, it's the deacons' responsibility." "The board of trustees needs to have the final say." "Maybe the bishop needs to be contacted." A common tactic within churches is to eliminate people from the power structure by calling them immoral. "He has been divorced." "He drinks too much." "She cheated on her husband." If a person can be tagged as immoral, he or she can be dismissed as unworthy of power. And, of course, all one has to do to gain power in this situation is to declare another person's sin greater than his own (and hope his is not revealed).

This method of the "immoral power play" has run rampant within our government. Politicians battle over "moral ground" as if it were possible for them to produce justice when the very way they obtained their offices was unjust. Somehow it is forgotten that the founding fathers of this country were all "lawbreakers," people whom the British crown would have hanged as traitors if our forefathers had not beaten them at another power game—war.

A favorite topic of many talk shows today is the schoolyard bully, who is accused of villainous acts. The guests on these shows lay the blame for their failed lives on the trauma suffered from this bully. Although this is true to some extent, it is also true that the bully, if asked, would say that he did what he did out of fear of becoming a victim himself. This does not justify the bully's actions, but it does let us know that fear is an important ingredient in all power games.

This brings us to the reason why most power struggles start—the belief that if a person does not take someone else's power, someone will get his. The amount of power, no matter how superficial, is not what matters. What matters is that it is his, and, to protect it, the person quickly moves to the offensive. It is the philosophy of "get them before they get you."

Even in small stores that only have a few employees, power games can be observed. The owner will try to capitalize on these power games by pitting one employee against another to find out who is stealing, who is leaving early, or who intends to quit and go elsewhere. Amazingly enough, in most cases the customers, whose patronage pays the bills, are seldom taken into consideration. We all, at one time or another, have been standing in a line while employees argue over who will wait on us. It is amazing how quickly a business group can lose tract of its main purpose—to take care of its customers and to make a profit.

I once went to a transportation meeting. Several years before, the group had formed a non-profit corporation to provide transportation for those in need. The group had had great success in its early years, but now, several years later, no one even considered the riders any more. Every conversation was about who on the board was going to get what and who was going to control what. The board did not care about the employees, and the employees showed their displeasure by taking the situation out on the clients. When the buses failed to pick up numerous riders, among whom were some elderly people totally dependent upon the system, the board blamed the staff, and the staff blamed the board. Yet, as individuals most board members and most staff members were committed to the idea that transportation was needed to get the clients to work, to medical appointments, and to grocery stores. Once the power games had begun, though, no one on the board or staff could find a way to move back to the main purpose. Therefore, within a few years of the initiation of the power games, the system collapsed, leaving the clients with no transportation at all.

We are a society that is addicted to power games, each of us playing them out in our various arenas. For many of us they start the second we awake, for most families are involved in their own power struggles. The mother might call several times before the child or teenager finally gets up to get ready for school. Husband and wife may play a power game about who has to take the children to school and pick them up or who is going to control the money.

There are some amazing statistics that reveal these power struggles in the family setting. In the year 2000 an estimated four million people were victims of spousal abuse, and more than 2,500 of these resulted in death. Arrests for domestic violence disputes have reached an epidemic level. In this same year, over three million cases of child abuse were reported, and over 2,000 children died as a result. The national divorce rate in the year 2000 was fifty percent. As family members play out power games, they become addicted to the power in the process and carry the addiction cycle back into the workplace and civic community.

After arriving at their jobs, power games often continue. In some cases a person's job, as defined by his employer, is "conquering" people. Getting control over others is the job of bill collectors, salespeople, social workers, policemen, judges, corporate presidents, and even teachers, just to name a few. And usually there is an ample supply of weapons to use to gain control. Court, jail, tests, added work, emotional explosions, suspension of licenses, and loss of benefits are just a few of a seemingly endless list. The control of others and the use of power are often necessary, but the abuse of power—sometimes the outrageous abuse of power—is unacceptable. A better method could always have been used.

After dealing with power struggles at home in the morning and at work during the day, a person might attend a club or church meeting in the evening, and the power games continue. Most of the time when a person pushes for power, he does it in the form of a question to disguise his intention. "Why should Mrs. Smith's daughter be able to have her wedding at the church? She hasn't attended for years." This is, of course, a way of saying, "My daughter comes to church every Sunday, so I am better and should be recognized more." Then, when we return home, the games begin again. The children argue about doing their homework and chores; husbands and wives argue about housework and errands. Most of the time family members play power games with each other instead of rationally discussing what is on their minds.

Are there people who have gotten beyond all of this? Sure, but sadly enough the number is too few, especially those who are totally free of power games. A few of us learn to do better at home; some of us even work in power-game-free environments. But, for most of us, the games are continuous, and we have no idea how to stop them.

A perfect example of this occurred at a business club meeting, which I attended several months ago. The guest speaker was an executive from a major electric power corporation. The man had a well-prepared slide show that explained how his company provided consumers with electricity. About mid-way in the presentation there was a slide with a picture of a shark swimming around a school of small fish. When the speaker announced that the sharks represented his company, the audience (about eighty people) burst out laughing—but it was an uneasy laugh. The speaker, realizing the slide revealed that his company was involved in power games with electric co-ops and municipal electric service, immediately tried to cover his blunder by saying, "But we're the good sharks!" This, of course, evoked more laughter, but everyone in the room knew that this revelation was "bad news" for them, the consumers.

This corporation had an established reputation for providing good service to its customers and excellent dividends to its investors. There was no need for any games, but temptation was too great. They had to control more so the power games began.

We can all use the power we have to do good or to do evil. The ability to act with authority forces us to make decisions about how we should act. The world would be much more harmonious if, when using our power, we remembered the commandment, "Thou shall love they neighbor as thyself."

Micro and Macro Power Warriors

Chapter 2
Addiction to Power

One definition of an addict is someone who is psychologically dependent, and certainly there are people who are psychologically dependent upon power. In *Potentates*, Margaret is not only addicted to power but also sweeps those around her into this addiction, turning them into effective enablers. Margaret seeks power for no other reason than to have it. This is different from a candidate or elected official who wants to hold a political office because he believes strongly in trying to accomplish a goal, whether it is related to education, capitalism, the environment, etc.

The addiction to power, which many of our political leaders today suffer from, is not a matter of the left opposing the right or Republicans opposing Democrats. Instead, it is a pure psychological dependence on power. The right and left issue or any other issue is just a means for politicians to reach their ends. For any candidate or official to be dedicated to a set of beliefs and to honestly try to enact these beliefs is certainly better for the welfare of our nation than to have candidates and officials who are addicted to power. Those addicted to power "sell out" just so that they can acquire more personal power.

We can take an example from history to illustrate these two extremely opposite states of mind. Hitler wanted power to achieve power. He used the issue of economic reform. The German people were suffering from an economic disaster caused by World War I. Hitler convinced the German people that he could change the situation, but once in control, his addiction to power became apparent. His concern for the citizenry of Germany turned cold as he had thousands upon thousands of people murdered and started ever-expanding wars. Hitler eventually carried his addiction to completion by committing suicide, thus controlling even his own demise.

On the other hand, in the United States President Franklin D. Roosevelt was also facing an economic depression. Every indication up until the time he became President showed that he supported a strong capitalistic system. His family had benefited from free enterprise, and he personally was a benefactor. As President, though, he realized that he would have to compromise. America needed programs to help people get back to work and to get economic recovery on its way. Roosevelt knew that if he failed in his efforts, his critics would hold him accountable in the next election, but he chose to go forward because he was committed to free enterprise more than he was to holding onto the power of the presidency. In the end, capitalism survived because Roosevelt shared the power that was in his hands, rather than being consumed with getting more. This, of course, eventually led to Roosevelt getting re-elected three more times. His ability to seize the moment, to compromise, so all could win or benefit not only saved the nation but also turned Roosevelt from a politician into a statesman.

In recent years we have seen a group called the Teleban use the Muslim faith to try to gain power by crashing planes into the Twin Towers and the Pentagon. This, of course, had nothing to do with the Muslim faith, but unfortunately, the Muslim faith became a cover for those who were addicted to raw power. If they wanted to get a message across to the American people, they could have chosen an array of other effective ways—television time, newspaper ads, radio stations, marches, demonstrations, or even boycotts. They could even have attempted to convince the Arab world not to sell the United States one more gallon of oil. All of these possibilities would have delivered a message, loud and clear, but, instead, they decided to create a war in the hope of becoming famous and powerful enough to be dictators in the Middle East.

Power games at some level can be amusing, even silly, but as in the case of September 11th, carried to the extreme, they can become deadly. In the years 1975 to 1979, Khmer Rouge ruled Cambodia. During this period 1.7 million people were murdered; that equaled 21% of the population. On December 13, 1937, the Chinese city of Nanking was taken by Japanese forces. In the massacre that followed, 300,000 Chinese were slaughtered, and 20,000 women were raped, including young girls less than ten years old and women over seventy.

Other examples of deadly power struggles can also be cited. Between 1981 and 1983 the right-wing Guatemalan military government targeted the Maya people, killing more than 85,000 of them. In 1994 in Rwanda, the Hutu militia and the Rwandan Armed Forces, which controlled the government, went on a murdering spree. Using machetes, they killed 800,000 Rwandans, mostly Tutsis and moderate Hutu government politicians. Babies were torn from their mothers' arms and thrown headfirst into pits.

Even more examples can be given of the atrocities that result from power games. In 1975, East Timor, a tiny country, was attacked by Indonesia. The Indonesian military murdered over 200,000 of the country's 700,000 people. In 1966 the Chinese government began a genocide of the Mongols. Over the next ten years, 200,000 died. Many of the Mongols suffered horrible deaths, being brutally tortured. Some were sliced apart piece by piece; others were burned until they died, being literally cooked alive. In 1971, Yahya Khan, president of Pakistan, ordered the Pakistani army to begin a genocide that would leave a quarter of a million Hindus dead. Once a house was marked with a yellow "H," the Hindus living there would be tortured and killed. The bayonet was the choice of weapon in this slaughter.

And, of course, the most widely known atrocity occurred in World War II. Between the years 1939 and 1944, the Germans, under the leadership of Adolph Hitler, tried to annihilate the European Jewish population, murdering approximately six million people. At least 750,000 Jews were killed in the Treblinka death camp; 550,000 Jews in the Belzec death camp; 200,000 Jews in the Sobibor death camp; 150,000 Jews at the Chelmno death camp; 50,000 Jews at the Lublin death camp; and 1,000,000 Jews and 1,000,000 non-Jews at the infamous Auschwitz death camp.

The committing of genocide is an addiction to power in one of its worst forms. Simply stated, the leaders who commit such an atrocity are refusing to compromise in any way. Their message is clear, "You do what I say or you will die and even if you do what I say, you may still die anyway." For leaders who sanction genocide, their addiction to power has become so complete that killing is "routine business." Slamming one baby against a hard wall or, for that matter, thousands of babies against a wall, will be done if that is what it takes to get more power. Power rules the life of those addicted to it—evil becomes good and righteousness becomes evil. The minds of these leaders become so twisted that they cannot understand what is logical to the rest of the world. The Apostle Paul wrote, "God gave them over to a reprobate mind...being filled with...murder." A person who is addicted to power has a reprobative mind, and, indeed, is a person who has lost his conscience.

Chapter 3
Power Addicts and Politics

In the political arena there are many power addicts that have obtained high offices. They will literally do anything to hold onto their power, even if it is illegal; consequently, good, honest people, whom we desperately need, will rarely submit themselves to the political process.

These political power addicts unfortunately have become pseudo-leaders. Their power games set the stage for the leaders in our professional and business communities, civic clubs, charitable organizations, and churches to mimic. Yes, even church leaders. Amazingly enough, greed for power has seeped into the church, a place one would think was beyond such behavior. I was at a church meeting once. For weeks a group of ladies had planned a celebration, which included a chicken dinner. When the pastor stood in front of the church and had what could only be called a "temper tantrum" because he did not like fried chicken, the event was cancelled. The "mistake" that the ladies had made was in not getting the pastor's approval and support of the event and menu ahead of time. The pastor, supposedly a good, decent, educated man, was so addicted to power that nothing, absolutely nothing, could happen in the church without his pre-approval.

17

If something were done without his knowledge, he would use all of his power to terrorize the offender.

In another instance, I saw a deacon insist that money specifically raised to send a youth group on a trip be spent instead on a new van. When another deacon said it would be wrong to spend the money raised for the youth group on something else, an unsavory incident that had happened several years before involving the protesting deacon was brought up. The protesting deacon was forced to resign. A new deacon, who just happened to be the brother of the church treasurer, was elected. Soon, a new van sat in the church parking lot, and the youth did not go on any trip.

These two examples are not typical, though, of most pastors who do, indeed, encourage the congregation to help in any way they can. These examples are important, though, because most people would think that the church would be a place of true community, a place beyond power games. The fact that power games have reached our spiritual lives speaks to how bad the quest for power has become.

This power addictive leadership has moved through our culture at a rapid rate. The question is from where does this behavior stem? Who are the culprits? The simple answer is that this nefarious behavior initiates from the "bad" behavior of our political leadership. Too often those who hold powerful positions in government are willing to do whatever it takes to achieve their ends. Lies, sixty-second ads filled with twisted truths, bribes, character assassination, "legal" trickery, distortion of the rules of order, and scare tactics that instill fear into the public (when, in truth, no serious danger is at hand) are all commonplace. The American public is so used to this type of behavior that we are immune to it and actually consider it "normal." Thus, bad behavior is now acceptable behavior.

These pseudo-leaders have almost completely taken over our national political process, as well as our state and local governments. Pseudo-leaders exist primarily because of the power brokers that give them large sums of money. These power brokers are fivefold: 1) the Political Action Committees (known as PAC's), comprised of lobbyists who work for large industries collectively; 2) individual mega-corporations; 3) individuals who want their personal agendas carried out; 4) businessmen looking for contracts; and 5) special interest groups. These power brokers contribute large sums or arrange to have money and other gifts given to candidates or a political party, which, in turn, gives the money to the candidates. Either way the results are the same—the power broker accomplishes his personal agenda or his organization's agenda to get some special treatment.

The Federal Election Commission (FEC) reported that during the 1999-2000 election cycle Senate candidates spent $437 million, an increase of 52% from the 1997-1998 cycle. The FEC cited a total of $1,006 billion being spent out of the $1,047 billion raised by congressional candidates in the 1999-2000 election. This is the highest recorded amount since the Federal Election Commission was initiated twenty-five years ago. The total dollars spent in the 1989-1990 cycle was just under $472 million.

In the 2000 Senate race in New Jersey, the FEC reported that $79.3 million was expended. In the 1999-2000 election cycle all federal candidates received contributions from Political Action Committees (PAC). These contributions totaled $245.4 million, up 19% from the $206.8 million in the 1997-1998 election. Political Action Committees gave $127.9 million to Republicans, $116.8 million to Democrats, and just under $631 thousand to third party candidates. Also, PAC contributions to incumbents far exceeded the contributions given to other candidates. The Commission's figures show incumbents receiving a whopping $184 million compared to the $27 million received by their opponents and just over $34 million went to open-seat races.

A political party itself also brings in millions of dollars for its candidates. This money is referred to as "soft dollars" and "hard dollars." A soft dollar is money spent for a candidate without the official campaign being directly involved. A hard dollar is money that goes directly into the candidate's political bank account. The Federal Election Commission reported an increase in fundraising efforts by both major political parties in the 1999-2000 election. Receipts reported by Republicans totaled almost $716 million for both soft dollars and hard dollars. On the other hand, Democrats reported funds of just over $520 million in both soft and hard dollars. Most of this money comes from donors who are looking for favors, and, beyond a doubt, these favors end up costing the rest of the American taxpayers billions of dollars.

It is easy to see how campaign contributions have bought certain industries enormous power. In the decade from 1990 to 2000, the accounting industry gave over $51 million to congressional candidates. These were the same years during which accounting practices became extremely lax, and the end result, as we now know, is that the industry has been left with little, if any, credibility. When the Securities and Exchange Commission (SEC) saw a conflict—the nation's five biggest accounting firms

(Arthur Anderson, Deloitte and Touche, Ernst and Young, KPMG, and Pricewaterhouse Coopers) were doing consulting work *and* audits for the same corporations—the commission proposed new rules that would end this absurd practice. The accounting industry immediately lobbied congressmen to call Arthur Levitt, chairman of the Securities and Exchange Commission, to protest the proposed changes and to threaten to cut off funds to the SEC. The commission was forced to give in and halt the new proposals.

Enron was one of the corporations for which Arthur Anderson provided consulting services worth $27 million. Later Arthur Anderson also did the audits, which we now know were deceptive, causing stockholders to lose millions. Enron, which had given over a million dollars to congressmen and senators, could move at will to block or create any law. Enron stockholders have paid dearly for those contributions and eventually the taxpayers will pay also.

Penelope Paturis, a reporter for *Forbes*, has written about allegations made against several mega-corporations in "The Corporate Scandal Sheet." These companies include Adelphia Communications, AOL/Time-Warner, Arthur Anderson, Bristol-Myers Squibb, CMS Energy, Duke Energy, Dynegy, El Paso, Enron, Global Crossing, Halliburton, Homestore.Com, K-Mart, Merck, Mirant, Nicor Energy, Peregrine Systems, Qwest Communications, Reliant Energy, Tyco, WorldCom, and Xerox. Each of these mega-corporations has been accused of being involved in unsavory activities. Inflating capital expenses and hiding debt, shredding documents, off-the-books partnerships, bribing foreign governments, inflating revenue, accounting practices that mislead investors, overstated assets, tax evasion, off-the-books loans, and falsifying financial documents are just some of the allegations.

Michael Dobbs, a reporter for the *Washington Post*, shows the irony about government interaction with Halliburton. The company is under investigation for unsavory practices, yet Halliburton, which just happened to be formerly headed by Vice-President Cheney, has been awarded government contracts for Operation Iraqi Freedom worth in excess of $1.7 billion. And Halliburton will make millions more on its "no bid" contracts which were handed to the company by the U.S. Army.

This is just another way that mega-corporations play the power game. They transplant their leadership into government offices, and these leaders, once they are in political office, transfer the power back to them. This is a two way street because when high-power government workers retire, they are given jobs in the mega-corporations for favors done while they were supposed to be serving the American people.

Another example of buying political influence is found in the telephone industry, which gave congressmen $65 million from 1990 to 2000 to take care of its special interests. WorldCom, the nation's second largest long distance carrier, is now bankrupt after overstating its income by four billion dollars. This four billion-dollar "misstatement" accrued while WorldCom leadership was lobbying to completely deregulate the long distance telephone business.

The Center for Responsive Politics reported that from 1989 to 2002 WorldCom spent more than $7.6 million in soft money. It had lobbying expenditures of $2.9 million in the year 2000 and over $3 million in 2001. The Center also reported that President Bush raised $41,601 from

WorldCom during the 2000 election cycle. WorldCom gave the TrentLott Leadership Institute at the University of Mississippi $1 million, a sum supposedly "off the books." This means that the money did not need to be disclosed to the Federal Election Commission.

When WorldCom went bankrupt, it was in total disgrace, yet this did not stop the politicians from doing favors for those who had paid them huge "contributions." In a move that can only be seen as a reward for terrible behavior, the Bush administration gave WorldCom a substantially lucrative contract to provide phone service in Iraq. Corporations that have acted ethically and used sound business practices did not even get a chance to bid on the contract.

Other industries spend big bucks, too. During 1990 to 2000 the tobacco industry contributed over $40 million to members of Congress to keep the sale of its products going strong and to continue the subsidies to tobacco farmers. The oil and gas industry "donated" over $120 million from 1990 to 2000 to members of Congress, and, as a result, prices to consumers have steadily risen. The pharmaceuticals and health products industry contributed over $70 million during this same ten year period to members of Congress to convince them that Americans should pay more for drugs than citizens in any other country. In 1990 this industry "donated" just over $3 million to political campaigns, but by the year 2000 this amount had increased to $26 million. Is it any wonder that Congress does not do anything about the prices Americans pay for prescription drugs?

Commercial banks and law firms are also large political contributors in the struggle for power. During this ten-year period (1990 to 2000), commercial banks gave $96 million to members of Congress. In 1990 commercial banks contributed just over $9 million, but by 2000 this amount had risen to over $24 million. From 1990 to 2000, law firms gave over $360 million. In 1990 law firms contributed a "paltry" 24 million; by 2000, this figure had reached over $112 million.

The result of all of these contributions is a "thank you" in the form of huge paybacks by government officials to these mega-industries. The paybacks amount to almost $125 billion a year. According to Chris Hartman in an article published in *Minuteman Media*, "two different sets of books" are maintained by these mega-corporations, "one [that] they show to their shareholders and one [that] they show to the government for tax purposes." Hartman also cites that a study conducted by the Internal Revenue Service revealed that the income reported to the corporations' stockholders was "24% higher than the income reported to the government."

In the year 2002, the total corporate income tax paid was $195 billion. Returning $125 billion to these industries is a huge give away when we consider that the Citizen's Guide to the Federal Budget estimates that the entire budget spent for education, training, employment, and social services programs is only $74 billion. After deducting paybacks, corporate America really contributes only $70 billion in taxes.

Compare this paltry $70 billion, to the $995 billion paid by individuals and the $712 billion paid in payroll taxes. For years our elected officials have been abusing their power so that the burden of taxes is on those who work. The income tax should rightfully be renamed the workers' tax, for earning money by working for it has become a taxable offense.

There are almost endless examples of these corporate paybacks. Over $5 billion goes to an export-import bank, which subsidizes corporations to make sales abroad. The assumption is that Americans will get jobs in the process. The truth is that many of these major corporations have been employing fewer American workers since receiving the funds. *Time* magazine reported in an article dated November 9, 1998, that the "five biggest beneficiaries—AT&T, Bechtel, Boeing, General Electric, and McDonnell Douglas—tell another story. At these companies, which account for about 40% of all loans, grants and long-term guarantees in this decade, overall employment has fallen 38% [and] more than a third of a million jobs have disappeared." Some other noteworthy corporations that have received large sums of money are Enron, Halliburton, Mobil, IBM, General Motors, and Raytheon.

An environmental group called L.E.A.N. reported that Borden Chemicals and Plastic received over $16 million in industrial tax exemptions in a ten-year period and only created four permanent jobs. These paybacks exist on the state and local levels, too. L.E.A.N. also reported that the state of Louisiana gave corporations $300 million in tax dollars but created only 6,250 jobs in return.

Another example of power broker paybacks involves the National Association of Broadcasters (NAB). NAB has lobbied successfully for television broadcasters to control digital television at no charge to them. License fees, which would have been worth about $70 billion, were given away free by the 1996 Congress. This means that the American taxpayers will pay $70 billion more in taxes to offset this deficit. The broadcasting industry donated almost $5 million in soft money contributions to the

Democratic and Republican parties to accomplish this. This is not a bad return on an investment, is it?

Many books have been written addressing the issue of the misuse of tax dollars to "pay back" corporations, individuals, and groups for their campaign contributions. Robert W. Benson, a law professor at Loyola, reported in his book, *Getting Business off the Public Dole,* that Sandia National Laboratories spends "$300,000 in federal tax dollars to show Disneyland how to shoot off fancier fireworks." He also documented that many states have huge giveaway programs for corporations. For instance, Illinois gave 240 million dollars' worth of land and bonuses to Sears; Kentucky gave $140 million in aid to Dofasco Inc. and Co-Steel; and New Mexico gave Intel $114 million in incentive programs, including a promise of no property taxes for thirty years. Benson's book is intriguing, for it not only states the problem but also gives solutions that will close the loopholes in our government laws. Unfortunately, Congress is not looking for solutions to close loopholes and to stop "give aways." On the contrary, it seems as if Congress seizes every opportunity possible to find new ways to give away the taxpayers' money.

Our nation's largest airline corporation failed to provide adequate security although it had been warned repeatedly by a government agency that it lacked proper security. This eventually led to the September 11th disaster, causing loss of life and billions of dollars in damage. For having contributed to the 9-11 disaster, the airline industry was given a $5 billion subsidy by the federal government. Of course, the airline workers who lost their jobs due to the crisis did not receive a dime.

Another book entitled *Take the Rich off Welfare* by Mark Zepezower and Arthur Naiman reported that in

1996 the Pentagon received $265 billion of our taxpayers' dollars. Much of this money went to corporations that greatly overcharged the military. Subsequently, many scandals have been uncovered, resulting in fines. For example, Grumman had to pay a fine of $20 million because it had forced various subcontractors "into making political contributions." Northrop paid a fine of $17 million for "falsifying test data on cruise missiles and fighter jets." Five corporations—RCA, Raytheon, Hughes, Grumman, and Boeing—were fined $15 million for "trafficking in classified documents," and Rockwell paid a $5.5 million fine for "committing criminal fraud" against the United States Air Force. These fines might sound like a lot of money; however, they are insubstantial compared to the total taxpayers' dollars these corporations received and the profits they made.

The United States' agriculture policy also costs American taxpayers millions of dollars. According to an article in the *Washington Times* written by John McCaslin, our government spends $20 million a year to warehouse a billion-dollar supply of powered milk which the government wants to keep off the market. The Heritage Foundation calls the United States' agriculture policy a "mistargeted system" and "America's largest corporate welfare program." The Environmental Working Group states that Westvaco, Chevron, and John Hancock Mutual Life Insurance [all Fortune 500 companies], are among the farm corporations that receive more than $1 million in subsidies. Over the next ten years, farm bills passed by Congress will cost the American taxpayers close to $171 billion in subsidies.

The 1996 Federal Agriculture Improvement and Reform Act sought to reduce subsidies over a seven-year period. Unfortunately, intense lobbying efforts made this act ineffectual since so many bills calling for supplemental spending were passed. Actually, direct subsidy payments, which averaged $9 billion a year in the early 1990's, are now up to $20 billion a year.

On its own web site, the USDA states that it has increased its need for funding sizably by expanding its existing programs and creating new ones. The Environmental Quality Incentives Program (EQIP) has marked 60% of its funding for livestock producers. This is up from 50% in the 1996 Farm Act, which allowed $450,000 per operation. The Farm Service Agency (FSA) funding for its guaranteed and direct loan programs is now set at $3.8 billion. Some of the crops which the government offers assistance programs for are corn, grains, such as wheat, barley, and oats, cotton, rice, soybeans, peanuts, wool, mohair, honey, small chickpeas, lentils, and dry peas.

All of these are examples of "pay backs" for political contributions and favors. Huge corporations "wheel and deal" in power. They spend millions having their lobbyists whine and dine politicians so that their corporate agendas can be met. Since these corporations contribute millions to political candidates on the national and state levels, they expect "their" candidates to support whatever legislation they suggest. Any candidate who doesn't go along with these corporations and who doesn't take their PAC money usually does not find himself elected. These corporations will do whatever they can to maintain and increase their power and have no conscience about anyone who suffers or gets hurt along the way.

Chapter 4
The CEO—the Biggest Power Player

No analysis of power can be complete without a discussion of chief executive officers, or CEO's. They are our nation's biggest power players. These men and a few women, who are the leaders of our largest corporations, rise to their position, in most cases, by being consumed with power wars. They take over competing companies, control government regulations and politicians, scheme against consumers to add hidden costs to products built to break down and scheme against their own stockholders, whom they are supposed to be serving, in some cases duping the investors out of their entire life savings. By the time these CEO's reach the top, they completely control who will sit on the corporate board, who the auditors will be, and what information will go into the annual report.

While corporate scandals abound in our nation, corporations continue to pay their CEO's higher and higher salaries. The average salary of a CEO is over $8 million a year. In the 1980's American CEO's got paid about forty-two times the hourly wage of an average worker. By the year 2000, the pay for a CEO had risen to three hundred times the hourly wage of an average worker. According to *Fair Economy*, from 2001 to 2002 the average salary for

CEO's at thirty-seven of the biggest defense contractors increased 79%.

Many CEO's receive much more than their base salary. The combined salary, stock-options, and bonuses for some have reached ridiculous proportions. In 2002, Milan Panic of ICN Pharmaceuticals, Inc. received more than $60 million in total compensations; Miles White of Abbott Labs received over 37 million; and Henry McKinnell of Pfizer, Inc. received over $33 million. Steven Jobs of Apple Computer received more than $89 million, and Craig Conway of PeopleSoft, Inc. more than $84 million. Ray Irani of Occidental Petroleum got over $32 million, and L.R. Raymond of Exxon Mobil Corp. almost $26 million.

No trade industry seems to be immune to these outrageous CEO salaries. Abercrombie and Fitch paid Michael S. Jeffries over $66 million, and Robert Nardelli received over $42 million from Home Depot. Exelon Corp. paid CEO Corbin McNeill $32 million, and Progress Energy, Inc. gave its CEO, William Cavanaugh, more than $15 million. Even the new CEO of "bankrupt" World-Com, Michael Capellas, is reported to have a three-year contract worth $26 million dollars. If you want to check the salary of a particular CEO, go to www.aflcio.org under 2002 Trend in Executive Pay. The same information can also be found in a corporation's proxy statement, which is filed with the Security Exchange Commission (SEC).

Interestingly enough, according to Standard and Poor, the companies which gave their CEO's the largest pay increases had poor stock performance. Some even lost a major portion of the stock's value. The October 2, 2002, publication of the *Minuteman Media* stated that the CEO's of twenty-three companies under investigation for accounting irregularities (three of which were Enron, WorldCom, and Tyco) "pocketed $1.4 billion over the last three years." While these individuals were getting outrageous paychecks, the companies' shareholders were suffering "massive losses," and "between January 1, 2001 and July 31, 2002, the value of the shares at these twenty-three firms plunged by $530 billion."

In an article he wrote entitled, "Everything in Excess for Shady CEOs," Don Hazen calculated that if the pay of an average worker had increased as rapidly as that of a CEO's, in 2001 that worker would have made $101,156 instead of $25,467. From another aspect, if minimum wage had increased as rapidly as the pay for a CEO, it would have been $21.41 an hour in 2001 instead of the $5.15 that it was.

The CEO's of these twenty-three large companies under investigation earned a yearly average of $62 million from 1999 to 2001. According to the survey on annual executive pay done by *Business Week*, CEO's of other corporations had an average salary of $36 million. While paying their CEO's these huge salaries, the twenty-three companies under investigation have also amassed a total of 162,000 layoffs since January 2001. Tyco, for example, laid off 18,400 workers during that time period. Another fact of interest is that at the thirty companies which have the greatest shortfall in their employees' pension fund, the CEO's made 59% more than the average CEO in *Business Week*'s survey.

Richard Grassor, chairman of the New York Stock Exchange, had to resign over a controversial salary and benefit package, which exceeded $139 million. It is the average taxpayer who suffers for these excessive CEO salaries, for at the same time the CEO's look to the government for subsidies and special favors to help pay for the excess. As a result, the average consumer and taxpayer get a "double whammy." We are all familiar with the old adage "the rich keep getting richer and the poor keep getting poorer."

All of this has happened while stockholders have lost over $5,000,000,000,000 (five trillion dollars) in the value of their stocks since the year 2000. At the same time, less than 50% of American workers have a retirement program paid for by their employers. These facts are ironic, are they not, when we consider court cases involving CEO's? The economy of the United States was on a downward spiral as jurors saw a videotape of a $2,000,000 party that L. Dennis Kozlowski, former CEO of Tyco International, had for his wife's birthday. The money was allegedly taken from the company, part of numerous millions of dollars used for his personal benefit.

At the same time that CEO's are receiving these astronomical salaries, the Agricultural Department reported that in 2002 approximately 12 million families in the United States were unsure of whether or not they would be able to buy sufficient food, and 32% of them actually experienced someone in their extended family going hungry. At the present time over a million people are in the throes of long-term unemployment (over twenty-six weeks). The consequences for the unemployed, who did their jobs and worked hard all their lives, are grave.

At mid-year in 2003, there were over 15 million people unemployed in our country, and the numbers are growing. America is losing over a million jobs a year, for statistics show that three million jobs have disappeared since the year 2000. The power games played by CEO's and mega-corporations have reached such an absurd state that our nation's very economic stability is in question.

Chapter 5
Power Scandals

Not all power addicts have escaped unscathed, however. Numerous scandals have been exposed over the last two decades. The Keating Five scandal is one of the most notorious. Five senators—Dennis DeConcini and John McCain both from Arizona, Alan Cranston from California, John Glenn from Ohio, and Don Riegle from Michigan—were persuaded by Charles Keating, Jr., owner of the Lincoln Savings and Loan Association, to meet with and ask federal regulators to loosen the rules regarding investments that the bank could make and to stop, or at least delay, legal action against the bank. Keating had made over a million dollars in contributions to these five senators between 1982 and 1987. In 1989 federal regulators seized the bank. When asked if the campaign contributions to the five senators were given in exchange for the passage of favorable federal banking regulations, Keating replied, "I want to say in the most forceful way I can, I certainly hope so!" We, the taxpayers, paid $3.4 billion to reimburse the depositors, and the whole Savings and Loan scandal cost the taxpayers over half a trillion dollars.

A plethora of other scandals exists, also. A retired lieutenant commander from the U.S. Naval Reserves has recently written a book entitled *The Conspirators: Secrets of an Iran Contra Insider.* The book describes government involvement he witnessed in illegal weapons deals, securities, real estate and insurance fraud, and drug trafficking, including the establishment of a gang to distribute drugs to children.

Another federal scandal deals with our corrupt bankruptcy system. A small computer software company called INSLAW developed a software called PROMIS, which helps attorneys to stay astride of cases. The U.S. Attorney used the software in several offices yet refused to pay for the service. INSLAW filed a lawsuit against the Justice Department. Journalist Harry V. Martin documents that when INSLAW filed bankruptcy, Anthony Pasciuto, who was the deputy director of the Executive Office of U.S. Trustees (which deals with bankruptcy), claimed that the Justice Department was improperly using its power to apply pressure to change INSLAW's Chapter 11 reorganization into a Chapter 7 liquidation. Doing so would mean that the rights to the software (which the Justice Department had been using illegally) would be sold at auction.

In the end, George Bason, Jr., a federal bankruptcy judge, ruled that the Justice Department had acted illegally, that "the department took, converted, [and] stole INSLAW's software by trickery, fraud and deceit." Judge Bason ordered the Justice Department to pay INSLAW $6.8 million, and the verdict was upheld on appeal. Martin reported, however, that three months later Judge Bason was denied reappointment and was out of a job.

The Nunn Committee conducted an investigation of the INSLAW scandal. It called the Justice Department "uncooperative" and said that the Department intimidated its employees who were called as witnesses so badly that they did not dare to testify "out of fear for their jobs."

According to Harry Martin, Texas Congressman Jack Brooks is reinvestigating the INSLAW case and the accusations that the "Justice Department officials, including Meese, conspired to force INSLAW into bankruptcy in order to deliver the firm's software to a rival company." Court records show that Earl W. Brian, the head of the rival firm, had given Meese a "$15,000 interest-free loan" and that Meese's wife was an investor in Brian's firm. The fingers of power are far-reaching.

ABSCAM was another famous scandal. Senator Harrison Williams and five congressmen—Richard Kelly, John Jenrette, Raymond Lederer, Frank Thompson, and Michael Myers—were convicted of bribery and conspiracy. FBI agents used a fictional business named Abdul Enterprises, LTD to offer bribes to these politicians; hence, the press dubbed the scandal ABSCAM. The conviction of Richard Kelly, however, was overturned on the premise that the FBI had unlawfully entrapped him.

In Operation Lost Trust, yet another scandal, a judge, lobbyists, and twenty-seven politicians were convicted of corruption and illegal drug deals. A lobbyist named Ron Cobb went undercover for the FBI after he was caught in a drug deal. Cobb told legislators that he was representing the Alpha Group, which was involved in trying to legalize dog track and horse track betting in South Carolina. Cobb then began to offer politicians bribe envelopes containing hundred dollar bills—and there were plenty who willingly accepted them. It became quite clear that bribes had become an integral part of the political system in Columbia, the capital of South Carolina.

In October of 2003, we saw yet another scandal unfolding in this seemingly never-ending array. R & V Warren Farms, a large tomato-growing operation in Candler,

North Carolina, was charged with filing fake crop reports and receiving more than $9,000,000 in insurance claims. According to news stories, ice cubes were thrown into the fields and the plants were beaten with sticks to make it appear as if a hailstorm had destroyed the tomato plants. Photos were taken of the fields to use as proof of damage to collect the insurance. A claim for 252 acres was filed but actually only a few acres were planted.

On November 10, 2003, Meg Scott Phipps, Secretary of Agriculture in North Carolina, pleaded guilty to five federal charges after originally being charged with thirty felonies by a federal grand jury. She also admitted to accepting illegal cash contributions and being involved in extortion and mail fraud. Assistant U.S. attorney Dennis Duffy was quoted as saying, "Mrs. Phipps literally sold her office." One of her crimes was awarding the state fair contract to one of her largest unrecorded donors. She literally sold the right to the midway. Even a state fair isn't sacred anymore when it comes to power hungry politicians!

These scandals, as well as a host of others, are a part of the addiction to power that dominates our political system from city hall to the White House. Some might say that it was the money that was the temptation, but almost all of the politicians involved had the capacity to earn a great deal of money legally and most were making six-figure incomes at the time they committed the crime. Power is what they were seeking. What they had was not enough.

Chapter 6
Is Democracy Still Alive?

If our government can be influenced by money in such a way, is democracy really still alive? Or has the nation been turned into a quasi dictatorship ruled by whoever can produce the most dollars to buy the election? Those who seize power may be corporate leaders looking for another tax break, political action committees seeking to have laws adjusted in their favor, or individuals lusting for raw power to sustain their addiction. Eventually someone truly sinister, a Hitler-type, will seize power and refuse to relinquish that power on Election Day. Could such a person not cancel an election, citing fear of a terrorist attack or create a war, as Hitler did? With so much money corrupting the system, does the vote of the individual really count?

If our vote is meaningless and does not affect the system in any real way, how long does it take before we do not even care whether or not we vote? In the 1998 national election less than 37% of the eligible voters voted. In the 2000 presidential election, less than 52% voted.

If the two major parties are not ruthlessly holding power, then why not level the playing field so that even those who do not agree with them have a chance of getting elected? Why not allow other candidates into the national television debates so that the public can see all candidates side-by-side, not just Republican and Democratic candidates?

For decades our nation openly criticized the Soviet Union. The United States called the Soviet Union a dictatorship because it only had one party and one set of candidates. The United States, however, has a system in which the candidates of just two parties, Republican and Democrat, get special treatment and guaranteed spots on the ballot. Every other candidate is forced to collect thousands of signatures (millions in the case of the presidency) and to have those signatures certified by the state election commission. Ironically, the members of the election commission are already compromised because they are appointed by Democrat and Republican officials, whose interests clearly oppose such a candidacy.

What makes the political system of the United States better than that of the Soviet Union? Are we saying that two parties are all it takes to make a democracy? Without a doubt, any nation could conjure up two parties to make an election appear "democratic." Should any country ever be controlled by just two parties?

Also, limitations should be placed on the amount of money a candidate can spend during any election cycle. Those opposed to this would say that such a law would limit free speech, but free speech is limited in many cases. For example, a person cannot yell "fire" in a movie theater. A United States citizen, unless by special invitation, cannot go onto the floor of the Senate and speak, even though his tax dollars paid for that building. A person cannot go into a public library, paid for by tax dollars, and create a disturbance by giving a speech. Nor can a person slander another person. These are just a few of the limitations that have already been placed on the right of free speech, limitations that protect all of us.

When elected officials take PAC money, they cast their votes directly in favor of the PAC's interests. That is nothing less than bribery. Why are prosecutors not prosecuting? Unfortunately the American people have been conned into believing that this is not a crime. Because politicians take PAC money **all the time**, we are brainwashed into thinking it is okay.

If politicians would get convicted for taking PAC money and voting the way the PAC group dictated—instead of in the interest of the constituents who elected them—we would not have to worry about money limitations anymore. The politicians would not take any of this "bribe" money because they would be afraid of getting indicted. And, special interest groups would not be able to give huge sums of money because they would be indicted for attempting to "bribe" a public official. Candidates would be forced to run their campaigns on small donations of less than one thousand dollars.

In reality, prohibiting politicians from accepting PAC money would turn America into a true democracy, one in which candidates were, indeed, free to vote as they, representing their true constituency, saw fit. And, if a politician really believed what a PAC was telling him, he should not need money to cast the "right" vote.

We, as a society, have learned our bad behavior of abusing power from our power-addicted leaders. Until we change our corrupt political system to a system of true democracy, we edge closer and closer toward collapse. The bottom line is that if people do not vigorously strive to maintain a true democracy, they will eventually lose their freedom. They could even wake up one day to find themselves under the abusive power of a dictator or to find their fellow countrymen turned on each other in civil war.

Chapter 7
The Power Addict and His Victim

Those who are addicted to power wish to control as many people as they can. They remind me of a man who once said to me, "I don't want any more land, just the land next to mine." Based on this theory, of course, the man would eventually own **all** of the land. The question is how do we deal with their behavior without getting involved in their power games and just becoming another player? The solution—do not allow others to use us in their power games.

The solution starts with introspection because sometimes we cause our own problems. We must learn to distinguish between those who are playing power games and those who are asking us to live up to commitments we have made. If a person signs up to take a course at a college and a ten-page paper is part of the course requirements, he can not blame the professor or the college if he decides not to do the paper and, as a result, receives a bad grade. The problem is not an over-controlling professor but a lack of living up to the contract. Another example would be a person who agrees to do a research survey for a business but then never makes the necessary calls. When the business owner calls to find out how the survey is going and gets upset when he finds out that it has not even been started, the owner is not a control freak. He is just a business professional who is trying to get the survey for which he has paid a retainer.

If a person agrees to "sell" his time and talent for a price, he has lost some control. People must accept the consequences of their decisions. For example, John has had a bagel and coffee with a friend at the same coffee shop at 8:30 A.M. for ten years. Then, John chooses to take a new job that requires him to be at work at 8:00 A.M. He has no reason to be upset with his new boss that he cannot be at the coffee shop at 8:30 any more. That was a choice that John made.

We must not give up control if we still want the control. We must ask ourselves, "What have I agreed to? Am I willing to agree to this loss of control?" Our choices are sometimes just that—our choices. We must be able to recognize and separate our good decisions from our bad decisions. These choices should be distinguished from the times when we come in contact with those who are addicted to power. When our choices have set us up to be dominated by power addicts, we must make new decisions to free ourselves.

When we go on a job interview, we should be interviewing our future boss as he interviews us. Are we really going to be accomplishing some worthy task that we will enjoy or are we going to become co-dependent in someone's power addiction and eventually addict ourselves to being victims? We need to listen carefully to how this potential new boss speaks to other people, and watch how he treats his secretary and other employees. If he speaks to them harshly or treats them with inferiority, we must not get lured into the idea that we are special and will receive better treatment.

Those addicted to power have many ways to lock us into their control. "You must be loyal." "Remember your past mistakes." "Your co-workers are doing much better than you." "Why do you act that way?" "Everyone else works as a team." These are just some of the phrases a power addict uses to control our behavior when we do not agree with him. The fact that the accusation is totally unfounded will be meaningless to the person addicted to power. He often feels justified in breaking any contract or any agreement. He sees himself as the supreme power, so any method of maintaining his power is seen as justified.

In *Potentates*, we saw how Margaret used people. She always made someone else the scapegoat for the problems she caused, and she often used Ren and Harry to carry out her vengeance. Her decisions were not based on some deep moral conviction but on who would vote for her and who would give her campaign funds. This, of course, was just another way of saying who would provide her with more power because the money would soon be used to obtain a higher position—which she believed would satisfy her thirst for power.

We must learn to recognize individuals, or even groups, that are addicted to power. And, we must make conscious decisions about our involvement with such people or groups. We must not ever think or expect that we can change power addicts. They themselves are the only ones who are warranted to do that. We should never expect a power addicted person to act in our best interest without getting something in return—and the cost will always be too high.

A person addicted to power is dangerous, but a group of power addicted people is even more dangerous. In a corporation, they find their victims, usually clients or customers, and use their power not to provide ethical, legitimate service but to manipulate and obstruct justice. In other organizations or clubs, they often find a power base within a key committee or connive to get one of their group elected president or chairman of the organization. A tiger will kill us if given the opportunity. The cute, seemingly harmless baby tiger will soon grow into a very dangerous animal. We must not delude ourselves into believing tigers are something they are not. They are not just cute cats; they are predators looking for prey. The same is true of power addicted people. Their addiction tends to get worse, not better.

Our first line of offense, then, against power addicts should always be to avoid them. Once we begin to have dealings with a power addict, he will do everything in his power to control us in a negative way. In *Potentates*, we saw that Ren tries to find another job in order to escape, but when Margaret finds out, she intimidates the congressman into retracting his offer. With this act, Margaret has tightened her grip on her total control of Ren. We must be careful when changing jobs, taking on new clients, or joining a club that we are not dealing with power-addicted people

Sometimes, however, we can not avoid power-addicted people. What do we do then? The most important thing is to always act assertively—be strong, be strong, be strong! We cannot let ourselves be intimidated. People who are addicted have much more respect for (and fear of) those who will not be pushed around or bullied. If we take on the role of a victim, the power abuser will make us have plenty to complain about. We must let the abuser know that we will not be victims and we will not play power games.

When dealing with a power addict, we must choose our words carefully so that we are clearly understood. Remember, if we choose to enter a power game or get conned into one, the abuser is always going to win because his whole life is based on these power games. Unless we are willing to give up our independence to play, we will lose. The dying thought of most power addicts is "I won." Sadly enough, most power addicts die still giving orders, manipulating, even working against the doctors and nurses that are trying to help them.

We need to rise above the power addict. We cannot let them drag us into their games. To do so is to give up our independence. We must not give any "secretive" or personal information to the abuser that may be used against us later. Our private life is ours. What we do when we are elsewhere is no one else's concern. We need to keep it that way because power addicts will use any information they get in a negative way. In *Potentates*, Margaret constantly sought negative information about people, information which she could use later to control them to accomplish her own devious schemes.

Also, we must not get conned into thinking that a person addicted to power is anything other than that—a power addict—or that they are suddenly going to change. Ren always thinks that Margaret is going to change. He thinks things will be different after she wins the Senate seat for a second term, after she becomes Lt. Governor, after her son dies. Ren is even conned into the extreme action of marrying her, believing that will change her. But, she is who she is—a power addict.

I once did volunteer counseling at a homeless shelter. Many of the men who ended up in the shelter were addicted to drugs. I was always amazed at the mothers, wives, and girlfriends who would visit and tell me in a shocked voice, "He spent his whole paycheck…he stole my jewelry…he stole my Social Security check." They should not be the least bit surprised. This is what drug addicts do. They will get their drug of choice any way they can. And one must never let his guard down around an addict, although it is easy to do. I once left a power drill on the seat of my car and left the door unlocked in a drug infested neighborhood. The only thing I needed to be surprised about when I returned a few minutes later was that the car was still there. Stealing my drill was not right, it was not justified, but it was an obvious act. I should have expected no less.

The same should be expected when we are dealing with a power addict. We should not look for justice; we should not look for what is right. We should not expect integrity or kindness. The only thing we will get is whatever the abuser believes will make him more powerful. We must understand that the abuser knows what the right thing to do is, but he will only do what is right when it will further his own cause.

When he is in the public's eye, the power addict will always seem to say or do the right thing. When someone dies, he will have flowers sent. Thank you notes are commonly sent, and gifts and awards are often given even when there is no special occasion. All of this transpires, however, so that the public sees the "right thing" being done, and this makes the person more powerful. However, because he has no real sympathy, thankfulness, or desire to give, all gifts come with a price, usually one too high to pay.

Power abusers, on the surface, can appear to be some of the nicest people we would ever meet. They teach themselves to be polite, to have good manners, and to put on a caring face. Typically, science students are nice to the frog, mouse, or rabbit—before they dissect it. Keep this in mind: when the power-addicted boss pats us on the back and says we have done a good job, we are probably closer to losing our jobs than when the boss was giving us a hard time. Power addicts always hide their true feelings.

Groups of people seeking control can act in this devious way also. I was once invited to speak at a celebration for a pastor at a local church. The congregation had decided to have the celebration to praise the pastor and his wife for the good work they were doing. When I arrived, however, I sensed something more was going on. For two hours the deacons and the congregation praised the pastor and his wife. Tables abounded with food and gifts. All I could think of was the similarity of this event to the Last Supper.

About a month later I was in the hardware store and saw the pastor. I asked him how everything was going. He looked at me with incredulous eyes and said that he had been fired the week before. He was devastated. He went on to tell me that he thought the board of deacons had decided to terminate him **before** the celebration. He knew there had been differences between himself and the chairman, but the deacons had showered him with so much praise, he thought things would work out.

I later learned what had really happened from a deacon of that church. The chairman of the deacons had ruled the church for twenty years. If anyone dared to disagree with him, he was "gone." The young pastor had had too many inventive ideas. The chairman had seized the opportunity the celebration would provide to carry out his scheme. He did not object because he did not want his eventual firing of the pastor to look personal. The chairman knew all of the congregation's positive energy for the pastor would be expended during the celebration, so he allowed it. Then, while the preparation for the celebration was going on, the chairman started to gather votes on the board of deacons for a new pastor, someone a little older, someone with a little more experience.

This, of course, should really be interpreted as "someone the chairman could control." And on the day of the celebration, early in the morning, the vote was taken. In two weeks, when a new pastor was found and ready to take up his duties, the present pastor would be "let go." The "good" part was that the congregation would not have to worry about a farewell party because the celebration had already taken place. Of course, when the new pastor was actually appointed, he was younger than his predecessor and easier to control.

We should never be deluded into thinking that we know what power abusers are thinking. We will always be surprised because their minds are so guileful. Their minds have so many twists and turns the average person just cannot think in those terms. A prime example of this is seen with the actions of the major leaders of Europe during World War II. As months passed, they continued to believe that Hitler would stop his aggression, that he would stop invading other countries. They could not fathom, until it was almost too late, that he was as evil as he was. This is not an uncommon mistake. We need to keep our guard up and always be prepared for the unexpected when we deal with power addicts.

Another pitfall to avoid is thinking that the organization or corporation is more important than we are as individuals. This is a trick power-addicted people like to use. They tell us that we have to be loyal, that we have to put the organization or company first. If our child is sick, their response is that we cannot run home every time our child has a runny nose. Power abusers will try to transform our moral values. They always want us to think that we exist to meet the organization's needs and that our whole lives should revolve around the company. If they can convince us of that, then they own us—which was their goal from the very beginning.

Remember, each of us is unique. What is most important about us is our individuality. We are not part of a big machine, just grinding out more pieces. We are individual people, who have the ability to love, the ability to have relationships, the ability to question, the ability to be creative, and the ability to influence others positively.

These attributes, in the long run, will be much more important than making one more sale, producing ten percent above a quota, or telling one more lie for the boss. Goals, production, and success on a job are relevant and part of a healthy life; however, when they dominate our lives and seriously hinder our freedom and individuality, our success in meeting these goals will produce a greater failure. Life will become hopeless and not worth living.

When dealing with power addicted people, we often find ourselves saying yes to what we really do not agree with. We need to be prepared to say no and to stand by our decision. If we stand firm, in most cases a power-addicted person will look for an easier target. There may be an initial explosion, but the power abuser is looking for a victim. Once we clearly define ourselves as people who will not be abused, the power addict will move on. The power addict is well aware that the world is full of easy prey.

I saw his happen when I volunteered at a shelter for abused women. When the wife or girlfriend finally stood firm and refused to return to the abusive situation, I was amazed to see how quickly the power-addicted man would find a new victim. This is not always true due to different types of mental disorders, but most power abusers want to totally dominate their victims. When their potential victim totally rejects being abused any longer, the abuser will seek out a weaker victim, one he can control. Amazingly enough, there seems to be an endless array of victims just waiting for the power addict.

Chapter 8
Coping with the Power Addict

There is specific behavior that we can use if we find ourselves working with or for a power addict or in a confrontation with one. First, we cannot act intimidated. We must perform our job to the best of our ability. That way, when a confrontation comes, we will be able to deal with it from a strong, solid position. When we are challenged by someone who is addicted to power, we will most likely be sitting because abusers feel much more comfortable attacking when the victim is "smaller." They also tend to loom directly over us. This gives them a psychological advantage, which they are well aware of.

So, stand up if they have positioned themselves in this way. Then, in a voice that is slightly above normal say, "Excuse me." We need to stand up straight, use body language that says we are in control, look them directly in the eyes, and then give the control addict our response. Remember that even people who are addicted to power need employees who will get the job done. They enjoy harassing employees, showing them who is the boss, but if we speak up with the strength of our convictions, they will most often find someone else to harass.

If we are a member of an organization in which someone is playing power games, we must prepare ourselves before all meetings. We need to make sure that we know the by-laws of the organization and bring a copy with us to the meetings. Most organizations go by *Rob-*

ert's Rules of Order, so it is a good idea to understand the basic rules of how to make a motion, how to move the question, etc. If we plan to make a motion, we need to have a person present who is willing to second the motion. This will clearly put the motion up for discussion. If possible, before the meeting prepare a concise statement of why the motion should be passed. If the power abuser asks us to change the wording and we do not think the new words meet our intent, politely say we would like the motion to stand as it is. If the power addict tries to filibuster, tiring everyone out, ask for the question to be moved.

In most cases the majority of the organization's members have been waiting for someone to stand up to the power addict. Even if we lose the vote, at least we will know that the members are rejecting our position because they truly do not agree with us, not because they were bullied into something by the control addict.

Again, to combat a power addict in an organization or club, we need to follow these steps: think out the motion in advance, decide if the motion is for the good of all of the members and fosters the objectives of the organization, present the motion without any malice, have someone ready to second the motion, and then explain the motion clearly and in detail. If we follow these steps, in most cases we will be able to overcome a control freak, who has been dominating the meetings.

Another type of power addict is the person who overpowers us with his problems. These people seem not to be as toxic as other power addicts and often seem pathetic because they have so many problems. In truth, however, they will create problems just to overpower anyone who is willing to listen or to get involved. Of course, because it is their problem, no one else can ever have the right solution. People who do this are not only addicted to power but also addicted to getting attention, usually because they have low self-esteem. Nevertheless, they will soon control us if we are not careful.

There is a way to deal with this type of addict when he comes to us with a problem. First, listen to his complaint very carefully. When he finishes, ask him what we can do. In most cases he will say there is nothing anyone can do. If he does ask us to do something, we must decide what we are willing to do and then stick to it. If the person begins to present the problem to us again later on, very politely, but firmly, we must interrupt and let him know that we have already discussed the problem with him. If he told us there was nothing we could do, remind him of this. If we told him that we would do something, remind him that we did it or are in the process of doing it. Then, we need to excuse ourselves and walk away.

Under no circumstances should we listen to the problem all over again because that is how this type of person gets power over us. As long as we listen, they are in control. Our refusal to listen may seem rude, but remember that we have already listened once (or even twice) and offered to help. The alternative to this is to be under the control of another, to give him the power to weigh us down mentally and physically with problems that we have absolutely no way of solving.

The reverse of the addict who tries to control us with his problems is just as malevolent—power addicts who try to convince us that we have a problem and that without them we will not survive. Of course, because they know all the answers, they want to totally control our lives. An example would be an employee who tells us that the company would not be able to survive or flourish without his special skills. If this was actually true and management believed it, that employee would have the final word at every meeting. Taken to the extreme, this addict could eventually manipulate the whole company and become a dictator over all discussion. The truth is that all people can be replaced, and when an individual is not willing to work with the team, the standards of the entire company are reduced.

This type of power addict tends to believe that he is irreplaceable while others who do work just as important are worthless. A clue that we are dealing with one of these power maniacs is that they are always demanding more resources. There is never enough; just a little bit more would bring about a great success. More resources for him equals more power for him, and fewer resources for everyone else means less power for everyone else. This is, of course, exactly what the power addict wants.

In *Potentates* there is a point when the office has so much money that Harry has to take extreme measures to hide it—he uses a pawnshop as a cover. Nevertheless, Margaret is still not satisfied; she wants more. She knows that more money can buy her a higher position, which, in turn, will allow her to control more people.

More power—that is what a power addict feeds on. People who are addicted to crack cocaine have this attitude. On one occasion when I was interviewing a client at a shelter, the man showed me his mouth. It was full of blisters from smoking crack. His eyes showed that he was in terrific pain. I asked him why he didn't stop when the heat from the crack was burning his mouth. He looked at me as if I had lost my mind and responded, "There is never enough." "Enough what," I asked, "crack or pain?" He just stared blankly at the desk with his head bowed.

Having dealt with all kinds of people who are addicted to many different substances—and crack is certainly a powerful addiction—I do not believe that even crack is more powerful and tragic than an addiction to power.

Some power addicts take their behavior to such an extreme that our only response is to completely avoid them. An example of this is spousal abuse. There is no excuse that can justify using physical, verbal, or emotional abuse to control someone. A power addicted person can become extremely dangerous, so we must not allow ourselves to be the victim.

Any one of these forms of power abuse that we have dealt with can be used against us in a variety of situations. These deadly power games can be launched against us in organizations, associations, churches, and even at the clubs to which our children belong. Even our families and extended families can be a source of these deadly games. I am referring to them as "deadly" games because they literally take the life out of the group. How many times have we said, "I never want to go back there again?" How many times have we gotten ready for a meeting and felt physically sick just thinking about having to deal with someone who is addicted to power? How many times have we heard a family member say or imply, "If you don't come, you must not love me," or "If you don't do this, you must not love me"?

The games go on and the pain and suffering are real. Indeed, our nation is affected. All we need to do is to look at our paycheck stubs, at the tax dollars extracted from our hard work. Are these tax dollars really dollars needed to maintain the nation or, in reality, are most of these deducted dollars just part of the biggest power game of all? When an individual, organization, business corporation, or political action committee gives money to a politician, that contributor expects a return on the "investment." So, the politician, in return, takes money from our paychecks and gives special favors to this individual or group in the form of tax breaks, government contracts, or special laws that benefit that person's or group's business interests.

In our grandparents' day this would have been called bribery and these power brokers and politicians would have been in jail. Today, however, these very politicians have us convinced that if they could not be bought and paid for, we would somehow lose our freedom of speech. Have we not already lost this freedom, though, when our money is taken from us without any real representation? There are exceptions—those politicians who refuse the money—but they are few and far in between. And, the price we might pay for these deadly power brokers feeding the power-addicted politician may one day be the death of our nation.

Can any nation or community survive when every person, every business, every association puts its self-interests first? This nation was not built on selfishness but on the toil of men and women who sacrificed, who gave their lives, so that the nation could grow and become a better place for its citizens. A patriot does not buy a politician to satisfy his own needs. Those people should be called traitors and thieves. We should not glorify them anymore or show any respect for what they do. A bribe by any other name is still a bribe, and those that accept them are dishonest.

Before the eve of the next Election Day, every newspaper in America ought to print how much money each candidate in its circulation area has accepted. This is, by law, public knowledge. Why should we not see this information in print? Are the candidates afraid that no one would show up to vote? And while the political leadership in our nation collapses in front of our very eyes, the leadership of the institutions that would normally sustain us—major corporations, accounting firms, legal firms, huge non-profit organizations, and mega-churches—is also collapsing into hopelessness. The only question left is whether we are to go the way of the Roman Empire or be saved by new leaders who will be willing to sacrifice and to avoid being self-serving so that they can bring about honest change and a new beginning?

Chapter 9
Management, the Alternative to Power Games

Webster's New World Dictionary defines management as skillful leading through careful, tactful treatment. Management, as described, is the use of control, which is probably how most people would define the word. However, the second part of the definition is very important—tactful treatment. These are the words that separate a true manager from people who direct power games for themselves or some specialized group. In our fiction story, *Potentates*, Ren is the office manager, but his real job is to use the power that his boss (Margaret) has gained from getting elected to a state office to get more power. This becomes an endless cycle.

Money is such an important part of the whole power game that Margaret's votes are up for sale. If Ren were truly a manager, Margaret's vote in the Senate would be decided by the will of her constituency or, at the very least, by her own judgment of what is best for her constituency.

Precisely the same is true of the Enron crisis. People who were called managers were really not "managers" at all, just highly skilled power game players who bilked the stockholders and employees out of billions of dollars. Aside from their high social position, they were nothing

59

more than what we commonly refer to as con men. But, we must remember that before Enron Corporation fell, these same people were held in high esteem. This should be a lesson to us all—not everything that is powerful is good, honest, or decent. Even when these people were caught and the whole world knew that their greed and lust for power had taken over the corporation, they were still so addicted to power that they did not repent. Not only did they not apologize but rather they had the audacity to start a new set of power games: they told us they did not personally have any money; they refused to testify; they expected immunity; and they arrogantly said they were not at fault.

If Enron was the only corporation using these tactics, we might say that corporate America was in good shape, that there was only one example in which an addiction to power made a business corrupt. The truth is, however, that we have many more major corporations that are playing these same games, deceiving stockholders, employees, and consumers with deceptive accounting practices.

Corporations must make a profit to stay in business. No one argues that. Management that tells the truth and uses proper accounting methods will, over time, prosper. This will benefit all of society, including the stockholders, who, after all, are the ones putting up the money. A corporation that is bankrupt can serve no one. We, as stockholders, employees, and consumers, must learn to recognize the managers, politicians, and businesses that are involved in these power games and move our money and votes to those who manage carefully and tactfully.

Also, if we ourselves are put into positions of power, we must always remember that we are strictly caretakers of that power. The power belongs to our constituency. For an elected office, the people in that voting district are the constituency. In a corporation, the constituency is made up of the stockholders, who invest their money; the employees, who provide the labor; and the consumers, who provide the profit by buying the merchandise or service. In a club or fraternal organization the power belongs to the members who strive to make it the best that it can be. In church, the power belongs to God and the entire congregation who serve Him. Finally, in our homes, the power belongs to the complete family, even the children, for if children do not share in the power when they are growing up and do not learn how to use it properly, what will they do when they reach adulthood?

Servant leadership represents our best chance to move away from our pattern of power-game leadership. Good servant leaders take into consideration the needs of everyone involved and use the power granted to them to maximize the opportunities of those they work with. Servant leaders find success by motivating others and view selfish self-promotion as a character flaw. Robert Greenleaf has written a great book about this topic called *Servant Leadership*; this book should definitely be on an informed person's "must read" list.

Another point to remember is that a person in power will get the maximum out of the people who work under his guidance when the workers are allowed to be creative. When a leader allows the people around him to be his helpers, he will soon see his problems disappear. However, when a person in power acts out of fear and mistrust, he will find that he will spend most of his time being angry, and the results will be unproductive.

A leader who projects the attitude of "let's work to-gether" will not only move himself closer to those who work under him but will also cause the workers them-selves to come together to find the necessary solutions to problems. When the leader says production needs to be increased and gives the necessary facts to back up his statement, the workers will realize they live in a competi-tive world and that more production is not only good for the company but will also mean that their jobs are more secure. If the company makes more money, they will share in the success. When everyone is connected to the goal in a real way, new solutions will appear from the creative minds of the workers.

A positive attitude can go full cycle. When workers see that their leadership is no longer angry and blaming the company's problems on them, the workers, in return, will stop getting angry and will stop blaming their prob-lems on the management and on each other. When the leaders start to forgive, so will the workers. This idea is not some kind of magic. It is obvious that when people are treated with respect, in most cases, they will respond in kind. In the process, an environment is created in which new leadership develops from within.

When the members of the group feel good about themselves, they will project this positiveness to the stockholders, customers, and other companies. The result will be stockholders who want more stock and are willing to pay more for it, customers who are satisfied and are eager to tell their friends to buy the product, and vendors who want to keep their quality high and their services su-perior in order to supply the company.

What we expect is what we get. The job of the servant leader, then, is to foster high expectations so that those who work with him produce the necessary creative ideas

to maximize success. A good servant leader always re-
members that there is never only one way to do something. The goal of servant leadership is to get co-workers
to be at ease with what they are doing so that the process
simply happens and the thought process is creative and
open to new insight. When we watch great ice skaters or
basketball players, they do not think about what they are
doing. They just do it. There is a natural, instinctive flow.
This is exactly the positive aura that will pervade businesses and organizations when there are no power addicts
in control but servant leaders.

Getting the job done should not take coercion. If a
person does not want to be a part of the team, for whatever reason, the servant leader helps him to find more suita-
ble employment. Time should not be wasted on destruc-
tive power games that choke the very life out of the company.

When servant leadership is successful, competition
moves beyond "what can we do to compete with others"
to "how can we do better than we did the last time." The
group sees itself as successful; therefore, it is successful.
Even the newest employee is a part of the team. The
servant leader nurtures everyone, brings them together,
encourages them to be creative, and moves them forward
to greater successes. Each member of the team is respect-
ed for his individuality. Each member can act assertively
to get his views heard without fear of being chastised by
other team members or the servant leader.

This type of leadership, free from power addicts, will
work not only for the business world but also for government, civic groups, churches, and homes. When we
can feel at ease enough to allow each person's opinion to
be heard and discussed, the power games will end, and
true democracy will take place.

Micro and Macro Power Warriors

Bibliography

"Abscam." 1994-2003: 2pp. *Awesome 80s.com*. Online. Internet. www.awesome80s.com/Awesome80s/News/1980/February/3-Abscam_Revealed.asp

AFL-CIO. "Douglas N. Daft." 2003: 2 pp. *Eye on Corporate America*. Online. Internet. www.aflcio.org/corporateamerica/paywatch/retirementsecurity/case_coke.cfm

AFL-CIO. "Durables." 2003: 11 pp. *Eye on Corporate America*. Online. Internet. www.aflcio.org/corporateamerica/paywatch/db_console_r.cfm?f=0&ind

AFL-CIO. "Edward M. Liddy." 2003: 2 pp. *Eye on Corporate America*. Online. Internet. www.aflcio.org/corporateamerica/paywatch/retirementsecurity/case_allstate.cfm

AFL-CIO. "Energy." 2003: 4 pp. *Eye on Corporate America*. Online. Internet.

www.aflcio.org/corporateamerica/paywatch/db_console_r.cfm?f=0&ind

AFL-CIO. "Financials." 2003:9 pp. *Eye on Corporate America*. Online. Internet.

www.aflcio.org/corporateamerica/paywatch/db_console_r.cfm?f=0&ind

AFL-CIO. "Health Care." 2003: 6 pp. *Eye on Corporate America*. Online. Internet. www.aflcio.org/corporateamerica/paywatch/db_console_r.cfm?f=0&ind

AFL-CIO. "H. Lee Scott, Jr." 2003: 2 pp. *Eye on Corporate America*. Online. Internet. www.aflcio.org/corporateamerica/paywatch/retirementsecurity/case_walmart.cfm.

AFL-CIO. "Information and Technology." 2003: 10 pp. *Eye on Corporate America*. Online. Internet. www.aflcio.org/corporateamerica/paywatch/db_console_r.cfm?f=0&ind

AFL-CIO. "Materials." 2003:5 pp. *Eye on Corporate America*. Online. Internet. www.aflcio.org/corporateamerica/paywatch/db_console_r.cfm?f=0&ind

AFL-CIO. "Richard M. Scrushy." 2003: 2 pp. *Eye on Corporate America*. Online. Internet. www.aflcio.org/corporateamerica/paywatch/retirementsecurity/case_healthsouth.cfm.

AFL-CIO. "2002 Trends in Executive Pay." 2003: 2 pp. *Eye on Corporate America*. Online. Internet. www.aflcio.org/corporateamerica/paywatch/pay/index.cfm?RenderForPrint=1

AFL-CIO. "Utilities." 2003: 4pp. *Eye on Corporate America*. Online. Internet. www.aflcio.org/corporateamerica/paywatch/db_console_r.cfm?f=0&ind

Backover, Andrew. "Judge Questions Incoming WorldCom CEO's Pay Plan." 11 December 2002: 2 pp. *USA Today, Money*. Online. Internet. www.usatoday.com/money/industries/telecom/2002-12-10-ceo-pay_x.htm.

Baden, John A. and Friends of the Earth. " More of Your Taxes Given Away to Welfare Queens." 1997: 3pp. *The Progress Report*. Online. Internet.

www.progress.org/archive/foe4

Baden, John A. "Using 'Green Scissors' to Cut Government Waste." 1997: 3pp. Online. Internet.

www.free-eco.org/pub/Scissors.ST1997.

"Bailout Watch." 2002: 3pp. *Taxpayers for Common Sense*. Online. Internet. www.bailoutwatch.org/index.htm

Bartlett, Donald L. and James B. Steele. "Special Report/ Corporate Welfare." *Time*. 9 November 1998.

Baue, William. "Huh?!?: CEO Pay Goes Up in 2002 While the Stock Market Goes Down."" 25 June 2003: 2 pp. *SocialFunds.com*. Online. Internet. www.socialfunds.com/news/article.cgi/1156.html.

Bivens, Matt. "In Down Economy, CEO Pay Continues to Rise." 2003: 1 p. *The WorldPaper*. Online. Internet. www.worldpaper.com/2003/april05/ceo1.html.

"Borden Chemicals and Plastics Receives Louisiana Quality of Life Campaign's Corporate Hog at the Trough Award." 30 November 2000: 3pp. *L.E.A.N. Louisiana Environmental Action Network*. Online. Internet. www.leanweb.org/qoflife/bordenpr

"Carrying a Big Stick: How Big Timber Triumphs in Washington." 1997: 5 pp. *Common Cause Report*. Online. Internet. www.commoncause.org/publications/timber%5F2.htm.

The Center for Responsive Politics. "Accountants: Long-Term Contribution Trends." 2002: 2pp. *Opensecrets.org*. Online. Internet. www.opensecrets.org/industries/indus.asp?Ind=F11

The Center for Responsive Politics. "Accounting Industry." 2002: 2pp. *Opensecrets.org*. Online. Internet. www.opensecrets.org/news/accountants/index.asp

The Center for Responsive Politics. "Andersen: Other Money in Politics Stats." 2002: 2pp. *Opensecrets.org*. Online. Internet. www.opensecrets.org./news/enron/andersen_other.asp

The Center for Responsive Politics. "Election Overview 2002 Cycle: Stats at a Glance." 2002: 2pp. *Opensecrets.org*. Online. Internet. www.opensecrets.org/overview/index.asp

The Center for Responsive Politics. "Election Overview 2002 Cycle: Who's Raised the Most." 2002: 2pp. *Opensecrets.org*. Online. Internet. www.opensecrets.org/overview/topraise.asp?cycle=2002

The Center for Responsive Politics. "Finance/Insurance/Real Estate: Top Contributors." 2002: 2pp. *Opensecrets.org*. Online. Internet. www.opensecrets.org/industries/contrib.asp?ind=F

The Center for Responsive Politics. "Securities & Investment: Long-Term Contribution Trends." 2002: 2pp. O*pensecrets.org*. www.opensecrets.org/industries/indus.asp?ind=F07

The Center for Responsive Politics. "Securities & Investment: Top Contributors. 2002: 2pp. *Opensecrets.org*. Online. Internet.
www.opensecrets.org/industries/contrib.asp?Ind=F07

The Center for Responsive Politics. "Top PACs." 2002: 2pp. *Opensecrets.org*. Online. Internet.
www.opensecrets.org/pacs/topacs.asp?txt=A&Cycle=2000

The Center for Responsive Politics. "WorldCom." 28 June 2002: 2pp. *Opensecrets.org*. Online. Internet.
www.opensecrets.org/news/worldcom/index.asp

"CEO Pay Peril." 2003: 2 pp. *The WorldPaper*. Online. Internet.
www.worldpaper.com/enewsletters/043003.html.

"CEOs at Defense Contractors Earn 45% More: Campaign Contributions Tied to Bigger Contracts." 28 April 2003: 1 p. *United for a Fair Economy-Press Room*. Online. Internet.
www.ufenet.org/press/2003/MoreBucksForBang_pr.html.

"CEOs Who Cook the Books Earn More: Accounting Scandals Hurt Workers, Shareholders, Taxpayers." 26 August 2002: 2pp. *United for a Fair Economy-Press Room*. Online. Internet.
www.faireconomy.org/press/2002/EE2002_pr.html

"Congressional Pork in the FY 1999 Supplemental Appropriations Bill (s.544)." 2002: 3 pp. *Public Citizen*. Online. Internet.
www.citizen.org/congress/welfare/articles.cfm?ID=1052.

"Corporate Welfare for the Politically Connected: The Story of Fannie Mae and Freddie Mac." 2002: 6pp. *Citizens Against Government Waste*. Online. Internet.
www.cagw.org/site/PageServer?pagename=reports_corporatewelfare

"Corporate Scandal Quick Sheet." 01 July 2003: 7 pp. *The Corporate Library*. Online. Internet.
www.thecorporatelibrary.com/spotlight/scandals/scandal-quicksheet.html

Crangle, John V. "Judicial Reform." 1995: 4 pp. *Point*. Online. Internet.
www.mindspring.com/~scpoint/point/9507/s04.html

Dobbs, Michael. "Halliburton Scores Big off Iraq." *The Washington Post* 28 August 2003: 7 pp. *MSNBC News*. Online. MSN.
www.msnbc.com/news/958312.asp?cp1=1.

Dowbenko, Uri. "New Book Reveals Secrets of Iran-Contra." 2000: 3pp. *Conspiracy Planet.* Online. Internet. www.conspiracyplanet.com/channel.cfm?channelid=43&contentid=6 9&page=2

Durhams, Sharif and Anna Griffin. "Phipps Pleads Guilty to 5 Federal Charges." *The Charlotte Observer.* 11 November 2003: 1A.

"Fact Sheets on Boeing and Proposed Deal to Lease 100 Tanker Jets." 2002: 3 pp. *Public Citizen.* Online. Internet. www.citizen.org/congress/welfare/articles.cfm?ID=6593.

"Farm Bill 2002: Analysis of Selected Provisions." 21 June 2002: 4 pp. *Economic Research Service U.S. Department of Agriculture.* Online. Internet. www.ers.usda.gov/Features/FarmBill/Analysis/sugar2002act.htm.

"FEC releases Congressional Fundraising Summary." 9 September 2002: 4 pp. *Federal Election Commission News Releases, Media Advisories.* Online. Internet. www.fec.gov/press/20020909canstats/20020909canstat.html.

"FEC Reports Increase in Party Fundraising for 2000." 15 May 2001: 4 pp. *Federal Election Commission News Releases, Media Advisories.* Online. Internet. www.fec.gov/press/051501partyfund/051501partyfund.html.

"FEC Reports on Congressional Financial Activity for 2000." 15 May 2001: 5 pp. *Federal Election Commission News Releases, Media Advisories.* Online. Internet. www.fec.gov/press/051501congfinact/051501congfinact.html.

"FEC Reports on Political Party Activity for 1997-98." 9 April 1999: 4 pp. *Federal Election Commission News Releases, Media Advisories.* Online. Internet. www.fec.gov/press/ptyye98.htm.

"Federal Spending & the Budget: Identifying Government Waste." 2001: 2pp. *National Center for Policy Analysis.* Online Internet. www.ncpa.org/pd/budget/pd071499d.html

Finlay, J. Richard. "Ending the Curse of the Disengaged Director: A Modest Prescription for Canadian Boardroom Reform After Enron and Other Corporate Scandals." 28 May 2003: 6 pp. *The Centre for Corporate & Public Governance.* Online. Internet.

Finley, Rick. "The Other "Welfare Queens."" 1996: 3pp. *The Written Word.* Online. Internet. www.mdle.com/WrittenWord/rfinley/finley20.htm

"404 Object Not Found." 8 September 2003: 4 pp. *Seattle Post-Intelligencer.* Online. Internet. www.seattlepi.nwsource.com/national/pot281.shtml

Friends of the Earth. "Corporate Welfare Scandals Analyzed and Exposed." 2pp. *The Progress Report.* Online. Internet. www.progress.org/archives/stadium

Gaul, Gilbert M. and Susan Q. Stranahan. "The Perils of Living Grant to Grant." 1996: 11 pp. *Corporate Welfare Information Center.* Online. Internet. www.corporations.org/welfare/inquirer7

Gough,Ph.D., Michael. "Funding at the National Institute of Standards and Technology." 10 April 1997: 15 pp. *Cato.org.* Online. Internet. www.cato.org/testimony/ct-mg041097

Hartman, Chris. "Facts and Figures: Part I: Wealth Patterns." 8 October 2002: 7 pp. *Inequality.org.* Online. Internet. www.inequality.org/facts2.html.

Hartman, Chris. "Facts and Figures: Part 2: Income Patterns." 8 October 2002: 7 pp. *Inequality.org.* Online. Internet. www.inequality.org/facts3.html.

Hartman, Chris. "High CEO Pay Is Costing U.S. Big Time." 2 October 2002: 2 pp. *Minuteman Media.* Online. Internet. www.opedresource.com/HARTMAN%20100202.htm.

Hazen, Don. "Everything in Excess for Shady CEOs." 2003: 3 pp. *AlterNet.org.* Online. Internet. www.alternet.org/story.html?StoryID=13932.

"John M. Murphy, U.S. Representative of New York, Defends Himself Against ABSCAM Charges." 2003: 1 p. *History Channel.Com.* Online. Internet. www.historychannel.com/speeches/archive/speech_197.html.

Kadlec, Daniel. "They're Getting Richer!" *Time.* 18 August 2003. "Keating Five." 1p. *Anecdotage.com.* Online. Google. www.anecdotage.com/index.php?aid=1774.

Klinger, Scott. "The Bigger They Come, The Harder They Fall: High Levels of CEO Pay and the Effect on Long-Term Stock." 6 April

2001: 10 pp. *United for a Fair Economy.* Online. Internet. www.ufenet.org

Kropf, Schuyler. "Cobb Finds Some Good in His Lost Trust Role." 1999: 3 pp. *Charleston.Net.* Online. Internet. www.archives.charleston.net/news/losttrust/cobb0823.htm

"Labor Day 'Executive Excess' Report: CEOs Profit from Layoffs, Pension Shortfalls, and Tax Dodges." 26 August 2003: 2pp. *Press Release from United for a Fair Economy & Institute for Policy Studies.* Online. Internet. www.Faireconomy.org/press/2003/EE2003_pr.html

Martin, Harry V. "Federal Corruption INSLAW." 1995: 48 pp. *Napa Sentinel, 1991.* Online. Internet. www.sonic.net/sentinel/gvcon7.

Muller, Bill. "Chapter V: The Keating Five." 2003: 8 pp. *Azcentral.com* [*The Arizona Republic*] Online. Internet. www.azcentral.com/specials/special39/articles/1003mccainbook5.html.

"National Parties Raise Record $107.2 Million in Soft Money." 9 February 2000: 4 pp. *Common Cause News.* Online. Internet. http://commoncause.org/publications/feb00/020800.htm

"New on *The Public i.*" 2003: 3 pp. *The Center for Public Integrity.* Online. Internet. www.publicintegrity.org/dtaweb/home.asp

"The 1997 Corporate Welfare Hit List." 6 pp. *Public Citizen.* Online. Internet. www.citizen.org/congress/welfare/articles.cfm?ID=1054.

O'Connor, Dr. Tom. "Abscam." 2003: 2pp. *American Government & Social Reform: a Glossary.* Online. Internet. http://faculty.ncwc.edu/toconnor/reform.htm

"Overall Campaign Spending at the Federal Level." 11 June 1999: 1 p. *Common Cause News* Online. Internet. www.commoncause.org/publications/cycle_total_cycle_facts.html.

"Party Fundraising Growth Continues." 19 September 2002: 2 pp. *Federal Election Commission News Releases, Media Advisories.* Online. Internet. www.fec.gov/press/20020919partyfund/20020919partyfund.html.

Patsuris, Penelope. "The Corporate Scandal Sheet." 26 August 2002: 8 pp. *Forbes. Com.* Online. Internet. www.forbes.com/2002/07/25/accountingtracker.html?partner=yahoo&referrer=

"Political Transformation." 2003: 3 pp. *Reclaim Democracy.org*. Online. Internet. www.reclaimdemocracy.org/political_reform/.

Randall, Kate. "CEO Pay Soars As US Stocks Plummet." 24 September 2001: 5 pp. *World Socialist Web Site*. Online. Internet. www.wsws.org/articles/2001/sep2001/ceos-s24.shtml

"Receipts of 1999-2000 Presidential Campaigns Through July 31, 2000." 2000: 2 pp. *Federal Election Commission News Releases, Media Advisories*. Online. Internet. www.fec.gov/finance/precm8.htm.

"Return on Investment: The Hidden Story of Soft Money, Corporate Welfare and the 1997 Budget & Tax Deal." 1997: 3pp. *Common Cause*. Online. Internet. www.commoncause.org/publications/return_3

Sanders, Bernie. "Stop Corporate Welfare at the Export-Import Bank." 2002: 1p. *Congressman Bernie Sanders' (I-VT) Website*. Online. Internet. www.bernie.house.gov/documents/releases/20020501150823.asp?print

Sanders, Bernie. "USA:Ex-Im Bank, Corporate Welfare at Its Worst." 15 May 2002: 2pp. *CorpWatch*. Online. Internet. www.corpwatch.org/news/PND.jsp?articleid=2570

Schooling, Ed. "Open Letter to Corrupt Criminal Cabal." 2000: 5 pp. *Conspiracy Planet*. Online. Internet. www.conspiracyplanet.com/channel.cfm?channelid=93&contentid=355&page=2.

Sklar, Holly. "CEO Pay Still Outrageous." 24 April 2003: 3 pp. *Knight Ridder/Tribune News Service*. Online. Internet. www.raisethefloor.org/press_ceo_oped.html.

"Spending in Presidential Election Cycles." 1999: 3 pp. *Common Cause News*. Online. Internet. www.commoncause.org/publications/cycle_party_pres_facts.html.

Stirton, Ian. "FEC Reports Increase in Party Fundraising for 2000-News Release." 15 May 2001: 4 pp. *Federal Election Commission*. Online. Internet. www.fec.gov/press/051501partyfund/051501partyfund.html.

"Statement on Corporate Welfare." 25 October 2002: 3pp. *Nader 2000*. Online. Internet. www.votenader.org/issues/corp_welfare

"Taxpayer Subsidies for Road Construction." 2002: 4 pp. *Lost in the Forest*. Online. Internet.

www.taxpayer.net/forest/lostintheforest.

"Trent Lott: Top Contributors." 2003: 2 pp. *Opensecrets.org*. Online. Internet.
www.opensecrets.org/politicians/contrib.asp?CID=N00003329&cycle=2002.

United States Department of Agriculture. "FY 2002 Budget Justification: Permanent Appropriations." 2002: 23 pp. *USDA Forest Service*. Online. Internet.

Vandeman, Mike. "Stop Corporate Welfare in Our Parks." 1998: 6 pp. *Communications for a Sustainable Future*. Online. Internet.
www.csf.colorado.edu/forums/deep-ecology/jul98/0040.

Walsh, Lawrence E. "Final Report of the Independent Counsel for Iran/Contra Matters: Volume 1, Part I." 4 August 1993: 30 pp. *Federation of American Scientists*. Online. Internet.
www.fas.org/irp/offdocs/walsh/part_i.htm.

"Waste Wire." 2002: 4pp. *Citizens Against Government Waste*. Online. Internet.
www.cagw.org/site/PageServer?pagename=news_Wastewire_MAY_2002

"What Is a Forest Road?" 2002: 3pp. *Wildlands Center for Preventing Roads*. Online. Internet.
www.wildlandscpr.org/resourcelibrary/faqs/roads_faq

Zepezauer, Mark and Arthur Naiman. "Take the Rich Off Welfare." 1997: 5pp. *Third World Traveler*. Online. Internet.
www.thirdworldtraveler.com/Pentagon_military/RichOffWelfare_EII

Helpful Information Sites

American Government & Social Reform: a Glossary
Compiled by Dr. Tom O'Connor
Justice Studies Department
North Carolina Wesleyan College
Rocky Mount, NC 27804
www.faculty.ncwc.edu/toconnor/reform.htm

Cato Institute
1000 Massachusetts Ave. WW
Washington, DC 20001-5403
202-842-0200
FAX: 202-842-3490

The Center for Responsive Politics
1101 14th St. NVV
Suite 1030
Washington, DC 20005-5635
202-857-0044
FAX: 202-857-7809
www.opensecrets.org

Citizens Against Government Waste
1301 Connecticut Avenue, NW
Suite 400
Washington, DC 20036
202-467-5300

Common Cause
1250 Connecticut Ave. NW 600
Washington, DC 20036
202-833-1200

Corporate Welfare Information Center
www.corporations.org/welfare/

Getting Business off the Public Dole by Robert W. Benson
Loyola Law School, Los Angeles, CA
Contact: International Law Center
8124 W. Third St.
Suite 201
Los Angeles, CA 90048
213-736-1094
FAX: 213-380-3769

The Heritage Foundation
214 Massachusetts Ave. NE
Washington, DC 20002-4999
202-546-4400
www.heritage.org

L.E.A.N.
Louisiana Environmental Action Network
P.O. Box 66323
Baton Rouge, LA 70806
225-928-1315
www.leanweb.org

Take the Rich off Welfare by Mark Zepezauer and Arthur Naiman
Odonian Press
Box 32375
Tucson, AZ 85751
520-296-4056
FAX: 520-296-0936

Time Magazine
www.time.com

United for a Fair Economy
37 Temple Place, 2nd Floor
Boston, MA 02111
617-423-2148
FAX: 617-423-0191
www.ufenet.org

USDA
United States Department of Agriculture
1400 Independence Ave. SW
Washington, DC 20250-1300
202-720-4623
www.usda.gov

Washington Times
c/o John McCaslin
202-636-4936
202-832-8285
www.washtimes.com

Visit our website at www.amosauthor.com